# MEDROMEDA

Lore Wren

Wordlark Publishing—Oklahoma City, OK
Paperback ISBN: 979-8-9903427-0-5
Hardcover ISBN: 979-8-9903427-1-2
eBook ISBN: 979-8-9903427-2-9
Library of Congress Control Number: 2024908494
Title: *MEDROMEDA*
Author: Lore Wren
Digital distribution | 2024
Hardcover | 2024
Paperback | 2024

This is a work of fiction. The characters, names, incidents, places, and dialogue are products of the author's imagination, and are not to be construed as real.

# Dedication

To Pompeii. Where a feather landed in the crossroads and the wind whispered, write.

# Preface

## The Greek Myth that inspired Medromeda

There are many versions of the myth of Medusa, but there are a few consistencies in all renditions, Medusa was turned into a monster by Athena and Perseus was the one to slay her. Medromeda intertwines the mythical tales of Medusa, Perseus, and Andromeda. I took my inspiration from the versions below and created a new myth that explores nature vs nurture and gives insight into who Medusa was before she was turned into a monster.

## The Myth of Medusa

Medusa was one of three Gorgons, daughters of the sea gods Phorcys and Ceto. Both of Medusa's sisters were monsters and immortal. Medusa was born mortal and with unsurpassed beauty. The sea god, Poseidon, could not resist the temptation and impregnated Medusa in the temple of Athena. Enraged, Athena transformed Medusa's hair into a sea of serpents, gave her fangs and talons and turned her into the legendary monster. Her face was so hideous and her gaze so piercing that the mere sight of her could turn men to stone.

## The Myth of Perseus

Perseus was the son of Zeus and Danaë. As an infant he and his mother were placed into a crate and cast into the sea by his grandfather who feared that one day the boy would kill him. Perseus grew up on the island of Seriphos. King Polydectes ruled Seriphos and wanted Perseus's mother, Danaë, to be his wife. Perseus was against this marriage. Polydectes tricked Perseus into promising to obtain the head of Medusa. He thought Perseus would die trying, leaving him free to marry Danaë.

Perseus received help on his quest to slay Medusa by the god

Hermes and the goddess Athena. He was given winged sandals and a sickle by Hermes, a shield from Athena, a sack known as a *kibisis* to store the head of Medusa, and the invisibility cap of Hades. Perseus arrived at the home of the Gorgons while they slept. Athena guided Perseus to look at Medusa's reflection in a shield so as not to be turned to stone by her gaze. He cut off the head of Medusa. From her severed head sprang Pegasus, the winged horse, and Chrysaor, a boar.

When Perseus was on his way home with Medusa's head, he rescued princess Andromeda. Andromeda's mother, Cassiopeia, had claimed to be more beautiful than the sea nymphs, so Poseidon had punished her land by flooding it and plaguing it with a sea monster. Andromeda's father, King Cepheus, was told that the floods would cease if he sacrificed Andromeda to the monster, which he did. Perseus, passing by, saw the princess tied to a rock in the sea and fell in love with her. He turned the sea monster to stone by showing it Medusa's head and afterward married Andromeda.

When Perseus returned to the Island of Seriphos, he turned Polydectes and his people to stone with Medusa's head and rescued his mother, Danaë. Then he gave the head of Medusa to Athena, who placed it in the center of her shield, to terrify her enemies.

# Part I
Raveled

# Chapter One
### Birds Eye - Seriphos Island

**B**OWED HEADS WEPT for eyes could not bear witness to what unfolded before them. The tragedy of life was nothing new but today it felt trans-formative. The island of Seriphos was an insignificant dot in the Aegean Sea blissfully unaware of the chaos of Athens. The dominion of gods over mortals escaped the inhabitants of this sleepy island until the birth of two girls and the arrival of a cast away boy who washed up on shore with his mother. Three innocent souls, unknown to all. Their innocence would not last long.

All lilted into the world on the same day, at the same hour, and with an ethereal beauty that surpassed that of the gods. For one, beauty would be their unraveling curse.

Days on Seriphos were tranquil. The sky was crystal blue with an occasional swath of white puffy clouds. The sea surrounding the island was also a translucent blue. It was hard to tell where sea and sky met most days. They existed in unison. The only time they felt separate was at sunrise and sunset when pink, coral and purple swept into blue and reminded the inhabitants of the passing of time. Without it, the languid hours would drift into one eternal day.

It was a period of calm for Greece. The country had been at war with the Persians for years and the people of Seriphos had fought tirelessly. Not a single inhabitant escaped loss. Twelve years ago, the fifty-year battle had ended and the children of Greece were spared of a future threat of invasion.

The weight of the war was fading but the people of Seriphos would protect the calm with all their might. Art, music, poetry, and philosophy were how they spent their days now. Out of darkness came appreciation of the things that mattered in life. Families spent more time together, neighbors helped each other, foes became friends and sunrises and sunsets were moments of reflection and gratitude. Kindness spread even to the animal kingdom.

An old crow sat on a rock and watched a fisherman abandon his net to free a boy and his mother from a crate that had washed up on shore. Two white owls, one male and one female flew overhead. They landed on the shore to search for fish. The male owl spotted a meal just feet away from his sister but what he did not see was that this meal was entrapped in a net. He too became entangled and his sister could not break him free. Her cries were heard by the lonely crow who heeded the call and went to help. At first the owls did not want help from a scraggly crow but his beak was sharp and the rope snapped easily. The male owl was free and the meal was shared between the glorious white owls of Athens and a banished black-winged crow.

Service to the good of all was paramount and there was no greater call than to be avowed to one of the gods. Greek children dreamed of living alongside the Olympians. Zeus, Hera, Poseidon, Demeter, Athena, Apollo, Artemis, Ares, Hephaestus, Aphrodite, Hermes, and Dionysus were universally adored.

Each god had a temple where families gathered and brought offerings of nourishment to please the gods. The Temple of Athena was a favorite among the girls of Seriphos. The goddess of wisdom and battle spoke to them. The stories of war from their grandparents fueled this affinity. The boys loved the stories of war battles at sea which sparked interest in Poseidon, the god of the seas. On any given day, you could watch boys using sticks as tridents and girls trying to tame an owl (or anything that looked like an owl) to sit on their shoulder like Athena's Owl.

The real-life Athena and Poseidon were anything but godlike. Their mythology left out the real-life events that transpired in Seriphos. Like mortals, they had a past and their past haunted them. Jealously was wrought between the gods of Olympus, but none had a rivalry as fierce as the one between Athena and Poseidon.

# Chapter Two
## The gods


## ATHENA

Athena walked with the confidence of someone who needed no-one. Wisps of long, light, peach-colored strands of silken hair framed her face. Sculpted cheekbones rested under golden eyes. Her lashes looked to be made of sunlight, they moved in a delicate fashion that contradicted the intensity of her gaze. Her stature alone commanded respect. She was the daughter of the most powerful god on Olympus, Zeus. Her beauty was made even more captivating by an ethereal glow that accentuated the rippling muscles concealed by her armor. She was not a delicate beauty; she was a warrior.

Athena presided over wisdom but her love of power fueled controversy. Her quick decisions on justice for minor infractions caused great suffering. She made land barren, devastated fleets of ships, sold women into slavery and sent down plagues. Her greatest controversy was the battle that ensued not over matters of wisdom but that of beauty. Her feud with Hera and Aphrodite over who was the most beautiful started the Trojan War. Her wrath became tempered after a white owl arrived at the temple. Before Athena had a white owl, she had a white crow. All crows were originally white. Athena had a secret that her crow unknowingly disclosed. She had a son that she put in a box and left with the daughters of Kekrops. She instructed them never to open it. Athena's crow saw the sisters open the box which revealed the child who had a snake's tail instead of legs. The crow flew to tell Athena. Athena was outraged and took it out on the crow. She punished the crow by turning his white feathers and the feathers of all crows into black and forbidding crows in the city of Athens. Athena replaced her crow with a white owl. Owl persuaded her to retrieve her son. On Owl's counsel, she brought the boy to the Acropolis and raised him with love and the gift of a warrior's heart.

The truth and wisdom Athena is known for comes from Owl. Owl is the source of her moral and creative decisions. Through Owl, Athena invented the plow, rake, yoke, chariot, and ship. With Owl's foresight, she was a dominant force. Owl encouraged peaceful resolutions over bloodshed, truth over righteousness, love above all, and sometimes, when Owl whispered in opposition to an unwise decision, Athena listened.

## POSEIDON

Poseidon was fathered by the Titan, Cronus. He had two brothers, Zeus, and Hades. Together, they killed their father and drew straws to divide power over the world. Zeus ruled the sky, Poseidon the sea and Hades became the god of the underworld.

While most gods lived under the command of Zeus on Mount Olympus, Poseidon created a castle made of gemstones, coral, and gold at the bottom of the sea. This magnificent palace was also home to the stables for the gods' white horses. Poseidon was an imposing looking god. His beard and hair were covered in barnacles and flowed to the middle of his chest and back. He carried a trident and rode in a golden chariot pulled by his hippocampus. These fish-tailed horses were as imposing as Poseidon. The trio made a statement.

He shared his underwater palace with his wife, Amphitrite and her sisters, the Nereids. His temperament was moody and unstable which made his violence unpredictable. The only thing predictable about him was his incessant desire to exert power over women and flaunt his larger-than-life masculinity. When he was not pursuing the favors of goddesses and mortals, he ruled over the oceans and sea creatures.

He also had powers on land where he lorded over horses and earthquakes. He had an ongoing rivalry with Zeus's daughter, Athena. Some say that it was over his jealously that his brother Zeus was a more powerful god than he was and since he could not fight Zeus, he took it out on the closest thing to him, Athena.

## THE RIVALRY

The contest over the sovereignty of Attica was the pinnacle of their feud. Both gods were vying to become the patron of the most affluent and desired city in Greece. They each believed themselves worthy of the title and more importantly they each wanted the glory that came with the title. Zeus intervened due to the caustic nature of their rivalry and suggested that each god offer a divine gift. The one with the best gift would win the city.

The Olympians and the citizens of the Attica met on a sacred hill at the top of the Acropolis to watch the competition. Poseidon went first. With a powerful blow, he struck his trident against a rock. The earth shook and from the rock, a stream emerged. The people were in awe until they realized that the stream was saltwater. The area already had many freshwater streams and was surrounded by ocean. A saltwater stream was useless to them. Athena moved next. She knelt on the ground and gently struck her spear which created a small hole in which she placed a seed. When she rose, so did an olive tree. The wood of the olive tree was strong and the fruit was nutritional and the oil useful. Athena was the clear winner. The city would be known as Athens from that moment on. This solidified her as more powerful than Poseidon. Poseidon's defeat resulted in tyrannical anger. He called for the sea to wash over and flood Athens.

When Poseidon's fury subsided over losing the naming rights of Athens, he realized something else, he admired Athena. He had met a woman that could beat him and he was impressed. He had conquered many women and was proud of his ability to charm even the hardest minds. This was not the case with Athena. The more he tried, the more she retreated.

Athena was enamored with Poseidon as well but hid it from all. Her wisdom on earthly things did not transcend into matters of water. She could learn from Poseidon and learning spoke to her soul. However, her choice of chastity elevated her among the immorality of mortals and of the other gods on Olympus. She was a warrior and unbreakable in matters of the heart.

The rift between Athena and Poseidon had just begun. The calm the inhabitants of Seriphos had enjoyed was about to be disrupted and no amount of interceding could prevent what was about to unfold.

# Chapter Three
## The Mortals

MEDUSA– Seriphos Island

Patrons filled the amphitheater from all over the island. The smell of jasmine permeated the air. Musicians played lyres and children skipped and laughed with their friends. A comedy was playing tonight, and Medusa was thrilled to be out of the house away from the daily chores of helping her mother. She watched the other kids play. Her mother nudged her to go join them. She was talking with other women about the theme of the show and Medusa could tell their conversation wanted to turn into something less appropriate for children. So, she took a deep breath and walked towards a group of girls sitting on a fountain. One had her hand draped around her friend and was whispering to her as Medusa approached.

"Hello," said Medusa. Her head was down but she was smiling. The girls, half-smiled back.

"I am so excited to see this play. Where are you sitting?" Medusa said as she sat down next to one of the girls.

The girls did not answer her. They continued talking as if she was not there. Medusa peered into the basin of the fountain. Her dark eyes shone in the reflection. The speckles of topaz and light that pierced her irises did not translate here in the water. Dark ringlet hair cascaded over her shoulders. It was so long that it skimmed the top of the water below. She brushed the tendrils over her shoulder and looked at her reflection.

*"What have I done to make them hate me so?"*

A group of boys were playing ball and with each toss, they got closer to the girls. One of them yelled out.

"Hey Thalia, who are you sitting with tonight?"

Thalia liked the boy but ignored him as young people do. He came closer but as he approached, he noticed Medusa sitting on the edge of the fountain still engulfed in her own thoughts. Thalia watched him watch her and fury rose inside her. She thought it was better that she did not let him see her squirm, so she tossed a pebble into the fountain and shattered Medusa's reflection and broke the boy's gaze.

Medusa was startled by the pebble and looked up to see who had thrown it. The boy caught her eye and took a few steps backwards before he ran away.

Thalia and the girls taunted Medusa. "You are so hideous no one can stand to look at you, not even your own reflection."

"Your shadow threw the rock." Said a younger girl. "You best go find your mother, so you'll have someone to sit with tonight."

The girls scurried off, leaving Medusa alone at the fountain. Dejected, she slid off the marble edge, walked past the girls, and ignored more snide remarks as she made her way to her mother.

"Someday I hope I'll have a friend." wished Medusa as she tossed a coin into the fountain.

It was a popular coin with children as it had the image of the double-headed golden eagle on its facade. Medusa loved the legend surrounding the coin. Golden double-headed eagles were common around her island, but elders foretold of an albino double-headed eagle with incredible powers that returned to the island every one-hundred years. If prophecy held correctly, that year would be the following year. Commencing on the summer solstice, which just so happened to be Medusa's 17th birthday. Since Medusa heard the story, she dreamed of this magical creature visiting her. Dreams come true if you try, her mother had always said. In a little less than a year, Medusa would know if her dream would come true. In her mind, she rode the albino eagle away from her island to a new land.

ANDROMEDA – Patmos Island

Andromeda was born into royalty on the neighboring island of Patmos, and nothing was spared to give her everything in life. She knew how to play instruments, was skilled in all areas of the arts, and spent her days torturing the servants. She was told how beautiful she was from the moment she was born. As an infant, her mother encouraged her vanity as she herself was vain.

Andromeda was free to go outside of her castle if she had her maiden, Vexia, with her. Today the pair left the castle in vastly different looking chitons. Andromeda's was embroidered in gold. She wore a golden laurel wreath crown and a gold snake shaped bracelet twisted around her arm. Its eye held a gleaming emerald much like the color of Andromeda's eyes. With the golden crown resting on top of her golden hair, she looked like a goddess, and she acted as one too. Andromeda had dressed Vexia in a plain linen chiton. Vexia was attractive and she could not have her upstaging in any way.

"Vexia, I need you to walk behind me now. You are too slow to keep up and the way you walk annoys me!" said Andromeda.

"Princess, what are you up to? I promised the King and Queen that I would prevent you from embarrassing the royal court." said Vexia.

"Me…get into trouble? You tease Vexia. I simply walk about being me and trouble whisks its way onto my path. My actions have nothing to do with it." Andromeda boasted and shooed Vexia away.

Andromeda floated down cobblestone roads as the inhabitants of Patmos curtsied and bowed in respect. Some shook their heads in disbelief at her brazen nature walking unaccompanied, but most looked on in admiration. Her beauty was other worldly. It was impossible to turn away without sneaking a glance, no matter your personal thoughts on her personality.

Throughout the village there were corners where food vendors set up daily. It was a social place and specific corners were known to be where the younger people frequented. Andromeda approached a food vendor where four boys sat. They all moved when she approached to make room. Grand gestures ensued, each boy trying to outdo the other. Andromeda played to their weakness in her presence and taunted them with casual but intentional flirty conversation. She gave them just enough to always want more.

"How am I to choose whom to sit next to today when you are all sooooo…she drew them into her mental web with a heavy sigh while biting her bottom lip…hmmmmmm," she trailed off, not finishing her sentence and not looking directly at any of the boys who had made room for her.

Her eyes were darting, ever so subtly, but often, to the boy assisting his father in the kitchen. The boy's name was Alcaeus.

"Father, please sit down, you have been working all morning. I will take over. Go home now and I will come and get you after work and you can join me in the bath house. This lot my age is here for that girl and not our food. They will not be ordering more. It will give me some time to start the soup for tomorrow and study a bit before I retrieve you for the bath house."

"You are a good son Alcaeus. Your mother would be so proud," said Argos, his father.

He beamed with pride. Alcaeus meant more to him than words could say. He placed his hand on the side of Alcaeus' cheek and looked directly into his eyes. Andromdea watched the scene unfold and tossed her hair a bit as she laughed. The father and son could not be distracted from their bond. Andromeda huffed and nodded to Vexia who was standing a few meters away.

Vexia scurried in. "It's time to head home now Princess Andromeda."

"If we must, we must. I am sorry gentlemen, but I shall depart now. I will count the minutes until I see you again."

With a coy smile she was off. The boys remained stuck in a stupor over being in her presence.

"What are you up to Andromeda?" said Vexia cursedly.

"Vexia, there is one boy in this entire world that does not know I exist. I plan to change that right now. Switch clothes with me!"

She was dragging Vexia down an alley and tearing at her clothes.

"Andromeda! Stop this instant or your mother will have us both imprisoned. You cannot possibly pursue this vendor boy. You could never make him yours." said a worried Vexia.

Andromeda slipped off her garment. Vexia's mouth dropped but Andromeda continued and removed the crown from her head and placed it under a laurel bush.

"My lady, you need to think this through. Your face is recognizable regardless of what clothes you wear." pipped Vexia.

Andromeda ripped a corner of Vexia's chiton and fashioned a headscarf that covered her hair. She placed laurel leaves in between the folds so that they framed her face and hid the general shape. She bent down and scooped up a sizable amount of dirt, opened her eyes wide and smeared it into her eyes and all over her face. Her eyes instantly turned red enough to hide the vibrant green. Vexia protested all along this plan as it unfolded but Andromeda was unstoppable in this endeavor much as she was in all she set her heart upon. What Andromeda wanted; Andromeda got. Today would be no different.

Andromeda tied Vexia to a laurel bush with the leather straps from her sandals. She placed a torn piece of her gilded toga into her mouth and kissed her on the cheek. Vexia watched her in disbelief as she skipped off to find the boy wearing the clothes of a royal servant and looking nothing like the ethereal being she was minutes ago.

She found the boy packing up the dishes and food from the vending site. She noticed a tipped over amphora and guessed that he would be filling it in the common fountain before heading home. Andromeda elbowed her way through the crowd until she spotted her target. She charged a large woman who toppled over and dropped her amphora. Andromeda scooped it up and ran off into the crowd before the women could tell who took it. She made her way down to the fountain spring and waited. Alcaeus arrived as she had predicted, and this is where her ruse began. Like a feline waiting to pounce she hid. Alcaeus filled his amphora and walked up the hill and sat beneath an oleander tree. He took out a scroll and a piece of bread and started reading. Children and dogs played disruptively nearby but nothing distracted him. Andromeda was annoyed at his ability to focus and wished for a child to throw a rock or something to get him to look her way. Then she remembered that earlier she was unable to distract him so if she could not do it how could she expect a child to. This thought made her happy. *No one should have power over him except me.* She would think of something. She moved closer and closer to the thoughtful boy and waited for him to look up from his scroll. When he did, she intentionally tripped on a stone and fell, spilling her water and breaking her amphora. She started to cry.

"Miss, miss, are you alright?" He said, offering a hand.

"Oh yes, I am fine. I am just careless and I should not have filled my jar so full. I overestimated my strength today. I need water for my family. My mother is not well and the only person she wants by her side is my father, so I offered to come and fetch the water for him."

"I am sorry your mother is ill. Mine suffered sickness and succumbed to her ailment a few months ago." He placed a hand on his heart and looked directly at Andromeda.

"I am not sure why I shared that? I have not spoken to anyone about it except my father." He shook his head and said, "I loved my mother." Though tear-stained eyes.

His sincerity struck a chord in Andromeda's tepid heart. She felt something she had never felt before. She did not know what it was, but she knew she wanted to know more about this boy.

# Chapter Four
## The Crow - Seriphos Island

THE SILVER GLINT of olive tree leaves shimmered in dappled sunlight. The leaves cast shadows along the path Medusa was walking. She hopped from shadowed leaf to shadowed leaf, careful not to drop the pomegranates she had gathered for gifts to present at Athena's Temple. As she approached the pond, the thick trees of the path opened and hugged the shoreline. Medusa was drawn to the water and knelt to touch its smooth face. Her touch sent ripples across the pond, and she sat admiring herself. She looked triumphantly into the ripples and thought her reflection was beautiful all stirred up and not so perfect. Her mother had told her she was beautiful, and she had believed her. It is just that others in the world did not hold the same opinion as her mother. She dipped her hand in the water again and broke the tension.

A rustling sound startled her, and she looked to see its source. Caws and chirps, squeals, and flapping were coming from a tiny island just below the bridge. She ran towards it frightened by what she heard. A double-headed eagle held a crow in its talons, its beak gripping feathers and tugging at black wings.

"Stop! Stop please! Somebody! Help!" she pleaded.

Another eagle approached and attacked the crow, then another swooped in. The eagles were known for their calm demeanor but all three were in warrior mode and the poor crow lay helpless. Medusa looked directly at the crow and seemed to understand his pain. She had been attacked too and she was not going to let him die without trying to save him. *If only I could swim*, she thought.

"Shoo!" She flapped her hands and pounded the water.

She waded in but could not get close enough to reach the birds. One of the eagles left the scene and flew straight towards her. He brushed past the top of her head. A warning. Medusa grabbed a branch and swung at the bird. During its next descent it plucked the branch from her hands and flew off. Medusa panicked. She was crying now and screaming for them to stop. The crow was bleeding and his cries had lessened. Medusa carried on.

"Help, help. Anyone! Please help!" she wailed through desperate breath.

Out of nowhere, an eagle fell just steps away from her. His heart pierced with an arrow. She heard the next arrow flying above. *It came from the bridge*, she thought. She looked up to see a boy. His hand holding a quiver taunt against his bow. He let go and dove from the bridge into the water. The arrow downed the second eagle. He swam to the crow who was still being held by the last surviving eagle. He grabbed the eagle with his hands and choked him until he released the crow. He reached back for his sword. It was different from any she had seen before. It was curved at the end like a sickle. He wielded the sword and pivoted around searching for other offenders.

Medusa wiped tears from her face as the eagle flew away. The boy placed the wounded crow on the nape of his neck and swam to the shore. When he reached Medusa, she was crestfallen. Her tears prevented any words from escaping her lips.

The boy gently took the crow from his neck and cradled him in his hands and reached out to Medusa. She had one hand covering her mouth as she stroked the somewhat featherless crow. The crow responded with a sigh of relief. He looked at his rescuers with admiration.

The boy and Medusa sat down with the bird and while Medusa consoled him, the boy consoled her. Tears dried, smiles returned, and an inseparable bond was woven between the three.

"Thank you for helping," said Medusa.

"My pleasure miss, I have an affinity for crows," said Perseus.

"I think we should name him said," said Medusa.

"I agree. This little fellow deserves a name fit for a warrior," said the boy. "I would first like to know your name, if you would care to share it with me?" asked the boy with a hopeful expression.

"Oh my, of course, how inconsiderate of me not to share my name with my rescuer. I go by Medusa. What name shall I call you boy? Surely your name is fit for a warrior as well." She smiled and at that moment the blue color of his eyes became a permanent memory for her.

"I am not much of a warrior, yet. I, and my sword, Harpe, have just begun our adventures. I have plans to be many things Medusa, but for now, I am simply Perseus."

*Perseus blue,* thought Medusa. *The sky matches his eyes. The sky is Perseus blue.*

"Well simply Perseus and Harpe, what shall we call our feathered friend?"

Perseus smirked at her quick wit and felt a little embarrassed that he did not think of something better to say. He had been so consumed with saving the crow, he had not noticed how light danced from her eyes or how her hair fell down her back. He watched as she brushed a stray curl away. Even her hands were perfect. Golden skin with a ring of Athena on the first finger of her right hand.

"You live in the temple?" asked Perseus touching Medusa's ring.

"I will, I am avowed to Athena as a priestess. I live to fulfill what the fates have predicted, I will go to serve Athena after my apprenticeship, in eight more full moons."

"Then I'll never see you again?" asked Perseus. "Athena's priestesses never marry."

"We do not. We only serve Athena. You may see me in the market or perhaps here again at the pond before I leave, but you are correct. I am required to take a vow of celibacy to serve our god. I will never marry."

Just then the crow tried to open his wings.

"There, there little friend," whispered Medusa. "You need to rest. We will have you mended and flying in no time."

Medusa gave an imploring look to Perseus. He stroked the bird's black wings, removed his sandal, and placed him inside and bound the straps around him to hold him snugly.

"If only your wings were gold, you would look just like the sandals that help Hermes fly," he said looking at the bird and then at Medusa. "I'll look after him Medusa, and when he's well, we will find you."

"Please, let's give him a name before I say goodbye." She looked lovingly at the now winged shoe. "You survived a great battle today little bird, and you are going home with an even greater man who has given up his shoe for you."

"That is, it! Scarpe is his name Medusa," Perseus said almost laughing.

"You are going to call him "shoe" Perseus? I do not see the nobility in that name. Please educate me."

"He won the day.... right?"

"You won the day. You seized it just like the saying, "Carpe Diem" or "Harpe" in your case. A moment of clarity came upon her. She looked at Perseus…

"Scarpe Diem!" they both said in unison. Laughter ensued.

"Scarpe it is then, it is settled," said Medusa with resounding confidence. "I will meet you here in one month, simply Perseus."

"I promise," said Perseus, making an "x" across his heart and grandiosely nodding Scarpe's entire strapped in body. "You may find me bold Medusa, but I see the sadness behind your smile. I will not betray you. I will look after what you love, and I will meet you here with a healed Scarpe. I hope to see your eyes shining as well by then. There is more to life than serving a flawed deity."

"You have already opened a small light in my heart through your kindness, Simply Perseus," said Medusa, shyly but confidently.

"One month from today then. That will be May 3rd. I will be here with Scarpe and a picnic perhaps. I will surprise you, Medusa. Make time for me. I feel we will have many things to discuss." An enthusiastic Perseus approached Medusa. "You have confirmed my courage. I have never met anyone I would risk my life for besides my mother. I feel we were destined to meet Medusa. I cannot wait until next month to see you again. Your time is limited. I would like to request to meet you once a week until you take your position in the temple."

The two were face to face now and their energy could light the entire island. Crow looked from one admirer to the other.

"I can Perseus, and I will…gladly…make...time, to spend with you." She smiled and looked directly into his Perseus blue eyes.

They touched their foreheads and laughed. He held her hand as they walked up the bridge and she stopped at the top. She handed him a coin with a double-headed eagle on its façade.

"Toss it in and make a wish," she said.

Perseus held the coin in one hand and her hand in the other which was wrapped around Scarpe. He paused and looked at them both for a moment and tossed the coin gallantly into the water.

"I think I know what you wished for," said Medusa.

"Do you want it to come true?" asked Perseus.

She looked deeply into his eyes. "I do. I will try Perseus…we will try."

"That is all I ask Medusa. I will see you next Wednesday. Come along Scarpe, we have lots of mending to do by next week."

With a wave and overflowing hope in their hearts, they parted.

# Chapter Five
## Perseus - Seriphos Island

"WHERE DID YOU come from little guy?" asked Perseus as he placed a new bandage over Scarpe's wounded wing.

The crow tilted his head as if to ask Perseus the same question.

"Who me? Ah, I am nobody Scarpe. Just a boy who arrived with his mother in a wooden chest on this island a few years ago."

Scarpe's head tilted again.

"Scarpe, I do not remember much. My grandfather was disappointed that he did not have a son, so he went to the Oracle at Delphi. The Oracle told him that my mother would have a son, me, and that I would kill him one day. My grandfather, Acrisius is his name, locked my mother in a bronze chamber open to the sky so that she could never marry. My mother, still to this day, is the most beautiful woman you could ever lay eyes on. So beautiful that the god Zeus came to visit my mother in the form of golden rain. He used the opening at the top of the chamber and his rain fell into my mother's lap. He is my father. My grandfather was furious that my mother had a son, but he was afraid to kill me for fear of the wrath of Zeus. So instead of death, he placed us in a wooden crate and cast us out to sea.

"We washed up on shore here. My mother speaks now of how the wind hissed and how bolts of fear overtook her during our time at sea. The only thing I remember about being in the chest is my mother holding me. She wore a silver crescent moon necklace. As she cradled me in a purple robe, I touched and turned the crescent towards fissures in our make-shift ship. I waited to catch the light as we crested a wave and used it to reflect the beams upwards illuminating my mother's beautiful face. The shiny necklace also attracted an orphaned looking crow. He tried to peck into the crate to retrieve the necklace but when he saw me, he flew off. He returned with tiny fish that fit through the slit perfectly. He continued to visit us every few days and brought us dates and figs and fish. Maybe it was your father Scarpe? We were at sea for months but I had no worries of salty brine, surges of waves or the howling racket of the wind. My mother was terrified, yet I never knew. She is what I hold the standard of a woman to be, someone who in their darkest hour can still be a light for those she loves.

"She risked her life to save me. I would do anything for my mother. She is still at risk today. When we landed in Seriphos, we were rescued by a fisherman named, Dictys. We were tangled in his net and he pulled us to shore. He pried the chest open and was astonished to find my mother and me in place of a treasure. He took us to his home. My mother instantly trusted him. He is a good man. His brother is King Polydectes. He informed us of the evilness of the king and instructed us to stay hidden. He told us many heartless stories and feared he would make us his servants or send us back to be killed by my grandfather. We spent our days getting to know each other. Dictys taught me all about weapons and how to defeat any enemy. He taught me about the sea and fishing. He gave me this sword, which I call, Harpe. It is what helped save you. Our lives were idyllic and my mother and Dictys grew to love each other. As time passed, we became a family and our fears of King Polydectes faded to the back of our minds. After being hated by our own blood and surviving our months in the chest, we deserved happiness. We found it with Dictys. With such happiness, you cannot imagine that anything bad could ever happen to you again. Our guards were down, and my mother and I ventured into town when Dictys was fishing one day."

"The king was alerted by one of his men that a beautiful woman was walking in the square. The king had his men take my mother to meet him. I was in tow but very unwelcome. When we reached the interior of the castle, I was pushed aside to wait with a servant who forbade me to speak. My mother was born of royalty, so she knew the proper decorum for such an encounter. She bowed deeply and eloquently. Her posture was perfect, just like her smile. She captivated all who saw her. Polydectes fell instantly in love with her. She loved Dictys. True to form, Polydectes ignored her pleas to return home and had her restrained. I could not watch anyone touch my mother."

"Stop now or I'll use force!" I said it before I thought.

"Who speaks?" asked Polydectes.

My mother and I answered at the same time.

"My son, Perseus," said my mother with imploring eyes.

"I am the son of Danaë," I said.

"Well, son of Danaë, come closer to me," said the king.

Scarpe blinked at Perseus.

"I walked up to the king, but I did not bow. I could feel my mother's eyes on my back, and I made myself bow. Scarpe, I did not want to bow to that man. No man should. He has destroyed my mother and I am the only one who can save her."

Perseus held onto Harpe and his eyes told a story filled with revenge. He ran his finger over the sharp edges of the sickle. Scarpe knew he saw the king's face being slashed with that blade.

"I told the king he had to go through me to win my mother's hand. He sneered at my statement. I should have known better but I was only 15 years old. My mother came to my rescue as she has so many times."

"My lord, please. My son and I have been through a tremendous ordeal. We were cast out of our home and only recently landed in Seriphos."

My mother was careful not to implement Dictys in anything concerning us," said Perseus to Scarpe.

"We would be most grateful to stay in your kingdom as we have nowhere to call home," said Danaë.

"We?" asked the king.

"Yes, we, my son Perseus and I would be most grateful to stay in your presence my king." Danaë bowed deeply with her eyes fixated on the king's.

"Then it shall be done. Show my lady and her son to the east wing. I expect to see you at dinner," said the king.

He looked on my mother as a possession. He never asked about our past and we were so hidden until that day that no one knew anything about us.

"I was never permitted to be alone with my mother again Scarpe. The king kept her locked away and wanted nothing to do with me. I only saw them at dinner. Her place at the table was next to him and mine was on the other end. We passed each other notes on occasion. Most were about concern over Dictys. We were prisoners in the castle. When I turned sixteen, I was allowed to go on a hunt with the king's guards. We passed along the shore, and I saw Dictys. His net in his hand, casting it effortlessly over his head. I wanted to go to him. I wanted to shout that we were alive, but I could not risk his life for my desires. We continued the hunt and I honored Dictys by using the skills he taught me. I bested everyone on the hunt, even the island's champion hunter, Simon. We went back to the castle with the greatest haul the guards had ever seen. A feast was made for the townspeople, and I was able to see my mother outside of the dining hall. She looked forlorn. I had never seen this look on her face before. She also had a scarf around her neck, and it was warm that evening. I was close enough that she could see my concern. I mouthed *Are you alright mother*? She did not answer. She did not need to. She lowered her head to one side and pulled the scarf down. I was happy to see her silver crescent moon necklace, but my happiness turned to sorrow when I saw the bruises. So deep was the hue that I could see them from where I stood. My pulse quickened. My body stiffened. She looked back up and mouthed these words to me. 'Do not fight for me. I would rather live in pain than lose you.' The king must have sensed our connection. He moved my mother out of sight and continued with his drink. I tried to be a part of the festivities since I had been the provider of much of the food, but I could not focus my mind on anything except what this man had done to my mother. The party went on for hours and the king had more than his fair share of libations. He was drunk. Scarpe, have you ever seen a drunk tyrant? Ah, of course you have not. Birds do not take part in such foolishness. I can tell you it is not a pretty sight. The king swayed up to the balcony with my mother. He addressed his loyal subjects."

"My people. Thank you for joining us today in these festivities. I take it you have all enjoyed yourselves?" The crowd cheered.

"Let's raise a glass to our hunters who spent the day capturing our meal."

The crowd cheered again.

"To the women, who cooked our meal."

He held out his glass and the crowd cheered once again.

"And, to my future bride, Danaë, who adores me above all others.

He put his arm around my mother and the scarf fell revealing the crescent moon necklace and bruises. The villagers could not see the bruises from where they stood but the silver gleamed in the torchlights. The king noticed the necklace and ripped it from her neck.

"Why do you insist on wearing this rubbish when you have a castle full of jewels?! It reminds you of him, doesn't it?! Doesn't it?!!!"

"Yes, my lord. Please, let me have it. I will not wear it again. Everyone is looking at us sir. Hand it to me and let us go on inside."

"Nonsense, no wife of mine will be caught wearing the jewels of a castaway nobody again."

"He tossed the necklace on the ground and whisked my mother away. I watched in shock with everyone else but soon they returned to their merriment. It was just one more thing to talk about for them after all. I grieved the pain my mother had endured that night. I searched for the necklace when I returned to the castle but could not find it. It represented all that my mother was to me…love, beauty, kindness, and strength. It belonged to her. It belonged to us. It was the only thing that gave us light and hope while we were locked in that crate. It was the only thing that connected her to me when we were apart. Now, she was truly alone with nothing to remind her of me or the strength of her convictions.

"I had to think of a way to connect with the king and save my mother without hurting Dictys. I am still trying to figure that part out Scarpe. Enough about me. Let us give a go at it, shall we?"

Perseus lifted Scarpe onto his arm and moved it up and down. Scarpe opened his wings and tried to catch air. He was too terrified to let go with his talons, but his wings were getting stronger. Perseus was persistent. He hid Scarpe in an alcove in the tower. He visited him at least three times a day. Within a week, Scarpe was lifting off Perseus' arm and taking mini leaps. Perseus could not wait to show Medusa.

# Chapter Six
## The Second Meeting - Seriphos Island

MEDUSA ARRIVED AT the pond before Perseus and Scarpe. She could hear them before she saw them. Perseus talked to Scarpe like an old friend and Scarpe gave him his undivided attention. They stopped at the top of the bridge and waved to Medusa. Scarpe unfolded his wings.

"Bravo, Scarpe!" she yelled.

The three sat together on a blanket made of lamb's wool. Perseus had brought figs and Medusa had brought some olives. Scarpe hopped with open wings in the grass searching for bugs. Every now and then he would look over at the two and a stray grasshopper leg would be sticking out. They laughed at him trying to chew with a still crooked and chipped beak.

"It sure doesn't slow him down much, does it?" asked Medusa.

"No, he would eat all day if I let him. I have been working him so much though; he needs the energy."

"You've done a wonderful job with him Perseus."

"Thank you, Medusa. I try and keep my promises."

Perseus disclosed to Medusa all the things that made him who he was. He told her everything that he shared with Scarpe during the week. Medusa was enthralled with every word.

"Now that you've heard my story, it's time to share yours," said Perseus.

"My story is not half as interesting as yours," said Medusa. "I have two sisters who are not like me. They are barely human. Have you heard of the Gorgons?"

"No," said Perseus.

"Well, most call them monsters. I know them as loving and loyal. We are from the same parents, but we are not the same. They are immortal. I am mortal. My parents hid all the polished metal in my house to spare my sisters the horror of their existence. I knew I looked differently than them, but I never saw my own face until I found a polished piece of obsidian outside on one of the few times I was allowed alone. My features were barely recognizable against the dark rock, but I could see that I did not have tusks protruding from my mouth as they did. My eyes did not look bewildered as theirs did. My skin was smooth. Their flesh was gray and full of welts like fish scales. I was embarrassed by my beauty but fascinated as well. Why should I be made in such a way? Why could I look upon my sisters and only see their beauty when others gasped in horror? Perseus, they have wings! Amid all that discombobulated contradiction of beauty, these glorious wings unfold like clouds protecting them from the sun. I have no clouds, only sun. Apollo has encased me with light and some days I want to hide beneath a real cloud instead of the clouds that float above my thoughts.

"At the age of twelve, my parents took me to be presented to Athena in the temple in Athens at her request. We walked along white marble paths adorned with blossoms of pink oleander trees. Statues of gods in polished white topped Doric columns and the sound of birds and water trickling from fountains filled the air. A man with a cart, wheeled by with an overflowing haul of all manner of fruit. My father told me it came from Africa. My mother whispered to me through a gritted smile to stop staring and close my dropped jaw. I could not help it. I was like a caged bird who had just taken its first flight and I wanted to experience it all! Even though I had never been a part of this world, I felt like I belonged to this place that was bigger than me and my cloud enshrined thoughts. My elation continued as we approached, Nike, the temple of Athena. The amount of white was made even more brilliant by the contrast of the vibrant mosaic tiles on the facade. A lapis blue sky showed the constellations on one part. On another, lapis blue represented the sea and Poseidon's world. All were intricately detailed and depicted important parts of Athena's story. Above the entry was a statue of Athena's owl. Her gaze looked out upon the town. Her wings folded behind in a resting position. She brought a sense of calm and order to the chaos of life outside the temple. An enormous gold statue of the goddess towered over me. I shivered at the sight of her, how was I going to stand before her this morning in the flesh? The closer we got to the temple; the more people filled the streets. My elation started to dissipate as I left my mind and realized the reality surrounding me. I began to feel stabbing glares from all who passed by me. Was I mistaken? Did that polished obsidian lie to me? Was I as horrific to look upon as my dear sisters? What had I done to warrant such looks? My mother whispered again through an even tighter gritted smile to stop my shocked look. I complied as well as I could. At one point, I looked over my shoulder and saw many of the people looking back over their shoulder as well. They looked away in shame at being caught staring at me.

"I questioned my purpose at that moment. Until then, I was a daughter that was loved by her parents and sisters. I had felt unseen but had never felt over-seen, exposed, or violated until that day. My fear of meeting Athena left. I was ready, nothing could make me feel worse than I already did.

"I entered the temple and was taken to the bath and given a fresh chiton to wear. There were six girls being presented that year as there were every year. The other girls were beautiful. I was the only girl from Seriphos. The other five were from neighboring islands. There was Cora, Rhea, Alexandra, Iris, and Daphne. All were twelve, just like me. I instantly liked Daphne. She had dark hair, like me, and I saw her look back at her mother when we entered the temple, just like me. I thought if she loved her mother, she must be kind and I was right. She sat next to me and shared her fears of meeting Athena. She did not want to be presented but her parents told her it was an honor and destined by the fates. She loved a boy at home named Castor. She wanted to be his wife and have children. I believed her. I told her I wanted to have adventures and see the world and fall in love with it all. I did not know about love and boys. My world was my family. Every time I saw a boy, he ran from me. It never entered my mind to try and have one of my own. We laughed at our differences and felt comfortable sharing them. I had a friend. At least one I would see every month during the waning crescent moon. If chosen today by Athena, we would begin coming to Athens monthly once we turned sixteen. If we passed our lessons and she deemed us worthy, at age 17 we would come to live full-time in the temple and serve our goddess. The first year we were there would be spent weaving the peplos that would be draped over Athena's statue. The peplos dress was blue and yellow and decorated with a scene depicting the fight against the Giants. Every year the golden statue was undressed, veiled, and carried to the sea to be washed. After it was cleaned, it was brought back for the festival of Panathenaia, where the new dress was placed on the statue. I imagined myself sitting next to Daphne weaving and laughing. I could see it as a good life.

"Our mentors arrived and we were given golden ties for our chitons and a simple laurel wreath for our hair. Our skin was coated in olive oil before we dressed. We followed an older priestess to the inner chamber of the temple. Athena sat on a silver throne. Along the back and sides were golden baskets. At the top of the throne was a violet crown made from blue lapis. The ends of the arms had figures that looked like my sisters except they were smiling. *This surely is my mind playing tricks on me*, I thought.

"The six of us were ushered in and placed on purple velvet cushions in front of Athena. Her owl flew over and around us making the initial inspection. She returned to Athena's shoulder and whispered in her ear. Athena called us up one by one. I was the last one called upon. She asked me one question.

'What do you have to offer me beyond your beauty?'

"I was doing that thing with my mouth that my mother was always trying to stop me from doing. I recognized it and slowly closed it and paused. In my head I was spinning but I heard my mother's voice and saw my sister's faces.

'I offer the ability to see beauty where there is none. I am a mortal, and my beauty will fade. To be absolutely beautiful, you must see the beauty in truth even if the truth is ugly. This goes for truth in humans as well as thoughts and events. Most human life is not beautiful. We make beautiful things like art and books and music to remind of us the beautiful times when things are not so beautiful. My beauty is not on the surface your highness. If you are looking for someone who is only beautiful on the outside, you should not choose me for my beauty resides within.'

"Athena snapped her fingers at her owl who instantly took flight. She raised her spear and struck it on the palace floor three times. I looked over at Daphne and the other girls who were all looking down at their velvet cushions. I watched the owl circle above us and then around us collectively, then individually. She stopped and hovered in front of my face a moment longer than she did the others. She flew back to Athena and whispered in her ear.

'You are all dismissed to go back to your parents. Report to the temple on the first crescent moon after your sixteenth birthday. You have all been accepted to serve. Although you have time until your service begins, your vow to me begins now in your hearts and minds.'

"I hugged Daphne and the other girls when we exited the temple. I ran to my parents and told them the news. They were elated that I had been accepted. We returned to Seriphos and I began my studies for entering the temple. I lived a quiet life until I met you and the crow."

# Chapter Seven
## Parchment - Patmos Island

LIGHT FILLED THE room when Vexia pulled open the curtains. Andromeda moaned and pulled the covers over her head.

"Stop that Vexia. There is no need to wake me in such a violent way."

"You need to rise my lady. Your mother calls."

"Fine. Gather my chiton," Andromeda replied resigned to the fact she has never been able to avoid her mother.

Her mother, Cassiopeia, was in the center courtyard of the palace. Lush landscaping filled the space. There was a mosaic of Echo, her dog, in the middle of the courtyard which was surrounded by reflection pools. Her favorite place to rest was here with Echo. She was seldom seen without her pup. He was more spoiled than Andromeda. Statues of the gods were located on the corners of the courtyard and caged birds sang from their willow prisons. A lone peacock wandered the garden. Cassiopeia was seated at a stone table with Echo on her lap. The small white dog was barking at the peacock.

"Hush now. Do not worry, Echo. My heart belongs to you. You are my favorite. I love only the most beautiful things and you, my pet, are my most precious possession."

Andromeda entered slowly looking over the courtyard. The peacock is a new addition. Her mother is so enthralled with Echo that she does not notice her right away. Andromeda tests this by jumping up and down and waving her arm. Nothing. Her mother does not break her connection with her dog who is now licking her face. Finally, Andromeda gives up and plops down heartily in the chair across from her mother.

"You called mama?"

"Oh Andromeda, look at Echo. Isn't he the most beautiful dog in the entire world?"

Cassiopeia holds the dog above her head and then squeezes him to her chest. Andromeda turns her head away from her mother and rolls her eyes. She turns back and gestures towards the peacock.

"What is this feathered beast you've acquired?" asks Andromeda.

"Oh, I am calling her Electra. Isn't she exquisite?" She says this in a sing song fashion while looking at Echo so not to alert the pup of a possible replacement.

"Lovely," says Andromeda flatly.

"I called for you because I have news to share. There is going to be a party at the palace to announce your engagement."

"Engagement? To whom?"

"Uncle Phineus."

"Phineus?! That old goat is no match for me mother."

Andromeda stands and leans in on the table with her palms spread wide against the tile surface.

"Darling, calm down and let me finish. Sit please."

Andromeda moves her hands off the table but does not sit.

"You see, being the most beautiful girl in all of Greece, next to me of course, has a downfall. Athena has summoned you to Athens to vie for a position as one of her priestesses. The only way out of it was to be betrothed. So, I spoke to your father and he spoke to his brother and it has been arrang—" Andromeda interrupts her mother.

"I would rather die than be in the arms of that old fat troll! I will not concede to this mother. I will throw myself off a mountain or jump into a river with rocks tied to my ankles."

She was pacing in a circle around the table with her arms flailing about.

"Stop this instant Andromeda, you are scaring Echo," she said as she covered the pup's ears.

"Me stop? You stop! Quit making decisions about my life without my consent."

Darling, hear me out. I have a plan you may be interested in learning about. I no more want you marrying that donkey of a human than I want to wear a linen chiton. Do you really think I would risk the chance of having troll-faced…what did you call him…oh yes, old-goat looking grandchildren?"

Andromeda laughs at the thought of her mother in a linen chiton chasing a brood of hideous toddlers. She softens.

"Do tell mother. I will listen to this plan. It had better be worth listening to." She sits down and places her elbows on the table and rests her chin in one hand and grabs a blackberry and places it in her mouth with the other.

"That's my girl. Andromeda, you truly get more beautiful every day."

"Tell me something I do not know mother. I am here for your newest scandal if you do not make me sleep outside like you did during the last one you schemed to catch father with drink. I itched for days from the bites. I take after you remember, and we were not made for sleeping with nature."

"Yes, you do take after me and I promise my plan does not involve the outdoors. I cannot bear to think of you leaving me and serving that Athena who thinks her beauty surpasses ours. This marriage is the only way. The party is set for three weeks from Saturday. Your engagement will be announced at the party as a surprise for the kingdom. I have already ordered a dress to be made that matches the green of your eyes." Andromeda claps excitedly.

"The entire kingdom will be elated with this news. Everyone loves a love story. It will bring our subjects a sense of hope. After the engagement, Phineus will want to spend time with you. I will only allow supervised visits so you will not be compromised physically with him."

"I assure you mother; my lips will never touch his." Andromeda makes a twisted face at the thought and so does Cassiopeia.

"A week after the engagement party we will host the wedding. It will be a small ceremony at the palace for our inner circle and family. You and Phineus will make an appearance on the balcony. I have hired a local food vendor, who knows nothing of our inner secrets, to prepare the meal. This is where you come in. I need you to use your charms to get access to the food being prepared and place this on the plate of food that will be served to that portly, old-goat Phineus." She holds up a piece of parchment paper tied with a red string.

"What is that mother?" she asked with the curiosity of a spider who has trapped their first insect.

"This my dear, is your freedom. One small sprinkle of this on anything Phineus ingests and he will fall asleep." She winks.

"Forever mama?"

Cassiopeia nods. Andromeda smiles. The pup barks. Mother and daughter grasp hands and dance in a circle around the peacock. Echo leaps and nips at their skirts. With a curtsy and a kiss on the cheek both leave the courtyard and carry on with their day as if this moment never happened.

# Chapter Eight
## Meda - Patmos Island

VEXIA DIDN'T KNOW why she tried to convince Andromeda to ever change her mind. Andromeda was head strong and drove home anything she set her mind to but Vexia felt a moral obligation to say something to try and stop her. Andromeda had her bring an extra set of servant's clothes disguised as layering in her market basket. "To protect the fruit," she had told the head of the kitchen. The maidens embarked on the road to town and as they approached, Andromeda pulled Vexia into the bushes from the path and changed into the servant's clothes and placed her silk garments into the market basket. She gave Vexia threatening looks every time the girl went to speak. Vexia bit her tongue for the time being but her body language told Andromeda that she was not amused. With arms crossed she marched next to Andromeda into the town center. They came upon the food vendor from last week and the same group of boys were sitting at the counter.

"I sure hope the princess comes today," said a handsome boy named Sebastian with sandy blond hair that dipped just over his eyebrows.

"I was the last one she looked upon last week," said a tall boy with dark eyes called Erik.

"You'd have better luck with a stallion than the princess, Erik." The boy named Sebastian whinnied like a horse which resulted in an eruption of laughter.

The girls approached and not one boy offered their seat.

"Ehhhh emmm," Andromeda said with her nose slightly elevated.

Vexia tried to contain her amusement. "Um, my lady, your request is pointless. They aren't going to move for the likes of us."

"Silence Vexia, I know what I'm doing." She continued "Pardon me, boys."

"Boys? Listen to this one…you should address us as Sirs? Boys! Ha! I should spit on you for that," said Sebastian.

More laughter came from the group of boys. Andromeda blinked hard trying to understand and when she did comprehend the truth, she gritted her teeth to try and control her anger at being treated like a commoner.

"What is your name, one that speaks out of turn?" asked Erik.

Andromeda was caught off guard. She fumbled a moment in her brain before she spoke.

"Meda," she said confidently.

"Ah Paps, could you bring us some more meat and a bone or two for our peasant friend here Meda?" said Erik slowly and irritatingly. "That's a good fellow."

"Why do you speak to him as if he is a pet?" asked Andromeda.

"Excuse me peasant. Did he ask you to speak?" asked Sebastian.

"I do not need permission to speak," said Andromeda.

Vexia was horrified at all that had transpired. She did not want to open her mouth but she could not let Andromeda draw this much attention. She interjected before another word could be uttered by either party.

"What my new kitchen maid means is that we do not need permission to speak outside of the palace gates. We came only to retrieve some fruit for the Queen and we will be on our way. We ask that you kindly let us in to serve our Queen," said Vexia without directly looking at anyone.

"Now there is the voice of a woman who knows her place. Brava peasant," said Sebastian while clapping. "What's Meda short for anyway…Med-iocracy?" The boys laughed and stood to make room for the girls.

"Thank you, Paps," was hollered as the boys made their way down the block.

"Don't mind them," said Argos, or Paps, as the boys like to call him. "The tongue has no bones, but bones it crushes. Only fools who have nothing to say feel they have to say something. Come now and sit and I will get you what you need for the Queen."

"Thank you, sir," said Vexia.

Andromeda looked around for Alcaeus but she did not see any sign of him. Vexia chatted with Argos. It was the end of the workday and people were going home to their families. Argos' eyes changed subtly but Andromeda noticed. She followed his gaze to a husband and wife who were passing by with a young boy and a dog. She wanted to ask him something to break his sadness but she did not want to ask him about his wife since she knew she had gone to live in the stars.

She said the first thing that came to mind. "Do you have a dog?"

Argos smiled. "Why yes, I do have a dog. He is probably a very hungry dog seeing I've been here at work all day miss. I have heard the Queen has a dog. Is this true?"

"Yes, it is true. His name is Echo and I think it a perfectly horrible name because it never leaves her side long enough to bounce back to her."

Vexia laughed and said, "True miss." Andromeda and Argos joined in the laughter.

"I am closing shop now misses. Off you go with fruit for the queen and please take this small bone to her Echo," said Argos.

"Thank you, sir. The queen will be delighted," said Vexia.

Andromeda looked in wild wonder as to how a man with so little could give her dog a bone when he had clearly saved it for his own dog.

The next day Andromeda and Vexia accompanied her mother to town to have a fitting for her wedding dress. Andromeda convinced Vexia to wear two linen chitons to town just in case she could make an escape to find Alcaeus. They passed through the kitchen on their way out the door. Echo lay under the table chewing Argos' bone. This made Andromeda smile.

They entered the seamstress's home through the main entrance. She had two servants that bowed when they entered. They were shown into a common room with natural light that illuminated the mosaic murals on the walls. They were composed of dolphins being ridden by the sea god, Poseidon. The light bounced off his trident and Andromeda thought it looked like he could strike her down at any moment. Kallirroi, the seamstress entered the room holding the adorned dress. It was white silk with jade-colored gems along the veil, hemline, and neckline. The beauty took everyone's breath away. Andromeda reached for the dress and Kallirroi took her to try it on.

While she was gone there was another visitor at the door. One of the servants went to answer the call. He returned with the visitor just as Andromeda was entering the room to show her mother and Vexia the dress. The visitor was Alcaeus who came to deliver fresh bread and vegetables to Kallirroi. As Andromeda turned the corner, Vexia gave her a look and Andromeda realized why. She quickly placed the veil over her face, took a deep breath and let her mother oooh and ahhh over her. Alcaeus was in the entryway but he could have easily seen her if he moved any closer inside.

"Your market items, handpicked by my father," said Alcaeus.

"Thank you, sir. We are always so pleased with his selections. We have guests now but do you have time to come back later for tea?" asked the head servant.

Alcaeus tried to look around the servant into the common room but he could only see the form of a woman in a dress.

"Not today, I have an engagement with the theater tonight and I want to read about it before I attend," I will be back next week with your order. Please send a message to my father with any changes."

Andromeda's eyes widened as she looked to Vexia who shook her head ever so slightly in a definitive, no. Andromeda nodded yes and mouthed, *We are going*.

Cassiopeia and Kallirroi were too engrossed in the dress to notice anything.

"Kallirroi, you have outdone yourself. I have half-a-mind to wear it myself," said Cassiopeia.

"Do not worry your majesty, I have something equally as beautiful for you. Consider it a wedding gift," said Kallirroi.

She left and returned with a light blue silk chiton covered in gold embroidered leaves along the sleeves. Cassiopeia was elated and hugged Kallirroi. She was all set now for the wedding. Andromeda was invisible yet again as her mother consorted with the seamstress. They did not even notice when she left and changed back into her royal street clothes because they were discussing how her mother should wear her hair for the wedding. Vexia noticed how invisible Andromeda felt and lifted a layer of her chiton to reveal the other chiton. Andromeda eyes lit up and Vexia winked and mouthed, *To the theater my lady?*

# Chapter Nine
### The Third Meeting - Seriphos Island

THE NEXT WEEK when Scarpe and Perseus stood on the bridge, Scarpe flew down to meet Medusa. Pure joy echoed at the pond that day. There was splashing and diving and storytelling. The chapter of a wounded Scarpe was ending. No one needed fixing today. Time was theirs for the taking. They enjoyed every moment as if it were their last. As the day wound to a close, their thoughts turned to the next chapter. Perseus and Medusa lay on their backs with hands interlocked at their sides. Each looking straight up into the Perseus blue sky. Too afraid to look at each other for fear the truth of their ill-fated union would shatter their glass hearts.

"How do you know me so well, Medusa? You say what I am thinking before I can say it."

"We see the world the same way, I guess. I do not have the answers Perseus. I just know," she said with a shrug.

"It is like when you first looked at me, your heart jumped into mine and mine jumped into yours. They are trapped now. We have no secrets, only understanding," said Perseus holding Medusa against his chest.

His hands held up one perfect coil of hair against the setting sun. He examined every inch of her to understand her. He wanted to know how her chest moved when she took a breath and how her wrist bent when she signed her name. In three weeks-time, he had memorized the curve of her body as she lay in meadows next to him. Medusa had taken a vow of chastity but their connection increased so rapidly that soon clothing fell among the flowers and eyes peeked at sun-kissed skin.

Medusa looked too at the indentions above his hip bones and the many ridges in his calves. His body was beautiful but she could not get past his eyes most days. These piercing blues had such depth, such light and such love emanating from them that she would get lost. They told her everything she needed to know. He was enough. Simply

Perseus was simply enough. She wished away the days between each Wednesday. There was never enough time when they met. The moments together were long, but the hours were short. Most encounters they spoke of life, love, and loss. They played like children and marveled about how each one saw the world. They loved that they were brought together by Scarpe who seemed to weave the two even tighter together. They were a team of misfits, each more in love with each other than the next. Where one hand (or wing) ended, the other began. It was just that way. Eventually, they stopped fighting their connection and rested in the fated glory that they shared.

"I cannot leave you today, Perseus. I know you are thinking the same thing that I am thinking."

"That we have limited Wednesdays before you leave for Athens to live in Athena's temple," he said with resigned torment. "There must be a way. I will not stop trying Medusa."

"Do you love me Perseus?"

"I do. You know I do."

"Why do you love me?"

"I have no choice Medusa. I loved you before I met you."

"And I you."

Medusa's hand began to lower across Perseus' chest.

"I love you Medusa and I want to make love to you but I will not let you break the vow you have made to Athena."

"I will not break that vow but I will make love to someday when you take me for your wife. I will make love to you over and over with the stars as our witness and you will sing to me as we become one. Then I will know I am complete."

"I will find a way to make you, my wife. I cannot offer you a temple to live in, but I can offer you a lifetime of truth."

"And I cannot offer you a lifetime of physical beauty, but I can offer you my intent to find beauty in the most illogical things."

"Then I think we are tied," said Perseus.

"We are written," said Medusa.

They turned their heads to look at each other. Love filled their eyes and tears punctured their veils of strength. They could not live without each other. They would find a way.

# Chapter Ten
## Deceived - Seriphos Island

THE SUNRISE WAKENED the mountain's hazy slumber. Jagged rocks reached into the sea. Several jutted out from its depths creating a cascade of shadows across the still celadon water. The path Medusa walked was seldom used. She removed her sandals and let her toes sink into the sand. Her thoughts were on Perseus, they had been since he saved the crow. His name became her daily prayer. She must have whispered *Perseus* one thousand times into the sky hoping somehow, he could hear her.

They were meeting at the pond later that morning. Her eyes were fixated on everything and nothing at once. The sea gently caressed the rocks. A flock of birds flew overheard. White puffs of clouds hung in the sky, still sprinkled with pink from the sunrise. The world around her did not matter. Only the thought of seeing Perseus again did.

She made her way down the shore to the water. Medusa could not resist taking another look at her appearance before she met Perseus. She approached the sea and gazed upon her perfect face. She touched her cheek and smiled thinking about how it felt the last time Perseus touched her. Warm. She ran her fingers down her neck just as he had and felt the same warm feeling, he gave her. She laid her head back and let the feeling wash over her body. A soft "mmmm" escaped her lips as she traced his steps down her neck to her clavicle.

Medusa was snapped out of her Perseus trance when the water started to ripple. Shimmering green and blue iridescent lights started to emerge on the surface of the water. They made a circular swirling pattern and began opening small vortexes in the water. Gently, mer-creatures appeared, with scales that Medusa recognized as the one that Scarpe brought her a week ago. Light was coming from within their bodies. Long hair adorned with shells and jewels captivated Medusa. They raised large golden Conch shells and blew a melody that would haunt Medusa forever.

The sea parted and giant seahorses pulling a chariot sashayed a top a wave carrying Poseidon. His hair fell below his waist and the strength of the god could not be ignored. The circumference of one arm dwarfed the circumference of Medusa's waist. His trident glowed a blinding gold. Medusa shielded her eyes from its invasiveness. The seahorses stopped just short of the shore and the water calmed once again. Shells gathered themselves to form circles that created a stepping path from the shore to the chariot. Poseidon looked through Medusa. His thoughts were confirmed with insincere warmth. He made a grand gesture with his trident and the mer-creatures retreated under the surface. All that remained was Poseidon and Medusa and the path of floating shells.

He spoke slowly and paused between each word while looking her up and down.

"I saw you looking at your reflection. I would be looking too if I were as exquisite as you."

"I was just trying to see if my hair was too—"

"Silence," he said abruptly.

"Silence," he said again more calmly after he caught himself. "I saw you looking at your reflection miss….?"

"Medusa, priestess to Athena," said Medusa.

Poseidon did not waiver with that disclosure. His intention had been set.

"What if I told you I had something much more rare and shinier than the sea in my lair which you could use to see yourself how others see you."

Medusa hesitated. She knew she must obey a god or fear some sort of wrath, but which god? Athena was who she was bound to by the fates. Her choices seemed doomed. She would be punished for what was about to transpire. She could not see a way out, so she knelt on one knee, bowed, and reached her tiny trembling hand towards the chariot.

"Come and I will show you. I mean you no harm. Athena will be pleased by how I have helped make you even more beautiful to serve her." His voice was commanding, and he turned away from Medusa.

Medusa dropped her hand and was contemplating her options when Poseidon glanced back and said, "You are invited but you don't have to come."

With that line, Medusa stepped onto the first shell stone. The lights became stronger with each step until she reached the chariot. The entire vessel was decorated in gold and lapis blue oceanic designs. The grandeur of it all took Medusa's breath away. Poseidon took her shaking hand when she reached the side of the chariot.

"That's a good girl. Your time has come," he whispered in a song like fashion.

As she stepped onto the chariot, the lights dissipated. Only the trident lit the way through the darkness.

"Where are you taking me?" asked Medusa.

"To show yourself in a beautiful way . . . The way I see you." Poseidon's words were lilting and melodic, they hypnotized the intended listener with ease.

"Take me then. I will go," Medusa said with an expressionless face.

With a final gesture, holding the trident above his head, and humming the haunting mer-music, they floated just above the water and went through an opening of a rock in the sea and entered Poseidon's lair.

The chamber was empty except for a few fires lit on the side of the rock walls. A large bed floated in the middle of the cave. Poseidon had his back turned away from Medusa. He was putting a large oval shaped necklace over his head and held another in his hand. He laid that one on the bed and went to retrieve Medusa.

The terrified girl went without a fight. She knew enough to know what was about to happen. There was no point in screaming. He was a god and could have his way with anyone he chose.

She tried to make Poseidon see the error of his ways.

"Poseidon, may I ask please, is this the place I am to see my beauty? I must be back soon to sail to Athena's temple. Please let me see what you have brought me here for and let me be on my way."

He said nothing. He approached her and placed her next to the large mirror-like necklace. He sat her down on the bed and hooked it over her head. The size engulfed her tiny neck. She held it with two hands and picked it up to see herself in it. Two horrified eyes filled the space. The mer-music began to play again.

"Take your hands off that mirror Medusa. That one is for me to see myself. The one around my neck is the one for you to see yourself the moment I enter you and then you will know that you are the most beautiful girl in all of Greece as I have chosen you."

"No!" she screamed. "Please no!"

She turned to crawl over the bed, but she was indeed no match for a god. Her tore at her chiton and flipped her onto her back and positioned himself above her. He could see his face in the necklace she wore, and she could see her entire bare torso in the one around his neck.

"The one I wear is magic. It will capture your response to this blessed affair, and you can live in happiness knowing that I will be watching you for eternity. Why do you cry? Serving me is the greatest achievement in your worthless mortal life. At least this moment will make you immortal in a small way." He whispered that last sentence into her ear and he touched her. Not as Perseus had touched her. All she could think of was the crow being pinned down and attacked.

"Poor crow," she muttered.

"What did you say child?" hissed Poseidon.

"Ooohhh Po." Despite her predicament she was still quick.

"How dare you use a nickname instead of my full name?" He pushed harder. "I will let it slide this time as I am having fun inside you. I am glad you are enjoying yourself. Truly, I do not know any who have not, but you are the loveliest my dear."

With that he smiled at himself in the mirror and pulled out. He removed the necklace from her neck and whistled. A sea horse appeared from under the bed.

"Take her to land."

Poseidon stood looking at the mirrored necklace. He said nothing to Medusa as she whimpered onto the back of the cold unloving seahorse. They sailed through the sea, and she walked off an unrolled tail to land. There she wept in the dark and straightened her chiton and tried to fix her hair. So many thoughts swirled inside her head. She could not decide as to what to do next. She thought she saw a white owl and a crow in a tree. Was that Scape talking to Athena's owl? She was too traumatized to comprehend what she saw or what had just happened to her.

She gathered what she could of her mind and willed herself to move. With quickened steps she found a secluded place to cry in a field of hemlock. How long was she there? It felt like hours in that lair, but the sun was just peeking over the top of the mountains. The next thing she knew she was draped in sunlight, the heat of the day upon her. She felt her skin and tried to wipe off the memory of foreign hands that took her innocence away. Raised indentations on her leg showed fish-like scale marks. The strap of one of her sandals was not tied and the rope around her chiton was missing. She reached for a coil of curls and covered her face to hide the sight of her tainted flesh. No good. The smell of sea and god-like wrath filled her senses. Medusa sat directly up and scraped at her scalp. Her hair felt alive, and she wanted to rip it all out of her head. She placed some strands in her mouth to chew it off, but the taste of sea salt repulsed her. She raked her curls with her fingers and out dropped an iridescent scale. It matched the one that Scarpe had brought her weeks ago. This beautiful object that was once a precious gift, was now a demonic reminder of Poseidon. She tossed the scale into the hemlock and continued her inspection of her body. She ran her fingers across her neck and tried to think of Perseus. Just hours ago, her neck was warm with his memory, now her own flesh felt foreign. She traced the curve of her neck down to her clavicle, over her breast and onto her stomach. She felt a raised area. Her mind flashed to the lair.

*Poseidon removed the cloak covering his groin. His manhood grew like a cobra from a basket and inched towards Medusa. His eyes were closed, and one hand was wrapped around himself. The other held the trident. He picked the trident up and turned it upside down. The point was pointed just below Medusa's belly button. A surge of electricity raced through her body as he entered her with such force that her head was pushed off the edge of the bed. Her hair dangling off into the water below. He grabbed at her hair and wrapped it around his hands like reins and pulled her back into position so that he could see himself in the mirror. Her tiny body burned all over. She tried to move her hands over her face, but Poseidon released one hand from her reins of hair, grabbed the trident and used it to move her hands away. She tried to close her eyes but when she did, he used trident to pry them back open, forcing her to look in the mirror around his neck.*

Medusa gasped at the memories that were flooding her consciousness. She ran her fingers over the scar again and forced herself to look down. It was raised and red and hot to the touch. The shape of a trident burned into her flesh. She heard the mer-music, covered the wound with her hand and drifted into the depth of her mind.

Minutes seemed like days. She had no concept of time. At dusk, Scarpe flew in and landed next to her limp body.

"Scarpe, it was you. You found me."

She simply shook her head back and forth as giant tears fell effortlessly from those brown eyes fire lit with topaz. Even tears could not put out that light. Scarpe nudged her hand open and laid his head in her palm. *He knows already.* Thought Medusa. *The entire town will know by morning, and I will be killed for what I have done. Is it better to speak or to die? Should I just taste these hemlock flowers and spare my Perseus from shame?*

Scarpe bellowed a loud caw and Athena's owl appeared. The white feathers illuminated a soft halo around the entire body of the bird. Crow and Owl spoke then Owl turned and spoke to Medusa.

"I know this crow and he has told me what he saw. I will do what I can to save you from death, but I cannot predict what Athena will do. The wisdom that is always available to her is not always taken. She is a flawed deity, but she holds the title, and her words are the final word."

"Why would you help me, Owl?" asked Medusa.

"I have an affinity for crows," she said looking at Scarpe. "Go to your Perseus and tell him. I will bide as much time as I can with Athena." Owl lifted directly up into the air and flew in the direction of the temple.

"Can you speak too Scarpe?" asked Medusa.

Scarpe shook his head.

"But you can understand?"

Scarpe nodded his head.

"You know what happened to me?"

Scarpe lowered his head and cautiously nodded. He placed his head back in Medusa's palm. She caressed his feathers and thanked him.

"You are my hero Scarpe. Thank you for looking out for me. I think I have the strength now to find Perseus. Come with me."

# Chapter Eleven
## The Fourth Meeting - Seriphos Island

PERSEUS HAD A plan he would present to Medusa today. He would ask her and Scarpe to run away with him. The three of them could start a new life in a faraway world. He had survived being cast out in a crate as a child and he knew how to fight and sail. He would take them as far away as he could go. Africa maybe. Many Greeks inhabited that world. He had a plan for how much food they would need, and he had been saving money. It was enough for them to get through a few months. He could teach weaponry. He would work three jobs if it meant Medusa would be by his side. She was the other half of the yoke he needed. He knew she knew it too. He could see her love dance for him in her eyes every time they met. All previous memories faded after he met her. His life began in her embrace. There was no turning back.

He waited at the pond for hours dreaming of their life together. He wove a garland of flowers into a crown and kissed each bud after he placed it. He waited. He planned some more. He said her name aloud. The moon began its accent into the night sky. He walked up to the bridge and wished for the same wish he had made with her by his side when he tossed the double-headed eagle coin over the edge. He fell asleep on the bridge with the thought of Medusa in his arms. He awoke at sunrise. She was not there.

# Chapter Twelve
### Intentions - Patmos Island

THE GIRLS ARRIVED at the amphitheater to watch the tragedy. They climbed up and down the large semi-circular structure looking for Alcaeus. The theater was built in a section of trampled earth set into an exposed hillside. There were some stone benches for the wealthier patrons but tonight the girls would be sitting at the top of the cave far from the stage below. The backdrop was the valley full of olive trees, and beyond that, the sea. Andromeda, Meda for the evening, and Vexia walked down the aisle to leave their offering for Poseidon on the altar in the middle of the front of the stage. All shows were dedicated to a god and tonight's show was to honor Poseidon. The play tonight was a tragedy by Euripides, called *Medea*. They continued to walk up and down the aisle until the show began looking for Alcaeus. They spotted him and slid in behind him just as the setting sun lit the stage right on cue.

Vexia had never attended a show before. She loved the costumes and over exaggerated masks worn by the male actors. It was comical at times to see a man try and portray a woman. Watching theatrical performances was a therapeutic outing for Seriphonians. Often, attending the theater was prescribed as a cure for the soul. Vexia was transfixed on the performance and Andromeda was transfixed on Alcaeus.

Alcaeus wept when Medea pleaded for her husband Jason to keep her one more day before he exiled her and took a new wife. Andromeda thought to herself that Medea should have just taken Jason out right then and there and stolen the crown. As the play progressed, she realizes that Jason lives but Medea kills the new wife. Andromeda looked over at Vexia who was wiping tears away. She then sneaked a peek at Alcaeus whose cheeks were also tear-stained. She looked around and saw that the entire audience was in various states of despair over Medea killing the new wife. Andromeda did not feel like crying then, nor did she cry real tears when Medea killed her two children to hurt Jason. She faked just enough tears at the end and wailed just loud enough that Alcaeus turned around to see who was as distraught as he was.

"Miss, it is you. How is your mother?" he asked.

*My mother?* thought Andromeda. "Oh, thank you for asking, she is… (Wiping a tear away) better, I think. At least in better spirits."

The play ended and the crowd rose to their feet. A standing ovation ensued and still many people wept at the calculated cruelty of Medea. Andromeda started to stand as people were now exiting the theater. She faked a stumble and fell forward just within Alcaeus' sight. He caught her.

"Sit a minute miss and calm yourself. I feel a bit lightheaded myself after watching the play. Can you imagine the nature of a person that would kill their own children just to spite an ex-lover?" asked Alcaeus.

"I can, a little bit." She wondered if she should say more. "I mean he hurt her. He told her he loved her. He married her. He had children with her then he found someone better to elevate his status so he tossed her away. I would be furious as well."

"Would you seek revenge by murdering your own children? She poisoned four innocent people for nothing."

"Not for nothing," she quickly interjected. "She got revenge."

"She tortured them, the poison consumed their bodies as if they were engulfed in fire from the inside. This goes beyond revenge; death does not hurt anyone but the living."

"Exactly my point. Jason must live alone with the memory of all he loved dying in a tortuous way."

"My point is stronger, revenge is wrong," said Alcaeus.

"He was wrong. He should have been loyal to Medea and none of this would have happened."

Alcaeus thought about that for a moment. Andromeda watched him think.

Andromeda broke the silence, "The problem is they did not love each other. They never should have gotten married. None of this would have happened if they loved each other."

"Very good point." She baffled him. He did not know what to say next so he said, "I was amiss to not get your name the last time we met. I am Alcaeus."

"And I am Meda."

"Well, that is a bit ironic. Mind if I add an 'e' and call you Medea?" asked Alcaeus.

"I do not mind one bit. Medea won in the end, didn't she? Jason was left in despair and she rode off in a golden chariot to start a new life."

"Do you have time for a walk Meda?"

"Oh, so you want to walk with Meda, what happened to Medea?"

"I think I would rather take my chances with you Meda. I know who Medea is and I try and stay far away from ladies like her. She reminds me of the queen's daughter. I watched her play with a pack of boys last week. She taunted them like a cat plays with a mouse."

"I work for the queen and I can say I have never seen her daughter act anything like what you are describing. She is beautiful and kind and treats me as an equal. She sent me and my kitchen mate Vexia to the theater tonight. That speaks volumes about her character. Where is Vexia?"

She looked around and spotted her hiding in a bush at the end of the row. One hand reached out with its thumb pointing straight up. *Good girl Vexia. Thank you,* she said to herself. She had time now with Alcaeus.

The duo walked in the gardens leading up to the theater. There were people still lingering around and the fires that lit the walkways were burning. The summer sky was full of stars that helped light the way.

Alcaeus still had wet eyes. He always looked like he was about to cry or that he just finished crying. Andromeda was attracted to him as most were. He wore his hair pushed back from his face and sometimes it fell over his right eye. He would push it back and it would fall again. Andromeda watched him long enough during the show that she had his hair-fall timed. Every seventeen minutes, it fell and every seventeen minutes and three seconds she watched his hand run over his head and wished it were she who had her hands and body entwined in all parts of him. They sat on a bench and he instinctively leaned over and laid his head in her lap. She took an uneasy breath and then relaxed. This is what she wanted after all.

"Do you think it's possible to love another for life?" asked Alcaeus.

"I hope so," answered Andromeda.

"Have you ever been in love?"

"Have you?"

"I asked you first Meda."

"I've been in love with the idea of being in love."

He took her hand and placed it on his chest. Her fingers clasped around his. He brought their held hands to his lips and kissed them.

"There, we are sealed."

"Sealed to what?"

"Sealed with a kiss."

Thankfully, it was dark enough that he couldn't see her blushing. She loved the softness of his lips on her hand and longed to feel them on her mouth. She was uncomfortable feeling this much.

"That sounds nothing like love. It sounds like ownership."

She diverted and took back her hand. He just smiled and said nothing. Before she knew it her hand was stroking his head and her eyes watched him smile. She could have stayed for hours in that moment but soon the guards would be looking for her. She had to leave in order to have the freedom to come again. She stood up letting Alcaeus' head bump onto the bench. He stood rubbing the back of his head.

"Let me walk you home."

"No, I have an escort, Vexia. I am fine to make it home. I am staying with my family tonight and not at the palace. It is just around the corner. My father is waiting up for me and I do not think he would like it if I showed up with a stranger."

"I hardly think we are strangers now, do you?"

"I will answer that when I see you again."

"So, there will be an again."

With a sigh, she said, "Yes" and smiled and waved as she walked back to retrieve Vexia from her bush.

Alcaeus walked as if on clouds. It was the first time he had smiled a pure smile since his mother had passed. The fragrance of jasmine was more alive tonight and the stars above twinkled brighter. "Thank you, mother and good night," he whispered.

# Chapter Thirteen
## Messenger - Athens

ATHENA WAS SITTING in her dressing room while her three favorite priestesses brushed her flaxen hair. She was talking about how she wanted to have the temple filled with flowers for the arrival of her newly appointed priestesses for their first lesson. Medusa was going to join the group of her favorites upon her graduation. Athena had hand-picked her for her beauty and delicate nature. She was good at her core and therefore easily manipulated. She had entrusted Medusa's parents to look after her before her appointment as priestess. She only required those girls who lived outside of Athens to come to the island on days with crescent moons. Medusa should arrive in three days' time and had promised to bring pomegranates from Seriphos. They were known for their sweetness. Athena smiled at the thought of all she could use Medusa for. Hiding her beauty here in the temple was paramount for she feared the gods would see her and snatch her up for themselves. She was wise to have her sealed as a priestess at an early age she thought. Once she had her in her possession, she could do with her what she pleased.

A guard interrupted her daydream with a peasant woman by his side.

"What is the meaning of this intrusion?" asked Athena.

"My apologies my most honored goddess. Please, I would not come if her message did not concern something particularly important to you. She says she comes from Seriphos," said the guard, taking a knee and lowering his head.

Athena motioned for the woman to approach. The woman was visibly shaking. Her words skipped meaning as they left her lips.

"Say what you came to say woman," said Athena.

"It is Poseidon my goddess and one of your priestesses. I saw them two weeks ago." The old woman ducked and covered her head as if bracing for a strike.

"Poseidon? And whom? This is not possible woman. Be gone and never return or I shall have you assigned to slavery on the north shore," said Athena.

The woman was escorted out and Athena called for Owl, who was nowhere to be found.

"Send the guards out to find my Owl." *She will help me find the traitor*, thought Athena. "Wait," she said. "There is no need to find Owl. Bring up my chariot."

The priestesses looked at Athena as she turned away from them. Under her breath one heard her say, "The old woman was from Seriphos…Medusa."

# Chapter Fourteen
### Seeds - Patmos Island

ALCAEUS'S HEART LONGED to see Meda again. Joy filled his soul and spilled into everything he did. He chopped celery happily. He filled baskets into the night for patrons with zeal. He tossed the ball to Daniel, his father's dog, with gusto. He read less and wrote more. He used to write to his mother, now, his words are about Meda. He felt like she needed to be seen and he was more than willing to be the one to see her. All of her if she would have him as her husband.

"What am I thinking Daniel?" he said tossing the ball for the 50th time. "Wife? Who would sign up for this life? I live with my dad and have no chance of leaving anytime soon. Plus, I cannot leave him, not now that mother is gone. He would have no one. Well, you Daniel, he would have you." He rubbed the dog on the head and left the house to meet his father in the market area.

"Alcaeus, my boy," said Argos.

"Dad! Hi, today is going to be a great day!" He hugged his father with such force that Argos' feet lifted off the ground.

"Steady there, steady son. What has gotten into you? I feel you are a new person with a new voice. Gone is the brooding intellect. Am I wrong?"

"I cannot lie to you father. I feel as if I have new skin. It is lighter and ready to take flight. Where shall we go father? I want to take you somewhere you have never been."

"When do you propose we make this journey? We have patrons to serve and orders to fill."

"Please father, tell me, where do you long to go?"

Argos planted his feet firmly on the ground and a serious look came upon his face.

"Alcaeus, I wish to see the place where I first saw your mother."

Alcaeus looked at his father with deep sincerity.

"Where is this place father? I will take you anywhere."

"Then take me to Livadi beach tonight and I will tell you a story or two about your mother. I am ready to feel a happy memory instead of sadness."

Father and son walked arm in arm across Livadi beach. The tide was low and crabs crawled frantically across the rocks. Alcaeus was holding a torch and Argos held tightly to Alcaeus as they made their way across the uneven terrain of the rocky beach.

"Over there Alcaeus." Argos pointed to a rock formation nestled between the lanes of the tamarisk trees. As they walked, they saw hundreds of sea daffodils dotting the landscape in perfect large groupings. Alcaeus had never seen so many in one place. Even in the dark their yellow faces glowed out of their wine-stained petals.

"Stop, right here Alcaeus. This is the place." Argos closed his eyes and took a deep breath and smiled before he exhaled.

He stood with his eyes closed for some time. His mouth was moving but no words left his lips. Alcaeus tried to read his lips but he could not make out what he was saying. It did not matter. His father was happy and that made him happy.

Argos opened his eyes and looked at his son.

"Alcaeus. Your mother and I planted all these flowers. You see, this is the spot where I first saw her. I was walking up this path between the tamarisk trees and she was walking down. She was laughing and I heard the sweetness of her voice and looked to find its source. When I saw her, I thought she was an angel. I truly did Alcaeus. I did not think anything as beautiful as her could exist in this world. She was picking flowers, so I started picking flowers. I had never picked flowers before, but by the gods, I would if she liked flowers. So, I gathered sea daffodils and she did not notice me. I kept gathering them and I had so many that I could not see over them. I was going to have to be bold if I were going to have a chance with her and in my uncouth way, I thought by picking more than her she would be impressed. I was showing her my manhood by beating her. Ha. What a fool I was. She did not even like sea daffodils Alcaeus but she grew to love them as she grew to love me. I ended up tripping over a stone and my hoard of sea daffodils spilled onto the hill. She heard me fall and came to see if I was all right. My ego was bruised but I played it up. She was in front of me and I was not going to let her go.

"I think it is my ankle. I am sorry to ask but could you help me up?" She helped me up.

"Your flowers, let me gather them back up for you. She said, "My you have so many. Who is the lucky lady?" she asked.

"You," I said. "I told you I was going to be bold Alcaeus."

"Wow father, what did she say?" asked Alcaeus.

"She simply said, 'thank you' and we walked back into town together.

I faked a hobble every now and then. When we arrived at her home, her mother invited me in. I ended up staying for dinner. It was that easy. We were together every day since the first time I saw her, right here."

"But why sea daffodils if she didn't like them?" asked Alcaeus.

"Ah, you were listening. Well, I took her sea daffodils every time I went to call on her, I even brought her one hundred stems on our wedding day.

Before we married, she said, 'I have one secret I've been keeping from you since we met.'

'You do?' I asked.

'Yes, and you are going to be furious. I apologize in advance but I do not like sea daffodils.' I roared with laughter. 'You don't?' I asked. She shook her head and watched me laugh until she finally joined in. Just thinking about the sound of her laugh melts my heart. My Calista." Argos leaned down and plucked a single sea daffodil. He placed it in Alcaeus' belt then looked around the fields. Flowers were everywhere. "I brought her here every year on the anniversary of the day we met and we planted seeds of sea daffodils. What you see here is our handy work over forty years of being together."

"It is beautiful father. Thank you for sharing this memory with me," said Alcaeus.

"It was a sacred place for us. This right here is the spot I proposed to her. It is also the place where I gave her this." He pulled out a necklace. I made this for your mother. The metal was brought to me by an old crow with a chipped beak. Well, I am not sure he meant it for me but you know how crows like shiny objects?"

Alcaeus nodded.

"This crow brought me all kinds of things, mostly seashells but one day he left me a shiny piece of silver metal. It was not much bigger than a rose petal but it was large enough that I was able to make a crescent moon. I chose the shape because the night I met your mother here there was a crescent moon, just like there is tonight."

"I remember this necklace father, I used to hold it when mother had it around her neck. I wondered where it went. I was afraid to ask. Why have you kept it hidden?" asked Alcaeus.

"I wanted to keep it for myself but now I want you to wear it. I would prefer to see it around someone's neck that I love instead of tangled up in my pocket." He placed the necklace around Alcaeus' neck.

"Thank you, father. I love it."

"Now when you find someone you love, I want you to give it to her, even if she does not like sea daffodils. Nobody is perfect Alcaeus. Your mother was close. What am I saying, she was perfect. . . at least to me she was."

"I love you Calista," he said while blowing a kiss into the night sky.

Alcaeus could have sworn he heard the necklace say, "I love you too my Argos."

"Let's head back Alcaeus."

"Father?"

"Yes, son?"

"Can we carry on your tradition? Can we plant sea daffodils together to honor mother?"

"I would like that very much and so would your mother. You are so much like her Alcaeus. Especially your laugh. It was good to hear you laugh today."

Argos smiled with more joy than he had felt since Calista had died. Alcaeus smiled too and father and son walked arm and arm under the waning crescent moon back to their home and the sweetest new memory, one of joy, carried them off to sleep.

# Chapter Fifteen
## Found - Seriphos Island

I WAS NOT looking for love when I met Perseus. I turned towards the sun, and love was there. I went about my days as I had before my time at the lair. Every sense seemed heightened. It had been two weeks and I had avoided Scarpe and Perseus. Now, I stood in the middle of a crowd, yet I was alone in my mind.

I felt him before my eyes beheld him. I was bending down to pick up my basket and remember feeling the warmth of the sun on my hair. Athena had asked me to bring pomegranates to the next crescent moon lesson. I would leave in three days for my lesson. I was admiring their pinkish hue as I rose to my feet. The rays of the sun felt different as I stood and turned towards the light. The light warmed me from the inside out. I froze like a startled deer at the sensation.

A man's form was eclipsing the setting sun. His gait shifted Apollo's glow peeking out behind his head. As he walked towards me, the edge of the sun occasionally created a crescent shaped halo. The serpent-like curls of his hair cast dark silhouettes within the golden crescent. With every step he came more into focus. I warmed to the point of fainting when our eyes met. He was looking at me as if I were not made of flesh. I dared not blink for fear that this feeling was a waking dream, and I did not want to wake. A gust of wind from the sea brushed my hair across my face and awakened me from my sunlight dream. He was now standing directly in front of me. I thought I was moving my arm to brush the wind-swept hair from my face, but it was his hand that tucked my straggling pieces behind my ear.

"Perseus," I smiled.

"Medusa," he whispered, and the corner of his lips turned up. "Medusa," he said again, this time louder and his celadon blue eyes smiled along with his lips.

I held his gaze, and he held mine. In that one moment a lifetime of words was said without speaking. I looked at him and saw myself. He loved me. With all his soul, he loved me, and I knew I would never doubt that love. He was more of a man than any man I had ever seen. His size alone was daunting. I would have thought him a god, but his eyes told a different story. He cared. I knew he had seen the world through a different lens and that he was following a path meant just for him. What part did I play on that path? It did not matter, I would follow him, but would he let me after I told him?

"Perseus, my Perseus," Medusa cried through wet eyes as she wrapped her arms around him.

"Medusa what is troubling you? Where's Scarpe? Please, tell me what is going on?"

"We need to get away. Athena is going to have me killed," she cried.

"Killed, for what?"

"It's Poseidon," she said shamefully. "He tricked me into going to his lair. I was walking to meet you. I am sorry Perseus." She crumbled into a heap, but Perseus caught her before she hit the ground.

"Medusa, say no more. I cannot bear to hear it. You poor girl. I will take care of you. We will run away. You and me and Scarpe. I planned to ask you to take a risk with me on the bridge weeks ago. I have a boat packed and enough money for two months. We can sail to Africa."

"Sail? That is not possible. Poseidon will find me."

"Then we will find another way."

"There is no other way Perseus. We live on an island. The only way off is by sea. I am doomed," said Medusa.

"We will fight Medusa. I will fight," said Perseus.

# Chapter Sixteen
### Athena's Wrath - Seriphos Island

MEDUSA AND PERSEUS held what they did not know was their last embrace. The air was still. It was as if time had stopped. Medusa noticed first that no birds were flying overheard. No crickets were singing their summer song and the oleander trees stood at attention. Their boughs still. She held onto Perseus even tighter. He was speaking to her, but she could not hear what he was saying. She knew the time had come.

The wind began to blow in from the direction of Athens. The usually gentle sea swelled with waves that toppled into the plaza. The streets became filled as people emerged from their houses to see what was happening. The clouds toppled over each other growing larger and larger. The blue of the sky darkened. Through the dark, sunbeams pierced the black clouds and a golden chariot being pulled by two dark horses and one white horse was emancipated from the depths of the storm. Athena held the reigns. Owl was on her shoulder, wings in full expanse. Athena wore a helmet and carried a spear with a serpent wound about its shaft.

As the chariot descended, the people of Seriphos stood in awe. Gods and goddesses rarely visited the island. The horses' hooves touched ground and the chariot came to a stop. Owl's wings folded to his sides and Athena removed her helmet.

"I come for Medusa," she bellowed while striking her spear on the ground.

Her eyes darted and she pointed her spear in the direction of the onlookers. Medusa looked at Perseus and tried to pull away. He held her closer and shielded her under his cape.

Athena's wrath was growing. "Quod Obstat Via Fit Via!" she roared.

"The obstacle becomes the way," said Medusa under the cape to herself. She closed her eyes and said a silent prayer. When she finished, she looked at her hand wrapped in Perseus.' She closed her eyes again and bit hard and fast. He let go and she dashed out from under the cloak running towards the chariot. Before Perseus could stop her, she screamed.

"I'm here your highness!"

"You dare to address me as one of my priestesses?" Athena cackled. "Medusa, your transgression has broken an oath promised to me. You owed me a life of service but now I will take your life for what you have done."

"I did not pursue Poseidon. HE took me. I tried to run! I tried! I have always been loyal to you, Athena. Please, I beg you. I must live!"

She looked for Perseus in the crowd. Their eyes met. He did not move. He did not blink. He stood expressionless. This hurt Medusa more than Athena's promise of death.

"Silence child! Look at me!" said Athena.

Three strikes of the spear and the entire crowd froze in time. Athena approached Medusa. She towered over her. Owl flew in and landed on her shoulder. He whispered in Athena's ear. She nodded with closed eyes and a tight lip. Owl whispered more. She nodded again. When she opened her eyes, she spoke.

"You have betrayed me Medusa. I blame you but my Owl has interceded in the fate I wished to dispose upon you."

Medusa's eyes were wet, and her body trembled. She dared not look away from Athena but she could feel Owl looking at her and wanted to turn to see her familiar eyes. She tried not to blink and took shallow breaths. With every exhale her heart dropped. She thought for certain that it would escape her body and she would have to walk over it. She would not bother to pick it up. It was no use to her anymore.

The topaz of her eyes was fire-lit and the sight of her alone could topple any onlooker. Athena almost cracked when she looked at her. So beautiful this child was, but beauty would be her gift no more.

"What is to become of me?" asked Medusa.

"Watch Medusa and you will see. Look around you. All are frozen. This is a preview of your destiny."

Her spear struck the ground six times, and the townspeople unfroze. Their speechless looks mimicked each other. Athena placed her helmet on her head and pointed her spear at Medusa.

"Let failure be your teacher Medusa. I warn you all to run away for what I am about to do will have dire consequences for all who stay."

Some ran, some stayed.

A bolt of light exited the tip of Athena's spear. She moved the tip up and down Medusa's body slowly torturing her. Medusa began to writhe in agony. Her body contorted. Light entered her body from the tip of the spear. She looked for Perseus one last time. He was still standing in the same place and looking at her with hopeless desperation. The light turned her skin darker, almost swampy. Scales appeared. In place of hair, vipers grew. Gruesome vipers with thick scales and sharp fangs. They circled together on top of her head to make a living crown. Her once brilliant smile now fanged. Her fire-lit eyes, now only fire. Her body was lying on the ground, motionless. The crowd thought she was surely dead. Athena stood over her diminutive body and made a final circle around her with her spear of light. Owl whispered in her ear again but Athena shooed her away.

She bent down next to the lifeless Medusa and whispered, "Only a monster could do what you have done to me. I do not have to kill you today. You will be the most feared and hated person the world has ever known. You will misstep and someone will complete the task I could not do today. My Owl is wise but she is not a god. Today I chose Owl over my own will but make no mistake, Medusa. I will win. Remember this. I will win."

Athena got into her chariot, removed her helmet, and snapped the reigns. The horses whinnied and with a kick of the dirt, they rose, out of sight.

A man approached Medusa with trepidation, he inched closer until he was three feet from her poison looking body. Another man handed him the branch of a laurel tree. He brushed the branch against her leg. Medusa sat up and looked at her legs. They were covered in scales. She felt the laurel branch and looked up to see the source. The man gasped and turned to stone. She stood up awkwardly in her new body.

She looked around at the crowd and said, "Why do you look at me so?"

Mothers and fathers, sisters, and brothers stopped moving. A young girl hiding behind her now stiff mother peeked around the hardened folds of her skirt and looked directly at Medusa. She turned to stone. Her face marred with terror. Medusa was horrified as she realized that she had committed this atrocity on this child. It was she who had turned all these people. She began to cry. She looked around and each soul who looked her way changed to stone. The horror of what was happening solidified in minds. People scattered. Window shutters shut. Cries came from behind every door. Arrows loaded into bows.

"Run!" Medusa heard Perseus' voice.

She dared not look in that direction. *He does care.* She closed her eyes and ran.

Those that remained in the square tending to their now frozen loved ones bowed their heads, for eyes could not bear witness to what unfolded before them.

# Part II
Unraveled

# Chapter Seventeen
## Seen - Seriphos Island

MEDUSA STOOD BEFORE an innocent soul that was a victim of her new self. He arrived early that morning. He was looking for a place to hide as he had stolen apples from the market. Her cave was dark. She was sleeping. Her swamp-colored skin camouflaged her against the rocks. He rested against her and startled her. She rose to her feet and he stood looking at her with a fearful expression. Once their eyes met, he was no longer made of flesh.

She circled the stone figure, running her fingers over the once warm body. Her hand was cupping the cheek of the male figure.

"I wonder if the mind freezes like the body. My powers for good are gone. Are you in there? Is your mind fixated on what you saw before you turned to stone? Did you see me as a monster, or did you see the crack in my forced facade? Could you feel that I still loved, and that I would gladly turn myself to stone if it meant I could see my love again if only for a moment."

Her thoughts turned to Perseus. *Oh, my Perseus, I wish this were you standing before me, and your eyes could gaze upon me now, and I could gaze upon yours, and together we could turn to stone and have our fleetingly adored faces ingrained in frozen memory forever.*

"Did you know love in your life? Did you know pain? I have known both."

"I reached for Perseus as I was being taken away for an offense I could not define. He looked at me, but he did not fight. *Fight for me.* He did not move. I am sure others were there frozen in time as Athena ripped the life I knew from my soul. Maybe that is what happens when you are faced with watching something you don't understand? You freeze. You do not react. You watch the scene unfold as an observer, so you do not have to feel. How many times had I committed the same offense? Did I help every time it was the right thing to do or stand in silent contemplation at the horror that was placed before me?

"What the crowd witnessed was horror. Why do I not feel vengeful?

Have I accepted this fate? What needs to happen for anger to overtake me? I am in disbelief. I know I must be, but something inside me knows this is not the end for me."

Medusa reaches her hand up to run her fingers through her hair. She feels snakes and her eyes harden. She curls her hands around the base of the head of one. She uncoils it until its face is directly in front of hers. The snake has its eyes closed. Medusa taunts it.

"Even you, part of my new flesh, abandons me. Look upon my face. I do not think it is possible for me to turn my own self to stone. If I could, believe me, I would and you, my friend, may be better off as stone as well. I do not know what our future holds, but you, like me, have no escape now. I do not want to hurt you, but I will if you betray me. It is not my pure nature, but it is what I am becoming. Open your eyes."

The snake does not. If a snake could tremble, this one was.

Medusa's voice became elevated. "All of you nesting in a crown of fear uncoil yourselves and come before me."

Slowly the snake in her grasp opened its eyes and nodded without losing his focus on Medusa. The other snakes followed suit and slithered around each other to position themselves in front of Medusa's face. They shook in terror and jostled around like bobbers on a lake being pulled slightly under by a nibbling fish. Some with both eyes open and some with one and some with eyes like slits barely looking at her. Each, in their own way, complied. They took their turn locking eyes with her and each other. An unspoken understanding transpired between them. They were separate, but one.

"My only sin was my beauty. I have no control over the juxtaposition of my nose in relationship to my eyes nor the size of my waist or how rounded my breasts are. I have been called vain. I do stop at the sight of my reflection and contemplate my appeal over others, but I am not vain. Why was a gifted this look? The inside does not match the outside. I am like a fine silk chiton draped over a rabid dog that has gone mad."

Medusa placed the stone man outside of her cave. She did not need a reminder of what she had become. The hollow provided solace for now. Alone with her thoughts she missed her parents, her sisters, Scarpe and of course Perseus. She would give anything to know he was safe. He had yelled at her to run. He must still care. She hoped he would not come looking for her. She could not bear to see him suffer the same fate as the man outside her cave. She resigned herself to isolation. The darkness of the day and her thoughts overtook her and she slept.

She was awakened by the sound of flapping. She brushed the snakes out of her face and peeked around the mouth of the cave. It was her Gorgon sisters! She had never seen them use their wings. It was more than Medusa could take to see them outside of their childhood home and flying! She wiped the tears from her eyes and then covered them as they landed. Steno and Euryale approached Medusa with wings wide open. They wrapped themselves around their sister. One of Medusa's snakes whispered in her ear.

"Master, you may open your eyes for they do not have any."

Medusa grabbed the snake and brought it before her face. The snake nodded.

"Ask them if you don't believe me," said the snake.

"They cannot speak," said Medusa.

The snake recoiled to the top of her head. Medusa unwrapped herself from her sister's embrace and placed her hands on their shoulders and held them at arm's length and touched their faces. Sure enough, there were empty sockets that used to hold eyes. She hugged them again. She could not believe their sacrifice. She would protect them.

The next weeks were hard as Medusa navigated her new life but with her sisters by her side, she felt empowered. She told them all about Scarpe and Perseus but she never knew if they understood anything she said. Their speech consisted mostly of grunts and ahhh sounds. They listened to their sister and gave her a safe place to fall when thoughts of never seeing Perseus again crept up on her. At night they took turns going out to hunt for food and gather water. During the day they wove baskets out of willow and reeds. Medusa tended to her snakes. Sometimes she let one go out on the hunt with her sisters. While she slept, her sisters, Steno and Euryale kept guard. The snakes ate the bugs and mice that co-habituated with them in the cave. They had a symbiotic relationship. Hours became days and days became weeks. Time was not a friend to anyone in captivity.

Medusa's mind began to change. She sometimes thought about biting through one of her snakes. Her sisters killed so easily. Could she be more like them? She had always had such compassion for animals and lost souls. Would she cry now like she did at the sight of the tormented crow? Would she call for help or watch it suffer until its last breath? She thought about that often now.

"What makes someone a monster?" she asked her snakes one night when the full moon shone into the opening of the cave during its accent.

"We are all monsters to someone," a snake hissed.

"Are we? If so, aren't we also a hero to someone?" asked Medusa.

"You are a hero to one," a voice said that was not coming from her slithering crown.

"Who speaks? Where are my sisters? Why didn't they stop you?" asked Medusa.

The light from the moon blinded Medusa as she walked out of the dark cave. She saw no one. She looked to the moon and saw a winged shadow fly past. It circled over her head and landed at the top of the opening to the cave. Medusa whipped around ready to pounce. Her eyes softened and her talons retreated. It was Owl.

"Owl, why can you look upon me and not turn to stone?" asked Medusa.

"I arranged it so your curse cannot work on animals. I am an animal am I not?" said Owl.

"Yes, one that I am incredibly happy to see. Where are my sisters, Owl?" asked Medusa.

"I put them in a sleeping trance over there." The owl motioned with his wing to point out the sleeping Gorgons.

"Why did you come? Please, can you tell me anything of Perseus and Scarpe?"

"This is why I came, Medusa. Perseus is in trouble. The king will ask him for your head to save his mother. Your crow has a daunting task ahead of him as well. You can help them."

Owl looked at Medusa. She stood stone-faced.

When she finally blinked Owl said, "Trust the crow, look through his eyes and help him fly to the moon and back Medusa. This will lead you to safety."

"I don't understand, Owl? Why are you helping me?" asked Medusa.

Owl bowed his head and blinked several times. He looked deeply into Medusa's eyes before he said, "I have an affinity for crows. I want the crow to live."

Medusa called out, "I already helped him fly! Come back Owl!"

Owl didn't respond. With a glorious beat of his wings, he was gone. The Gorgons awoke confused as to why their sister was crying. They carried her to the back of the cave and positioned the snakes into a pillow for her head. Medusa stared blankly at the stalactites above her. The Gorgons went to their post outside of the cave and listened to the sounds of the night. The hunt could wait. They would not leave their sister tonight.

# Chapter Eighteen
## Peasant Gold - Patmos Island

IT WAS THE night before the wedding. Cassiopeia and King Cepheus were finishing the final instructions to the staff. After the wedding there will be a reception for the townspeople followed by an intimate dinner with the family. Firm instructions were given that no outsiders were to remain in the palace after the public reception. The bride and groom wished some time to celebrate their union in privacy. The staff understood. There had been no privacy since the engagement had been announced. Hundreds of flowers and gifts arrived daily at the palace. Most were thrown away by Cassiopeia except for the flowers. Andromeda's room was covered in color. Exotic flowers not found on Seriphos were her favorite. She loved an orchid sent by African royalty. Its green hue reminded her of her own eyes. She placed them by her bedside. She lay on her side looking at them.

"I have everything, yet I still feel alone," she said aloud.

Cassiopeia knocked on her door.

"Andromeda, may I come in?" She was carrying yet another bouquet of flowers but this one was wrapped in market paper.

"Yes, of course mama."

"I have one final delivery for you before wedding. I would have thrown it out due to the inferior wrapping but the servant told me that the man who delivered it had walked all this way in the night to make sure you received them before your wedding and well, the note is sweet." She read it out loud.

*Your Highness,*

*We send this gift not because of its value but because of its symbolism. My love for a woman started with a sea daffodil and our marriage was blessed. It is my hope that you will find as much happiness in your marriage as I did in mine.*

*In reverence,*

*Argos and Alcaeus Aetos*

"Sweet, isn't it? Who knew sea daffodils could ignite love? I always thought of them as more of a weed. Peasants can be so charming."

"They are not peasants; they are people just like you and me and they hurt and they love and they laugh and they give mother. They give just to give, not for anything in return."

"My, my, this wedding has you on your toes. I am simply saying we are fortunate to have our way of life. I cannot imagine being delighted over a sea daffodil, but to some, as we have learned through this letter, they mean the world."

"Don't you want to think more about things beyond your hair and wardrobe? Would it hurt you to look outside of your mirror?"

Andromeda rose from her bed and removed the green colored orchid from the vase on her side table. She walked to the window and threw them out. She then took the sea daffodils from her mother and gently placed them into a vase. She crumbled up the market paper but tucked the note into her nightgown as sneakily as a fox.

"Andromeda, what has gotten into you? Of course, I want to feel more. I do feel more. My desires are for you, my darling. Oh, I think I understand, you are nervous about our little plan for after the ceremony. Let me remind you, you have no choice but to go through with it. You will walk into the kitchen just before serving time to thank the staff for the amazing work they have done. They will be elated by your visit and bow most devotedly. When they bow, you will take this and sprinkle it on the meal for Phineus. You cannot fail me on this Andromeda."

Andromeda is lost in her mind. Her mother snaps.

"Andromeda! Do you understand?"

"I understand mother and I will comply on one condition."

"Do tell."

"After Phineus is dead, release me to marry whom I chose."

"Oh, I have already chosen Andromeda. You need not worry."

"What? Who? When were you going to tell me?"

"In one month, you will be sent to live abroad with the kind king who sent you the delightful green orchids you just threw out. Our kingdoms will unite and we will rule with more strength than all the other kingdoms combined. You will have everything you ever wished for."

"I do now and I am miserable mother." After a long pause, she reveals. "I love...," she stops.

"Another, who? There is no suitor worthy of you anywhere on the island."

"It does not matter. I am a prisoner in my own mind and you have always had the key."

"Take this boy you've met as a lover Andromeda."

"I do not think he will follow me to wherever you are sending me and I do not want him as a lover mother. I want him to plant sea daffodils with. I want to wake up and know that someone loves me for just being me."

"I love you Andromeda. I have done everything for you!" exclaimed Cassiopeia.

"You love what I can do for you mother and once I surpass you in beauty, you won't love me anymore."

"I have no fear of that my dear," she said through fearful eyes.

"You have made me to be just like you, mother. I know no other way. I will hurt you just as you have hurt me."

"There, there now my love, calm down. Mother has everything under control. I have saved you from having to spend the rest of your days with Phineus. You will have one kiss at the altar and be done with him. I am saving you from service at Athena's temple too where you would have no chance of being with this love you talk about. Do this one little thing for me tomorrow and I will see what I can do about keeping this pet you have found."

"He's not a…" she stopped. She knew when she was beaten. "You are right mother. If you can promise me a chance no matter how small that I can chose who I marry, then I will complete the task you ask of me."

"I promise you a chance," Cassiopeia said and left Andromeda.

When the door shut behind her, she whispered, "A chance in Hades."

It was ten hours before the wedding.

# Chapter Nineteen
### Willow Tree - Seriphos Island

DANAE AND PERSEUS were in the palace gardens. Scarpe was resting on a branch above them. Danaë had been alerted to the king's morning meeting and knew she had time to sneak away and find Perseus. She found him in the garden. Mother and son embraced without words and snuck under a willow tree where they would be hidden from the windows of the palace.

"My son, we don't have much time but I need to know that you are alright."

"I am mother, are you?"

"I am trying to be Perseus. Have you heard anything about Dictys?" Danaë's eyes welled with tears.

"I saw him fishing mother. He was casting a net over his head and I wished to be in that net again rescued by his loving hands." Perseus tightened his grip on his mother's hands and thought about the last hand he had held; her bite marks were still there.

"Ah this makes my heart happy Perseus. Just knowing he is alive brings me joy."

"I fell in love mother," said Perseus, running his fingers over Medusa's bite marks.

"In love? With whom child?"

"Medusa," he said. Crow shook his head.

"The monster that turned our friends to stone?" asked his mother.

"She is not a monster mother. She is like you, lovely and strong and intelligent. She loves with all her heart even in her darkest hour . . . just like you."

"Whatever she was, she is no more Perseus. She will never be what you want her to be now. You must understand."

"I can save her and I can save you."

"I cannot be saved Perseus and neither can she."

Perseus began to weep and his mother held him just like she had in the crate. A wave of conviction washed over Perseus and he stopped crying and sat upright and held his mother's face in his hands.

"I will not stop fighting for you. I watched how he treated you on the balcony and I cannot turn away from this injustice. He ripped your crescent necklace off your neck and with that, he took my childhood and he took the last of the old you. There is no turning back. The path has been set. If I die trying at least I tried. I will not let you suffer mother, nor will I let Medusa suffer. I will find a way. Trust me. You will be free to love Dictys again."

Danaë was now the one crying. She had never let Perseus see her cry before and it felt liberating. The child had become the parent and Danaë was relieved to pass the torch. She had raised him with all the love she had and he was now a man. Dictys taught him all the things she could not. He was free to choose his path. He knew what he stood for. He knew what he loved and he knew what he would fight for. She was worth fighting for and she wept out of gratitude.

# Chapter Twenty
## Mercurial - Patmos Island

AT FOUR O'CLOCK, Vexia helped the bride put on the dress that Kallirroi had made. Andromeda waited for her mother to come and help her with her hair and veil. At 5:00 she sent Vexia to check on her whereabouts. Vexia returned to say that an entourage was working on her mother's hair and that they would be here by 5:30. At 6:00, Andromeda held a sea daffodil while Vexia lovingly braided her flaxen strands and wove them around an exquisite golden crown.

"My lady, there is not a lovelier work of art in all of Greece. You are perfection," said Vexia.

She walked to retrieve the veil and placed it on Andromeda's head.

"The last time I wore this, Alcaeus was only a room away from me," said Andromeda.

"What were you thinking when you saw him that day?"

"I was thinking to hide."

"I saw this heartache before you first spoke to him princess. Your worlds are too different. He was never meant to belong to you. Phineus is a match for your status princess."

"My status? If you have not noticed, NOBODY notices me around here and Phineus is a fat beast," Andromeda said in anger full of hurt.

"I do miss. If I honestly thought it would fix your problems, I would switch with you for real tonight, I would," said Vexia.

"Why are you so good to me Vexia? I treat you like those boys treated Argos."

"We are what we know. I know nothing else," said Vexia.

Andromeda looked at Vexia in a new light. She hugged her and upon realizing what she was doing, she pulled away.

"My dress has a crease in it now. Fix it Vexia, before mother comes to take me. Tonight, is going to be torture. All I can think about is Alcaeus. Do you think one can endure any heartache if you feel loved? I feel loved by Alcaeus."

Andromeda says this as if to convince herself of something. Vexia watches her as she rubs her fingers over the petals of a sea daffodil. She sees the torment in Andromeda's eyes as she kneels at her feet and works on getting the creases out of her dress. She spends more time than necessary while she thinks of what to say next.

"Alcaeus loves Meda. Meda is not you, miss. I may be a servant but I have been a shadow in your life. I know this hurts you but you must let go of what you cannot change."

"Are you saying I am incapable of love? Tell me the truth Vexia. Who am I? I truly do not know. I want to escape out of that window and run to Alcaeus and tell him everything."

"But you won't because you fear once you get what you want you won't want it anymore."

"You do know me Vexia." A resigned Andromeda relents.

"It is all you have been taught. To take and move on. One dress. One pet. One flower…then the next and the next and the next. Once the new thing appears the love of the past loved thing fades."

"So, you think I do not truly love Alcaeus?"

"If you must ask the question, I think you know the answer. You want what you cannot have and the only thing you cannot possess is Alcaeus."

"When did you get so wise, Vexia?" asked Andromeda with a shaking voice.

"I have watched you make many mistakes. Today is not one of them. Go and marry Phineus and take your place in the world."

The palace bells were ringing. The temple would be full soon. Andromeda looked out of the window and saw her chariot waiting. It was covered in green leaves and white flowers. The horses' coats were shimmering and their bridles and reins were jeweled in jade green. Hundreds of torches lit the path leading to the temple.

"Vexia, look!" Andromeda's eyes danced.

Vexia gasped, "I've never seen it's equal."

"It is all for me! Let us find mother. I cannot wait here one more minute around those dreadful sea daffodils."

The opulence was shocking even to Andromeda. The halls were covered in white petals and white candles lined the walls. Garlands of exotic white flowers interlaced in green laurel wound around columns and arched over doorways. Once in the garden, the peacock sashayed between topiaries. Bunnies and lambs with green ribbons around their necks hopped about the white petals that had been sprinkled along the path Andromeda walked. Lilies floated in the fountains. Even the gardeners were dressed in linen and silk. They stood in two lines along the path and bowed as Andromeda passed. They were thrilled with how elated she looked taking in all their handy work. The vista was impeccable. In true Cassiopeia form, every detail was orchestrated to perfection. She was standing just outside the garden gates in her light blue chiton. The golden embroidered leaves were illuminated by the torchlight. Her hair was twisted in an elaborate way on top of her head. She looked more regal than Andromeda had ever seen her. *I will be just like her, only better, one day,* she thought.

"Mother." Andromeda curtsied.

"Andromeda, your beauty outshines even the brightest stars." She took Andromeda's hand, smiling. "Are you ready?"

"I am ready mother." Andromeda returned the smile.

The two entered the chariot and sat hand in hand looking straight ahead. Cassiopeia was thinking about herself. She could not bear to look at Andromeda again for fear that she was more beautiful than her tonight. Andromeda's thoughts skipped from the torchlights along the path, to her dress, to what else her mother could have planned for her. Her senses were overwhelmed. This is where she belonged. She felt stronger and more beautiful than ever before. The chariot stopped at the temple. Thunderous cheers greeted them. Andromeda stepped out of the chariot after her mother. When she did, the town simmered to a lull. Andromeda looked around and began to wave. The town awoke and joyful sounds filled the air. The more she waved the louder they cheered. It was exhilarating.

"Andromeda, that is more than enough, walk slowly, do not wave until we get to the temple doors, then turn and wave once more," instructed Cassiopeia.

Andromeda did exactly what her mother said. As she stood at the temple doors and turned to wave, she thought of nothing other than how this feeling filled her like nothing else had before. She was adored and adoration by many was better than adoration by one.

# Chapter Twenty-One
## Sight - Seriphos Island

KING POLYDECTES ROSE with a splitting headache from the drama that surrounded Athena's visit to Seriphos. Danaë was nowhere to be found nor was her man-child Perseus. He had to calm the fears that were rampant in his town after a known monster was on the loose. He was set to meet with his most trusted counsel at ten that morning. The five of them were impatiently waiting on the king when he arrived thirty minutes late without so much as a plan.

"Have you seen Danaë?" he asked.

"No, your highness. I have not. Have you looked outside the castle walls yet this morning?" asked his most trusted knight, Hector.

"How would I have done that, Hector? I came straight here after I rose from slumber. You called this meeting at this ungodly hour. What do you need from me?" asked the king gruffly.

"I, I mean, we your highness, we need a heading." Hector gestured to the other four knights in the room.

"The kingdom is distraught over Athena's visit. You must do something," said a dark-haired knight that was missing a finger named Linus.

"The town is outside the castle and demanding answers," said a chubby knight named Jason.

"Well, go and find this monster and bring her to me," said Polydectes.

"Sire, we lost nineteen men already this morning trying to find her," Alexander, a kind-faced knight chimed in.

"Nineteen! How?" asked the king.

"All eaten or turned to stone," said Linus.

"Eaten?" asked the king.

"Yes, eaten. We sent twenty men this morning to find Medusa and her sisters were guarding the cave where she dwells. These sisters are more sinister than Medusa your grace. There are two of them but they fight like a hundred men. They ripped the limbs off four men in seconds. The men had arrows and blades but none could compete with their strength or instincts. When the men at a distance went to draw a bow, they flew to them and ripped their eyes out and ate them before they could release the arrows," said Hector shaking at the thought of it all.

"Out of twenty men, only one returned. He said there were three that made it past the Gorgons and entered the cave. He was frozen in terror watching from a tree. In mere seconds he said he saw their stone bodies being thrown out of the cave and left in a heap at the door. The Gorgons grabbed the stone figures and flew with them to the sea and dropped them in. He stayed in the tree all night and just arrived in Seriphos this morning. It took him two hours to relay these events due to the terror he expressed while telling it. He shook and cried. He is resting now at home with his family," said Alexander.

The king sat in silence for a long time. He placed his hands on the table and said with resounding confidence. "Gather volunteers. We need all the able-bodied men of Seriphos who are not afraid to fight. We leave at midnight."

The men gathered around the gates of the palace. There were fewer than 50 men that were brave enough to show. Most Seriphonians only left the house now out of necessity after what they witnessed during Athena's wrath. Wives pleaded with husbands to stay back. Most listened. The palace guards could barely force them to fight after what they had seen or heard about the first group of men that had tried to reach Medusa. It was a small group but they were armed and ready. The men stood outside the palace gates for instruction. Torches lit their armed bodies and melee of weapons. The men were wearing bronze armor leftover from the war with Persia. Helmets, chest plates and shin guards protected them. Most had a bronze shield which would be their chief defense. The largest weapon was a ten ft thrusting spear with an iron tip and butt. Men on horses carried these. The least prepared carried sling-propelled pellets and doru and xiphos swords. Among the men carrying a sling was a boy who knew Perseus, Simon. The boys met during the hunt on Perseus' sixteenth birthday. They only saw each other once but what Perseus shared stuck with Simon.

*"I must say sir, your hunting skills surpass mine," said Simon.*

*"That is very kind, thank you. My name is Perseus."*

*"Yes, of course I know your name sir, you are to be the new son of*

*the king. My name is Simon."*

*"Ah yes, Simon, but I am not suited for royalty. I much prefer my time outdoors."*

*"I felt that when I saw you looking at that fisherman when we passed by the sea."*

*"I spent a lot of time fishing and hunting growing up. It has been a while since I fished."*

*"Perhaps we could go sometime and I could test your skills against mine?" offered Simon.*

*"If you are as proficient at fishing as you are at hunting, I fear I may win," joked Perseus.*

*"Challenge accepted," a puffed-up Simon said with a wink.*

During the ride back the two boys competed for the smallest of things. They raced from tree to tree, rode backwards until one of them fell off and told each other tall tales about wrestling wild animals to the death. Perseus and Simon laughed the entire ride back from the hunt. The boys planned their fishing expedition but it never happened. Once home, Perseus went back to isolation and dreamed of Medusa and how to save her and his mother.

When Perseus heard of the plan to slay Medusa, he made his way out to the palace gates where he saw Simon. He called for him and Simon came straight away.

"Perseus, where is your armor? Come join us. We can finally have a go at fishing after I beat you in slaying that monster. We can use her flesh as bait."

"You cannot! Simon, do you trust me?"

"Why yes Perseus, I do. What has you troubled? Where is my jovial friend with the fire to hunt?" Simon holds his sling and pellets up but lowers them when he sees a very different side of Perseus.

"I am not allowed to accompany the group tonight by order of the king, nor could I slay what you hunt. Simon, I know Medusa... I love her."

"What do you mean love? She's a monster that has killed many already. She's not capable of love."

"She is made only of love Simon. I know there is a way to change her back. I just need time to figure it out. Please don't go tonight. I could not go on if my only friend killed what makes me whole. We all have cracks in our soul but her cracks were inflicted upon her by Athena. I tell you before Athena's unjust punishment, she saw every broken piece of me and took the pieces I was afraid to show and held them and gave them back to me and said 'keep them' they are also parts of you I love. If you've ever looked inside yourself and felt the darkness you know that there is always light. There is still light in her. I implore you, Simon. I will bestow upon you any favor you ask in exchange for your promise not be the one that strikes her down tonight."

"I cannot promise what will happen in the heat of battle. A great love is worth fighting for but look around me Perseus. These men are also fighting to protect what they love. When the time comes, I will have to ask myself whose love is more worth dying for."

Perseus placed his hand on Simon's shoulder. Simon returned the gesture. They locked eyes. It was midnight and the king had appeared on the balcony to address the men.

"The threat to peace on our island ends tonight. Those of you who have shown the courage to fight the beast will be rewarded with a promise of gold and a lifetime of protection for your families. We are a people of strength and cannot let our ancestor's sacrifice during the war with the Persians be in vain. We must fight to protect future loss of life and restore this beautiful land we call ours to a time of peace. This can only be done through war, but this war men, is only against three women. You are fifty men. This is an easy fight. Are you ready?"

Victory cries of "Yes!" echoed off the palace walls.

"Then fight! The…time…is…now!" The king's commanding voice reached deep into the night. He pointed his hand towards the direction of Medusa's cave bellowing; "Fight, Fight, Fight!" The men charged off into the night, Simon brought up the rear questioning the role he would play tonight.

〰〰

The battle cries waned as they approached the area known to be where Medusa was hiding. The night sounds diminished the closer they got. Crickets were not humming. Double-headed eagles did not fly overhead. The nocturnal jackal and wild goats were not grazing. The wolves did not howl. The stillness made the hair on the back of their necks rise. Simon thought how odd it was to feel a chill when the heat of summer was still upon them. With each step closer, Perseus' words haunted him. What they were approaching felt like evil. He looked at his fellow fighters and saw terror behind their stoic faces. He decided to look only straight ahead until the end was clear.

Mist rested in the valley. The men made their way through, slowly losing sight of each other. Only the flickering torchlights could be seen under the weight of the translucent blanket of fog. The sightless journey crept along. Every step seemed longer than the last. Fearful anticipation took hold of the men. Midway through the valley, they put out their lights to conceal their approach. The next leg in their journey would be in total darkness. They had one obstacle left once they emerged from the hollow, the climb up the hill towards their enemy.

Medusa was sleeping and the Gorgons guarded the cave. They had already finished their hunt and were feasting on deer. Without sight they did not see the men approach but they smelled their horses and took position for a fight. The snakes awoke from slumber sensing unrest. They left their sleeping host and slithered into the night past the Gorgons.

"Separate and search. The air smells of harm," said one snake to the rest.

The snakes went in all directions down the hill. One signaled the others when the group of men was found and they silently approached the slow-moving caravan of fighters. The first to fall was a horse that was bitten. The rider was spooked and slashed at the horse; blood spilled into the night. The cries and blood drew the Gorgons who attacked from the air. Every man on horse was destroyed in an instant. The now unmanned horses retreated into the valley. The remaining men took shelter where they could find it. The snakes found them by heat and strangled or bit them in silent death strikes. The screams began and arrows and pellets flew. Medusa awoke to the sounds and sensing a chill on her head she reached and realized her family of scales were missing. Her only friends inside of the cave were gone as were her sisters. She ventured outside into the night air. The smell of blood rushed through her veins. She could see wings flapping in the distance and her instinct for sisterly protection kicked in. She moved with lightning speed that caught her off guard but it was exhilarating. She toppled over trees on her way to save her sisters. Her strength was otherworldly, so was her rage. She used the pain inside to fuel her quest. It was liberating. The Gorgons sensed her approach and grunted in both concern and delight. Together the three were unstoppable. Men fell or turned to stone. Medusa's snakes returned to their host and wound themselves into an impenetrable living crown. Their reunification bought some time for men to flee. The women were unconcerned with the cowards. There were still warriors to defeat in their midst. A wave of silence filled the land. Those that were gone did not suffer. Death by Gorgon was swift.

Simon lost sight of the group ahead of him. He was trapped. The only way out left him exposed to his hunters. He held tight to his sword and his sling and pellets. He felt a shiver through his entire body. He froze in fright. A female figure stood before him. He closed his eyes and braced for death.

"He loves you," trickled out of his mouth as Medusa made her first kill by ripping his eyes from their sockets and eating them.

She then slashed him through the heart and decimated his hollow body with teeth and talons. Every ounce of pain she felt she hurled onto the flesh of Simon. When her ravaging stopped her heart heard what blind rage could not see.

*He loves you.* She heard it over and over again and then she began to see what Simon had seen.

*A hunting trip flashed before her eyes, there was Perseus on horseback. Then again, Perseus at the palace gates. The look on his face was painful to see but the words she heard hit her hardest.*

*"She is made only of love Simon. I know there is a way to change her back. I just need time to figure it out. Please do not go tonight. I could not go on if my only friend killed what makes me whole. We all have cracks in our soul but her cracks were inflicted upon her by Athena. I tell you before Athena's unjust punishment, she saw every broken piece of me and took the pieces I was afraid to show and held them and gave them back to me and said 'keep them' they are also parts of you I love. If you have ever looked inside yourself and felt the darkness you know that there is always light. There is still light in her. I implore you, Simon. I will bestow upon you any favor you ask in exchange for your promise not be the one that strikes her down tonight."*

These visions faded from her mind but the words lingered. She had killed and she knew she would do it again. She would try not to look at what she had done. Only pieces remained of the boy she now knew was named Simon. Perseus' friend was nothing now because of her. The only light was the knowledge that Perseus loved her. He had said it this very night. Would he know it was she who killed Simon? She took an un-launched pellet out of his sling and carried it home stepping over the bodies of headless or stone men and vowed to kill no more.

# Chapter Twenty-Two
### The Task - Patmos Island

THE CELEBRATION WAS over and Andromeda and Phineus left the temple as husband and wife. All eyes were on them; they were the epitome of royal elegance. The month leading up to the ceremony had given a new purpose to the inhabitants of Patmos. Cassiopeia saw to it that every resident felt as if they were a part of the wedding. She had even hired peasants to work the private dinner for the newlyweds. The palace staff would be given the night off since they too deserved a break after the month of arduous work leading up to the wedding. Even Vexia would be released for the night after dinner. Andromeda only needed her to help her change out of her wedding attire and into something more appropriate for poisoning someone.

Andromeda had forgotten all about her mother's task, until that fat troll Phineus whispered into her ear during the ceremony.

"Today, I make you a queen. Tonight, I make you a woman. My hands will be on what you hide under that silk in hours," he whispered.

Andromeda wanted to gag with the smell coming from his mouth. It was a mixture of rotting guts and stagnant swamp. The stench matched his demeanor. Even silk and gold could not hide the visual and verbal atrocity that was him. She could not wait to poison him.

When Vexia removed the layers of silk and jade, Andromeda took them from her and tossed them into a corner.

"Bring me my dinner dress Vexia and take that reminder of today laying in that corner out and burn it with the other rubbish."

"Yes, my lady. Do you need anything else before I go?"

"No, thank you Vexia," said Andromeda.

"Thank you, queen."

*Queen* thought Andromeda. *Yes, I love the sound of that.*

"I hear the dinner chimes," said Vexia.

"Wait six minutes and we will head down. Now that I am queen, they can wait on me. I do not need to scurry down like a tamed rat to please them."

Andromeda knew her mother would cover for her. She would do anything for her tonight if she wanted her parchment wrapped gift to find its intended recipient. Her mother did not need to know that Andromeda would strangle Phineus with her own bare hands tonight if the poison failed to work.

Vexia waited outside of the intimate dining hall until Andromeda gave her the cue to go. The only closed door to the room was the one to the kitchen. The others were flanked by draperies that could be open or closed. Tonight, they were closed. The king and Cassiopeia sat at the ends of the table and Phineus and Andromeda were at the center with their backs to the kitchen. The only other guests were the king's sister, Jerica and her husband, Oscar and the queen's parents, Queen Crysabel and King Orane.

The group's mood was casual. A stark contrast to all the pomp and circumstance of the day's events. A carved statue of the bride and groom stood at the center of the table surrounded by fruits and nuts and cheese. Andromeda laughed when she saw the statue, the artist had cut off a good portion of Phineus' belly. She looked over at him just as he was shoving in a handful of cheese. She rolled her eyes. Jerica broke the casual conversation between the small groups with a toast.

"To my brothers King Cepheus and King Phineus, may your rule expand beyond Patmos. We all know a good man is only as good as the woman behind him. If Andromeda proves to be a force even half as strong as yours Cassiopeia, then the people are in capable hands."

"I'll raise a glass to that," said King Cepheus. "My wife and my daughter have won me great favor. Their beauty opens many doors."

"But one's beauty only opens a door; it cannot buy it," chimed in Cassiopeia.

"Gold is the true king," said King Orane.

"I prefer to wear it than fight for it," said Queen Crysabel.

The dinner guests all laughed.

"Some things are worth fighting for," Andromeda spoke out of turn and all eyes were on her.

"What things are you talking about my bold, new queen?" asked Phineus.

"I know . . . She is going to fight you for your—"

"No one is going to be fighting for anything," Cassiopeia

interrupted Oscar.

In her opinion, he shouldn't be allowed to speak. Nothing noble ever had left his lips.

"The bride has had a trying day. We are family now. We should feel free to make errors without retribution. Come with me Andromeda, before the meal is served, let us go and thank the kitchen. It will give them a thrill to see the bride in person."

Andromeda followed her mother. As she took her hand, she felt something…parchment. When they exited the dining hall, her mother locked eyes with her and both nodded. Cassiopeia stopped just beyond the door. Andromeda cracked open the last door that led into the kitchen. What she saw devastated her to her core. Argos.

She looked back at her mother and then forced herself to re-play the words that Phineus had said to her at the altar…My hands will be on what you hide. She said to herself over and over…*It will be done, it will be done, it will be done.* She opened a corner of the parchment paper. She put her shoulders back. She smiled with radiance and pushed down any feelings she had about anyone. Rage, she kept and stored behind her smile. Rage against her mother and Phineus would fuel this task. She opened the door and walked to the table that held the plates. Argos and his three helpers were putting on the finishing touches and were so engrossed they did not notice her entry.

"It smells heavenly. If it tastes anything close to as good as this aroma, I cannot wait for it to enter my mouth," Andromeda said with quiet enthusiasm.

"Your highness!" they gasped and curtsied.

"Please rise, and show me what you have prepared," said Andromeda.

"We hope it is to your liking. We have sea bass for every plate, with tarhana and arugula drizzled with olive oil and asparagus picked fresh just hours ago," said Argos.

"It is lovely. What else?" gushed Andromeda.

A young women said, "Over here I am making carrots and right over there are the plates that are about to go in."

"I have made the bread to go with the cheese and fruit your highness. We have figs and grapes, raisins, and pomegranates," said another young woman.

"And I oversee the seasoning. Your meal will be dusted with fresh coriander, oregano, mint and saffron and thyme," a young man said proudly.

"It's all glorious!" said Andromeda.

"We welcome your approval," said Argos as he motioned for the staff to begin plating. "We have one more surprise."

"I adore surprises," said Andromeda.

"A special arrival meant only for the happy couple." Argos brought out freshly prepared eels. "These are delicacies that arrived moments ago. They came from a messenger from Lake Copais. We prepared them with care."

He placed the eels on two plates alongside the seabass. The plates were ready to enter the dining hall. Andromeda had only moments to spare.

"Thank you for making my day so special," she said.

"It has been an honor," said Argos. The kitchen staff nodded in agreement.

Andromeda was right in front of the plates meant for her and Phineus. She made a grand curtsy and when she did the others returned with bows. Andromeda rose quickly and sprinkled the eel on one plate with the substance given to her by her mother. She tossed the opened parchment under the table careful not to touch any residue. The task was complete.

"Thank you," she said as she left the kitchen.

"I hope you have a long and wonderful marriage," said Argos.

'I strive for quality over quantity," replied Andromeda.

"Then my wish for you is that he brings you as much joy as your visit to us has," Argos said with another bow.

Andromeda smiled and met her mother outside of the curtains leading to the dining hall. She took her mother's hand and squeezed it tightly. A sign to confirm the question before she could ask.

Cassiopeia opened the curtain and said, "The meal is complete. Let us all prepare for its arrival."

Phineus was salivating at the thought of the meal. Andromeda sat next to him and placed her hand on top of his.

She whispered. "I have been thinking about what you said and I feel ready for what lies ahead tonight."

Phineus placed his other hand on top of hers and gave her a knowing look. Little did he know that his fall to the ground filled her thoughts and not the fall of his clothes.

Servants stood at the side of each guest and placed the plates on the table in unison. The plates with eel were in front of the bride and groom. The servants returned to the kitchen. When they arrived, they wiped sweat from their brows and hugged Argos. Alcaeus was at his side. He had returned from checking on their dog, Daniel, at home.

"Alcaeus you missed the new queen, she actually was standing right where you stand," said one of the young ladies.

"As Apollo shines, so did she," a young boy said dreamily.

"It was as if she was one of us," the other woman replied.

"Well, I am sorry I missed all the excitement. I met the queen a few months back. Do you remember father? She sat at our corner in town and enjoyed the company of a few of the boys. I am sure they are wallowing in sorrow tonight after missing their chance at the altar." Alcaeus grabbed a carrot and took a chomp.

"You also missed the fly," said one of the women.

"Yes, it landed on the eel right after the queen left."

"I had taken a bow of reverence and heard it buzzing next to my ear, I raised my eyes ever so slightly to follow its path but the buzzing stopped and I returned my gaze at the tile floor. Thankfully, the queen did not see it stuck there in the eel. Luckily, I saw it before it was taken out to the bride and groom. I was able to rescue its sticky carcass. I wrapped it in a piece of parchment I found there under the table and tossed it in the rubbish outside. Can you imagine? Our reputation would be destroyed if the new groom ate a fly because of our carelessness. My fingers are still sticky from the darn thing." Argos licked his fingers and the group laughed.

It was a joyous day.

Inside the dining hall the exuberance was contagious. Phineus had cleaned his plate and most of Andromeda's. He was thrilled to hear that she did not want to try the eel. Andromeda kept her palate to the scores of breads and fruit under the mis-represented statue. She thought she should just go ahead and topple it over as a kind of foreshadowing for what was to come. Cassiopeia's eyes darted between Phineus and Andromeda and then the king. Echo joined the party and sat on her lap. She sneaked tiny bites of food to him.

The king told stories from victories past and everyone pacified his need for attention. King Orane mentioned the matter of the monster, Medusa over on neighboring Seriphos. Everyone shouted names of people they would like to see turned to stone.

"The cobbler, now there's a man that would have more personality as stone," laughed Cassiopeia's mother.

"His wife too," said her father.

"Wasn't this Medusa girl vowed to Athena?" asked Jerica.

"Yes, she was set to leave this month. Poor girl, she thought herself beautiful enough to surpass Athena is my guess," said Cassiopeia.

"I hear she is guarded by the Gorgons that eat anyone who approaches."

"Remind me to send a message to Seriphos that Patmos is wishing them the best in their fight against these monsters. We can send weapons to help," said the king.

"That is very kind of you my darling," said Cassiopeia. "Has anyone seen Echo?" Echo had disappeared from her lap and that was usually a cause for great distress but more was on her mind tonight. Echo could wait.

Phineus began to sweat. Andromeda noticed it first. His fork was still making its way from the plate to his mouth. He did not chew his food. He swallowed each full bite in its entirety. The thought of what was going on in his stomach made Andromeda sick. His fork was stacked so tall that morsels fell off onto his lap. With every bolt of laughter, the scraps bounced off his lap onto the floor. The mice are going to have a feast tonight, thought Andromeda.

"Ahhhhhh! Help please!" The cry came from the kitchen. Andromeda recognized the voice and stood to go.

"Let the men go my dear," said Cassiopeia.

"I'll go," said the king. "Carry on, this should only take a moment. The cooks are probably fighting over the leftovers."

When the king entered the kitchen, Argos was laying on the floor with his head in Alcaeus' lap. Sweat was seeping through his clothes. Alcaeus was removing his father's hat and unbuttoning his shirt.

"Bring me some cold water," he calmly demanded. "I am here father; I will not leave."

"Alcaeus, I see you. I see you son," Argos said as his eyes slowly closed.

Alcaeus was silent. He stroked his father's head and placed kisses gently on his cheek. He placed his head on his chest. There was a heartbeat. Relief came over his face.

"What happened when I was gone? Does anyone know anything?" asked Alcaeus.

"He was jovial. He was strong. He was good Alcaeus. He complained of nothing," said the boy who oversaw seasoning.

"Ahhhhh," Argos moaned.

"Father, I am here." Alcaeus turned to the boy. "Will you help me get him up?"

A scream came from the dining hall. The king froze at the sound of his wife's voice. Cassiopeia flew into the kitchen. She was holding a limp Echo.

"Which one of you did this to me!?" she hissed.

Rage filled her eyes as she shook Echo in front of the faces of all who were in the kitchen. Andromeda was two steps behind her.

"I will find out and you will pay for this!"

Andromeda looked confused. She had never seen her mother out of control. She did not know what to do. She was so concerned with her mother and Echo that she did not notice Alcaeus on the ground with Argos. Her eyes darted around the room several times before what she saw registered in her brain.

*No, no, no,* she thought.

Andromeda left her mother in the kitchen with her father, the king. She closed the door and leaned against it with a face full of regret and uncertainty. She bit her lip and reached into the depths of her soul to find the strength to walk away from Alcaeus and Argos. With one foot in front of the other, she returned to the dining hall.

"There's been an accident in the kitchen," she said.

No one heard her speak. No one cared what she thought. The chaos in the dining hall surpassed the chaos in the kitchen. Crysabel was blaming Phineus for Echo's death.

"You dropped so much food under the table with your horrid eating habits that the poor dog gouged himself to death."

"Cassiopeia was feeding that thing from the table. She is the one that killed that white ball of fluff," said Phineus.

He coughed and crumbs flew out of his mouth. Andromeda shuddered at the sight. More screaming came from the kitchen. Andromeda grew more anxious wondering if Argos was all right. She wished Vexia were there so she could send her in to ascertain the situation. All she could hear was her mother carrying on about Echo. She interrupted the debate between Phineus and Crysabel about who killed Echo.

"Phineus dear, would you go and check on mother and father in the kitchen? It would mean the world to me." She stroked his arm as she spoke.

With hesitation, Phineus replied, "Why yes, of course I will. I can check on desert while in there."

When Phineus entered, the kitchen help was bouncing off the walls trying to dodge accusations from Cassiopeia. The king was trying to console his wife. Alcaeus and the boy were holding Argos up. He was conscious and with great effort and assistance, he was walking out the back door. Phineus walked around the prepping table grazing on the piles of leftover scraps.

"Do you need help, Cepheus?" asked Phineus.

"Send everyone home. We have a dog to bury."

Phineus went to reply and the words would not form. He stood there, mouth agape. The room started to tilt. He grabbed onto the table for support.

"Are you alright brother?" asked Cepheus.

"Wedding jitters, I think. You take care of Cassiopeia and I will close the dining hall."

Phineus informed the guests that the kitchen staff was fine. The man who had prepared the meal fell ill and startled the staff. He was headed home and was expected to make a full recovery.

"Goodnight and thank you for the gift of your company. My wife and I will continue our celebration upstairs."

Phineus bowed to the table and extended a hand to Andromeda. She stood reluctantly and placed her hand in his. It was clammy and her tiny hand looked horrible against his pudgy fingers. She smiled and curtsied to the table. She and Phineus walked hand in hand up the winding stairs to the honeymoon suite. The candles were still burning along the carpet of white petals. With every step Andromeda crushed the petals smearing them into the cold floor. She imagined each one was Phineus' face. They made it to the top of the steps and turned right down the hallway. They did not speak but the monologue inside Andromeda's head was rampant.

*Fall…die…choke…bleed…now please…you pig faced baffoon…I can't do this…I hate you mother…you didn't account for the size of this beast when you got the poison…I could push him down the staircase…I could jump myself…end this now…not one more step…you must fall…she promised me that you will fall…*

The door opened to their room. Phineus closed the door. He removed his sash and wetness filled the space where the sash had been. His entire body was covered in sweat.

"Phineus?"

He did not answer.

"Phineus?"

Andromeda waved her hand in front of his face…no reaction. She smiled at him.

"Time for bed darling."

She let her dress slide off her shoulders, revealing unblemished skin. Phineus did not react. His eyes were glazed over and fixed to one spot. She squealed.

"You can thank my mother. Oh wait, I will have to. You will not be able to." She said the last line poignantly while poking his chest.

Phineus slumped to the ground. Andromeda walked around him slowly watching his labored breaths. She counted to one hundred. She applied olive oil and water under her eyes. She removed her sandals. She pinched her cheeks. She opened her eyes and rubbed the edge of her chiton against them so they appeared red. She tapped his body with her foot. She grabbed a satchel full of servant's clothing to change into to find Alcaeus as soon as possible. She flung open the door and screamed.

"Help! Help! Phineus has fallen!!!"

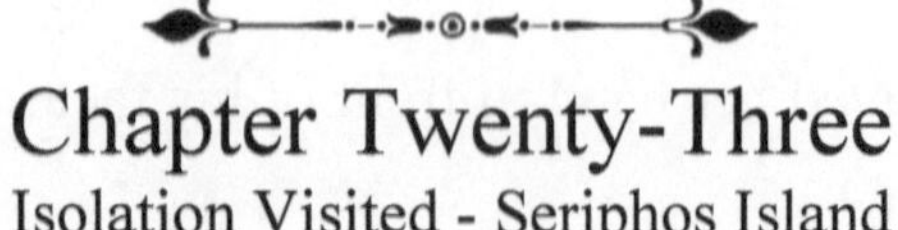

# Chapter Twenty-Three
## Isolation Visited - Seriphos Island

MEDUSA WAS USED to her sisters causing a ruckus. They would howl and chirp and growl at anything that came close. They understood each other. Medusa had no one that understood her. She became increasingly isolated, rarely venturing out of the dark recesses of the cave. She also cared less if her snakes untangled themselves from the hair on her head. They got annoying sometimes, always writhing about eating bugs and mice here and there. Their chomping and digesting made noises so close to her ears that she started humming to block them out. Medusa could not bear to eat the meat her sisters had brought home. Cooking the meat was not an option. Fire would send a signal alerting more men to their location. Her snakes would bring her fruit but she missed the fresh goat milk and fish from home. She missed many things from home. Most of all Perseus and crow. She hoped they were together. The thought of them brought her both comfort and pain. The more time she was alone, the more she became accustomed to her new life. She soon began eating the spiders and roaches that shared her domain. Her sisters would eat anything and they never got sick. Her snakes ate centipedes and scorpions and they never got sick either.

"I'm more like a snake than a human these days," said Medusa as she brought her snakes down from her head.

She laid them on her chest and touched their cold skin. She too had become cold. She could not remember the last time she felt hot. She could not remember the last time she felt cold.

"I myself am stone," she said to her nest of snakes. "At least you have each other. I have no one. I never will. I know not my limits. How am I defined? I think now as if I am entirely a new creature. I almost forget I was human."

She laid back on the ground and reached a hand to the earth. She took a handful of dirt and slowly let it fall through her grasp like an hourglass.

"Time is a horrid beast."

When the last speck of dirt fell, she rested the back of her hand on the cave floor and gently opened her fingers. Her mind swirled to a memory. She saw Perseus swimming towards her with a crow on his shoulders. Then there was Perseus at the top of the bridge making a wish with a coin. She could not remember the sound of his voice but she could feel him and she could feel crow in her hands. Gnawed on wet feathers, then dry feathers. She could smell him. She wished for Perseus' blue eyes to look at her like they did that first day when he handed her crow. She remembered what trust felt like. She remembered what hope felt like. She remembered what love felt like. She went to close her hand into an actual fist when she awakened from her daydream. She hurt and she wanted to hurt something. Her hand closed on…feathers? The cave was so dark, she could not see and she was afraid to move too quickly in case her sense of touch lied to her. She felt a head nuzzling her palm and she moved her ring fingers over the head and down the beak. She felt two tiny chips.

"Scarpe? Is it you?" she asked.

More nuzzling. She picked him up and moved towards the mouth of the cave where there was some light coming in. As she emerged from the shadows, so did the outline of a bird with dark wings. She raised the crow and held him to her chest. His feathers tickled her neck. The Gorgons moved swiftly to her side sniffing the crow in her hands.

"Sisters, this is a friend. I helped save him from certain death. We know each other. Do not harm him. Do you understand me?"

They nodded in agreement and went back to gnawing on the bones of the boar.

"How did you get past them?" she asked Scarpe.

Scarpe tried to gesture with his wings and caw his story but he could not make Medusa understand that he had flown to the top of the mountain and walked with such trepidation that even a field mouse could not hear him. He waited at the top of the cave until the Gorgons returned from their hunt. Once they started eating, he dropped onto the ground behind them and into the cave. He was not too worried about them eating him since his slight body made him nothing to be trifled with compared to the boar they were feasting on. He entered the cave as carefully as he had walked down the mountain. Every step revealed something new about Medusa's new home. There were so many insects that the walls seemed alive. Shadows scurried across the floor. His sight failed as he traversed into the deep abyss of the cave. The last thing he could make out was a small pile of bones along the rock walls. The deeper he went, the colder it got. The only sound came from the water dripping off the stalactites. He put one claw directly in front of the other until he could hear breathing. Medusa was lying on the ground. He inched closer without breathing until he touched her. It was her hand he ran into. Her palm was open. Scarpe blinked twice. It looked like home. It smelled like home. He placed his head in its familiar shape, said a prayer that she would recognize him, held his breath, and waited. All worry faded when she ran her fingers along his chipped beak and recognition set in.

"It doesn't matter, you are here!" Medusa said while kissing the top of his head.

Scarpe flapped his wings and tugged at her chiton with his beak.

"What is it, Scarpe? Are you trying to take me somewhere?"

The crow opened his chipped beak and made a chirp.

"Please, take me," Medusa said as she placed him on the ground.

She nodded to her sisters to let them know she would be safe. Scarpe hopped to a spot not too far from the top of the cave. He had placed what he brought there just in case he was eaten, trying to get it to her. He had hung it on a branch that he thought would be at her eye level. He hoped that she would find it if he could not give it to her. Luckily, he was not an appetizer tonight for the Gorgons. He flew to the branch and jumped up and down.

"Scarpe, what? I do not know what you want me to do?"

Scarpe jumped harder and the gift fell. Still Medusa did not see it. An exasperated Scarpe flew off the branch, onto the ground and picked up the gift with his beak and flew directly in front of Medusa's face. He was transfixed by her eyes. Her iris's looked more like a diamond shape now. The fire-glazed topaz that shone out from them before was amplified. He dangled the necklace back and forth until it registered in her memory. It did not take long; her eyes renewed their color and glowed when she saw what he was holding.

"Put it around my neck Scarpe. Vipers move to help him."

The snakes coiled as tightly as they could to her scalp and Scarpe flew above her head and gently placed the necklace around Medusa's frail neck.

"Perseus. Perseus. Perseus," she said his name and wrapped her hand around the crescent shape and kissed the tip. "Moonlight feels like home on my lips." She held back tears and Scarpe gave her this moment.

Now that his mission was complete, he had time to really look at her. He did not like what he saw.

She was thin, skeletal thin. The bones in her hands and wrists looked as if they had been sucked dry like the carcass the Gorgons were working on. The crescent moon fit perfectly inside the hollow of her collar bone. The bones were so pronounced, it looked like the crescent was resting inside of a full moon. At the end of her fingers, were talons, larger than those of the double-headed eagles that ripped at Scarpe the day they met. Her once rose bitten lips were gray and small fangs rested on the bottom lip when she sealed them closed. Her dark symphony of curls replaced by snakes the color of olives with eyes as fierce as Hades himself. This gift brought her a sense of hope. Scarpe was overjoyed to see some light escape her darkened heart. He could not make sense as to why this diminutive broken body, that once held the heart of Perseus so perfectly, now only held the reign over nine heartless snakes.

"I wish you could tell me the story of how you came to acquire this necklace Scarpe."

Scarpe nodded and then shook his head then nodded and nudged her mouth with his head.

"Ahhhh, I remember now, you can understand me."

The crow nodded.

"Yes! Scarpe, did Perseus give you this necklace?"

Crow nodded and shook his head.

"So, he didn't give it to you?"

Crow nodded.

"Did you find it?"

Crow nodded excitedly.

"Did Perseus lose it?"

More nodding from Scarpe ensued.

"Does he know you found it?"

He shook his head.

"Is he looking for it?"

He nodded his head.

"Then take it back to him."

He shook his head.

"Scarpe, is he in trouble?"
He nodded his head.
"Take me to him!"
He shook his head and made an "X" with his wings.
"I will be killed?"
He nodded.
"Does he want to see me?"
He nodded.
"I want to see him too. Is his mother all right?"
He shook his head. Medusa gasped.
"Can he help her?"
He nodded and then shook his head.
"Can you help him?"
He nodded his head.
"Can I help him?"
He nodded his head.
"How? Tell me how, I will do anything Scarpe."
The crow looked puzzled and then started scratching in the dirt. He drew a sundial and then made a series of sun shapes over and over along a half-moon shape and then a small moon.
"Time?"
He nodded.
"I should wait?"
He nodded again and flapped his wings.
"How long do I wait?"
He hopped back and forth along the half-moon shape and pointed to the sky with his wings.
"How many days?
He looked up to the sky again and pointed to the rising moon. He held his wings out in full span and then closed them until there was only an inch between the tips of his wings."
"Wait until a small moon?"
Scarpe nodded. Medusa looked at her necklace.
"A crescent?!"
Scarpe shook his head.
A defeated Medusa looked at the scratched-out image and rubbed her forefinger and thumb over the silver crescent around her neck.
"Scarpe, I have it! The Solstice! My birthday!"
Scarpe flew to her shoulder and rubbed his head against her cheek.

"Thank you Scarpe. I have something to hold onto now. Do you have to go?"

Medusa could feel Scarpe nodding against her cheek. More words would just prolong the inevitable. She took him in her hands and held him in front of her eyes. She turned him from side to side to look into each eye.

"The Owl visited me as well."

Scarpe tiled his head.

"He told me to trust you. He did not need to tell me that Scarpe. I always have and I always will. I love you."

She kissed his head a final time, lifted her hands to the sky and loosened her grip. Scarpe flew towards the stars. He circled her three times and headed towards the town of Seriphos.

"Caw, caw, caw," he cried.

Medusa stood and watched him go until she saw his obsidian feathers fade into the night sky.

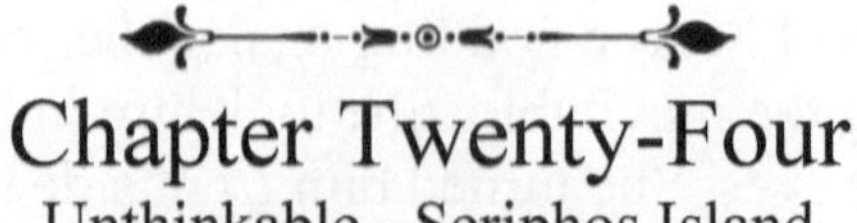

# Chapter Twenty-Four
## Unthinkable - Seriphos Island

PERSEUS WAS IN the palace when all were summoned for a proclamation from the king. He walked down the halls feeling eyes upon him which was not uncommon but today it felt weighted. He knew he needed to brace himself for something, he only hoped that something had nothing to do with the safety of his mother. He made his way into the great courtyard and took his place in the back of the enclosure. King Polydectes and his mother entered from a balcony. Danaë was dressed in a light pink gown. Her hair was pulled back in a low chignon. Golden combs in the shape of eagles decorated one side. She looked so different than the mother he knew at their home with Dictys. There her hair flowed freely and the only adornment she needed was the wind blowing it away from her perfect face. As a child he liked to be held on a windy day. The breeze grabbed the long strands and they looked like a cape flowing behind her. In his mind's eye they flew away together sailing on wind that caught the imagined cape. His mother's eyes searched the room for him. They landed perfectly upon his and both hearts rested at the sight of each other.

"My people, today I have gathered you here for an announcement worthy of a kingdom-wide celebration. Please make way for the palace guards," said King Polydectes.

The crowd dispersed to the sides of the hall and the gates opened. A hoard of men marched into the space covered in armor. Horses pulled wheeled cages full of wild beasts. There were lions and wolves. Their paws swiped through bars as they passed. The crowd murmured suspiciously.

"I bring you a new army made up of prisoners from the islands of Patmos, Kos and Leros. Their kingdoms have sent the men and the armor to help us end the terror of Medusa."

The crowd began to cheer. They stomped their feet in unison. The army pounded their spears on the ground. The sound reverberated off the palace walls. The pounding and the animal sounds overtook Perseus' senses. His mind swirled.

"I vow to put an end to this monster and restore a sense of peace and hope to our land. Our neighbors are feeling the unrest as well and fear she may escape Seriphos to terrorize their islands. If any man wishes to join, we welcome you. These forces will be training on palace grounds. They will be working with the animals that came as a gift from King Cepheus of Patmos. They arrived on boat all the way from Africa last night. With man and beast, our enemy does not stand a chance."

The crowd cheered and more stomping ensued.

"During the next few weeks, I invite you to bring your children and admire the animals and watch the daily battles in preparation for the war we will unleash on these women. Our men will bring back the head of Medusa and her sisters. When they do, the palace will celebrate with a wedding."

The crowd hushed to curious whispers.

"My Danaë and I will wed as a symbol of optimism and a vow of our love for each other and the people of Seriphos. Together, our union will be a beacon of hope for all to see. A light after the darkness of Medusa."

"Hooray for King Polydectes!" yelled a spectator.

The rest of the spectators joined in celebration. The Salpinx blew in unison, a feast was brought in and all but two celebrated in joyous merriment. Perseus fought his way through the crowd to the king.

"A word your highness?" It was more of a statement than a question. "Alone."

On Danaë's persuasion, the King agreed. The men retreated to a smaller chamber. Two guards were positioned at the doors.

"What brings you to seek my counsel, Perseus."

"I cannot let you marry my mother nor can I let you slay Medusa."

"I just made a promise to the entire kingdom, Perseus. The army is set to train and in three weeks they will make another attempt at slaying the monster. As for your mother, she will be my wife."

Perseus paced around the room. His torment was palatable.

"If I slay Medusa, will you release my mother?" Perseus asked.

The King laughs condescendingly. "But of course, Perseus. If you bring me the head of Medusa with no help from the palace, no armor, no horses, no torches, and no map, I will give your mother back to you."

He slaps Perseus on the back and guides him to the door.

"If you fail, your head belongs to me…if you still have one after your visit to Medusa. Good luck Perseus. You are going to need it."

Before Perseus could say another word, the guards surrounded Polydectes and walked away. Perseus held his head in his hands.

"What have I done? I have dammed one love to rescue another. Oh, Dictys, I need your help," he said to the excitement filled air.

The festivities lasted until the wee hours of the night. Perseus watched from a distance and searched his mind for a way to free his mother and Medusa. Every thought ended with somebody dead. Most likely him. Simon's words echoed in his thoughts. *When the time comes, I will have to ask myself whose love is more worth dying for.*

# Chapter Twenty-Five
### Eschewal - Patmos Island

"**M**EDA, YOU ARE all I have left. My father is one step closer to joining my mother in the stars and I have nothing but a place to sell food and this. He pulls a necklace out of a satchel tied around his waist. I used to wear this necklace but the dreams it gave me were too much for my heart to take. It was my mother's. Holding it while she held me is one of my first memories. My father asked me to give to someone I loved. I feel I am looking at its new home. It is time to start making new happy memories. I would be honored if you would be my wife and wear this necklace as a symbol of our love."

Andromeda's trembling hands are comforted by Alcaeus.

"There is no need to fear my love. I am here and I will take care of you. I see you, Meda. Please let me place this around your neck."

Andromeda nods and lifts her hair so Alcaeus can fasten the necklace. When it is clasped, he holds her face in his hands and kisses her gently on the lips. Andromeda holds one hand on the necklace and looks down. It is made of silver and in the shape of a crescent moon.

"Will you marry me, Meda?" asks Alcaeus.

"I cannot. I am not who you think I am. I love you Alcaeus but…" She takes his hand and takes him to the alleyway where Vexia is waiting tied to a tree and wearing royal clothing.

"Who is this, Meda? Have you kidnapped a royal?"

"No Alcaeus, I am the royal. This is my servant, Vexia. I have deceived you. I am the daughter of Queen Cassiopeia and King Cepheus. I am Princess Andromeda."

She removes her head covering and moves her sleeve up her arm. Her upper arm is pure white, she has never worked in the sun. She brushes off the dirt she intentionally placed on her arms. Bone white. The part of her hair covered by her cloth is shiny and clean, not like the ends which she had covered in earth.

Alcaeus looks at her in disbelief. He now places her at the wedding dinner.

"Phineus…you?" Horror fills his eyes. "My father. You were there. You did nothing. He may die! You saw me holding him in your kitchen and yet you looked away from him and from me! In my darkest hour you abandoned me. Even a stranger would have done more. They did do more. Your kitchen staff even…Arrgggghhhh…on all that is true and holy…Med…Andromeda, how could you?"

A new realization washed over him.

"Your mother is not sick! I consoled you on lies. Shame on you Andromeda. I wish I could have seen you for what you truly are before I fell in love with you. You are a monster and unworthy of my love."

Andromeda reaches for him with eyes full of tears. His eyes are full too but he backs away unwilling to let her touch him.

"Stay away. AWAY with you and keep that necklace, I do not want it back since it has touched the skin of a traitor. You have tainted my mother's memory and my father is near death because of you and your unblessed wedding."

"I only got married so I could be with you Alcaeus. I had to do it to be free. Don't you understand? I have no freedom as a royal, not like you do. I cannot go about freely loving who I choose. I must serve in the capacity best for the monarchy and you were not on their list of qualified suitors. You must see this as a path. Now that Phineus is dead, I can choose my partner, and I choose you. I do Alcaeus. I choose you."

Andromeda is convincing but Alcaeus is wounded.

"I only see the truth Andromeda and your truth is all lies."

Alcaeus rips the satchel that held his mother's necklace off his waist and throws it on the ground. He backs away from Andromeda clutching his hands over his heart. In moments he is out of sight. Andromeda falls to the ground at Vexia's feet.

"My lady, you surprise me. I thought you were playing sport with this boy but I can see you do care about him."

"Of course, I do. What did you all think? I would not have you sneaking around switching clothes with me every week for fun, Vexia. Do you really think I enjoy frolicking around in these linen rags?"

Her attempt at channeling her inner princess is met with more tears. She cannot stop the truth from escaping her soul. She thought these feelings must be love. Maybe she loved him as much as her mother had loved Echo. Maybe more but the truth of her love for him was revealed when she could not bear to lie once more. He loved her and she caused him pain. She would find a way to win him back.

# Chapter Twenty-Six
### Argos - Patmos Island

"**M**Y SON, TAKE me to the daffodils. I wish to die there."

"You are not dying father," said Alcaeus.

"Please," Argos said as he squeezed Alcaeus' hand.

The grip was weak and his skin felt thin against Alcaeus's firm hand.

"Anything for you father."

Alcaeus lifted his father from the bed. Argos groaned in pain. Alcaeus cradled him in his arms and walked towards the door. He kicked it open and Daniel followed his masters down the cobblestone streets towards the sea. It was nearing sunset. The days were long. The summer solstice was fast approaching and Alcaeus would turn seventeen. He thought about his life as he carried his lifeless father. Argos weighed nothing. He had not been able to keep anything down since the wedding three days ago. He regretted going to check on Daniel. If he had been there this would not have happened, he thought. He played the scene over and over in his mind.

"Alcaeus. Did the dog recover?" asked Argos.

"The dog is fine father. Daniel is right here. He is skipping right alongside of me just like you will be in no time."

"No, not Daniel. The queen's dog, Echo."

Alcaeus knew the dog had died and he knew his father had to have heard Cassiopeia ranting that night in the kitchen but he must have forgotten.

"Ah, the white pup. Yes father, the pup is in good hands."

"Ah good. Please send a bone with her kitchen girl next time she comes to town," said Argos.

"Which kitchen girl father?"

"There is a golden-haired girl who always has red eyes. She is kind to me."

"This girl father…do you know her name?" asked Alcaeus.

"She made me laugh one day. She stood up for your old man against those boys with the cruel words."

"Did she tell you, her name?" asked Alcaeus again.

"It starts with an M. something like Meta. No, that is not it…Meda. That sounds right. Yes, Meda is her name. I gave her a bone for the white dog." Argos's voice was weak.

"Rest father. I promise to send a bone with Meda."

Alcaeus was tormented by this story. He tried to push the idea that Meda was anything but pure evil out of his mind but he trusted his father. Argos knew good people when he saw them. His intuition was something that Alcaeus admired. His father never questioned his instincts. If he thought you were good, you were good in his eyes and nothing could change it. He had seen something in Meda. Alcaeus had as well. He forced himself to stop thinking about Andromeda. She had betrayed him and when his father recovered, he would tell him the story of the real Meda. All that mattered was getting his father to the daffodils so he could ease his mind. He hoped that taking him there would in some small way help with his recovery.

Daniel led the way up the hill to the spot where Argos like to sit when they went for walks. Alcaeus found the rock his father had shown him as the spot where he first met Calista. He gently knelt and placed his father on the ground next to a full patch of sea daffodils.

"Thank you, Alcaeus. I can smell your mother from here," Argos said with closed eyes.

Daniel laid down next to Argos and took a large sigh. Alcaeus simply sat and waited for his father's next request. Argos was quietly breathing in and out. Alcaeus watched his chest go up and down. His eyes constantly searching for a sign of need. He had brought water and some food and of course a seed to plant. He was waiting for the right time to plant the seed with his father.

"Alcaeus?"

"Yes, father."

"Will you leave me for a moment?"

There was a long pause and then reluctance.

"I should not – but yes, of course I will father. We can watch the sunset from the beach when you are done. I will walk down and find a spot for us. I will be back in less than ten minutes."

"That would be perfect my son."

Alcaeus walked slowly down the hill towards the sea. Daniel

looked up but stayed with Argos. Alcaeus tried to hold onto hope but tears were escaping his locked lids. They seeped out and fell to the ground, he tried to position himself above a sea daffodil when they fell so at least they were not wasted. He could use his pain to feed the flowers that brought his parents together. His vision was blurry when he looked out over the water. The sun was still bright but low and glistening over the water. It looked like diamonds being skipped over the gentle waves. He reached for his mother's necklace and remembered it was gone. Thoughts of Andromeda filled his head. The tears fell faster into the sea. He was far from the flowers now. The sea doesn't need any more water, he thought. He let his mind drift to a future with Andromeda. Could she love him like his mother loved his father? He knew he would have loved her with all that he had and poured his life into giving her everything. He knew the moment she challenged him after the play and then so effortlessly ran her fingers through his hair like she had been doing it for years. Her touch was electrifying, knowing, and loving.

"Andromeda, how could you have lied so profoundly," he asked the sea. "I loved Meda. The heart of a man in my profession could never belong to a princess. Our star was blighted from the start. So why did I think in poetry when I was with you? Blue was brighter. Night was lighter. Hearts succumbed to thoughtful gaze. I would have stayed in your love. Mine has yet to wane. Now I look out to the sea and question this pain."

"Woof! Woof! Aoooohhhhh!" came from the hill. Alcaeus ran with the speed of Hermes to his father. Alcaeus was fine. He was sleeping but Daniel continued to whimper. Alcaeus looked around and made out a female figure in the shadows under a tree. She was bending over and looked to be planting something.

"Stay here Daniel. Watch over father," Alcaeus said while patting Daniel on the head.

Alcaeus walked towards the figure. Her back was towards him and she was digging. There was a golden satchel on the ground and a horse tied to the tree. The horse's saddle was embossed with the markings of the palace. When she turned around, the crescent moon around her neck caught the sunlight. Alcaeus stiffened.

"What are you doing here?" He was half angry, half happy to see her.

"I'm planting seeds." Her eyes were red, not from dirt this time but from grief.

Alcaeus watched her as she took seed after seed and covered them with dirt. She was relentless in her task.

"I'm sorry Alcaeus."

She planted a seed, and another, and another. He did not respond. He looked at her inquisitively. She kept planting. Her hands were dirty from digging in the earth. Her hair was tied up high on her head. Wisps fell and blew away from her face. They looked like lashing tongues, thought Alcaeus.

"Stop Andromeda."

"I cannot stop. He sent me sea daffodils for my wedding. It was my favorite gift."

She was sobbing and planting. "When they died, I went looking for more. We did not have any on the palace grounds. I wanted to plant the seeds from the dead flowers but my mother would not let me since she considers them weeds, so I went looking for them and found this hill. I brought the seeds from the flowers he sent. I wanted to plant more so that I could share them with someone I loved someday and tell them the story of the poor man who gave my mother's dog a bone instead of his own dog and walked in the night after a long day of work just to give a spoiled aristocrat a gift for an ill-fated wedding.

I never dreamed that my actions could have caused him or you so much pain. Forgive me Alcaeus. Forgive me. He is the only profoundly good person I have ever met. It hurts me to know that I caused this. I would switch places with him if I could."

"I want to forgive you Andromeda. I want to love you. I want to believe you. I do. On my fragile heart, I want to hold onto to you. I wish it were you I loved but it is only the thought of you. You are not who I shared secrets with at the theatre. The woman I loved would have run to me not away from me that night in the kitchen. Yes, I know you were there. You say you love me. You say my father was good. You turned away. You cannot save yourself from what I saw with my own eyes."

"What could I do to change your heart?"

"Save my father."

The words were inaudible but Andromeda knew his heart's desire. The two looked down at the ground too hurt to move. Too uncertain of what to do next. Too broken to speak another word. Too blind by grief. Their trance was broken by another bark. Alcaeus and

Andromeda looked towards the sound of the bark but it was not near Argos. Daniel had moved and what he was chasing was unexpected. There above the field of love-planted sea daffodils soared a glorious bird whose details in legend paled in comparison to what flew above them. The translucent wings were in full expanse. The bird's shadow washed over Argos and then over Daniel. The double-heads moved in unison surveying the land. Their beaks, a golden color, blended with the setting sun, the bird made a grand bank against the crest of the hill and circled around back towards the star-crossed lovers.

Alcaeus motioned for Daniel to return to Argos. The pup obeyed. Andromeda and Alcaeus watched in wild wonder as the Albino flapped three glorious beats and floated down into the field of sea daffodils.

"Alcaeus, the legend. You can save him."

"I would rather rip my own arm off than kill that majestic animal," said Alcaeus.

"You only need one feather Alcaeus. One."

"How do you know this Andromeda and why would I trust you?"

"I know it because the palace records are true. I read every word about the history of the Albino's arrival passed down from oral tradition. Its powers are magnificent. He can tame the gods. He can save Argos. You should trust me because I love your father and I am cold and harsh and he made me see what love truly is. Please go and take a feather and save your father. I will leave if it makes you happy. Let this be a small amends for all that I have taken from you."

"Andromeda." Alcaeus shakes his head. His lips are red from holding them tersely. The truth spills from his eyes. He bends to plant his seed and whispers words she cannot hear into the earth. He kisses his palm and places the kiss on top of the covered seed.

"I am sorry mother. I need father a little while longer." He rises to face Andromeda. "Go. This is a sacred spot and your presence brings no love, only tarnish."

Andromeda does not try to change his mind. She backs away and slowly unties her horse. She looks back and watches as Alcaeus approaches the Albino. She mounts her horse and searches for the strength to not turn around again. She wants a new final memory, a happy one. She wants to see Argos recover. She wants hope. Andromeda's wants overcome reason. She gives her horse a kick and pulls the reins to turn him around. She heads directly towards Alcaeus and the Albino. The thundering hooves startle the eagle and it starts to take flight. Alcaeus lurches towards the scared bird and catches it by the legs. It was in mid-flight when Alcaeus pulled it to the ground. Daniel barked and ran towards them. Andromeda pulled an arrow from her saddle; she placed it into her bow and pulled the quiver tightly. If Alcaeus lost grip, she would stop the eagle.

"Daniel, stop her!" screams Alcaeus.

Daniel ran towards the horse and rider. Suddenly the Albino stopped fighting. It laid still and looked directly at Alcaeus. The boy faltered only for a second. He looked at Andromeda and could not bear to think of her arrow taking another life. He pinched a wing feather in between his thumb and forefinger.

"I am sorry but I take this to save you from her arrow."

He pulled and the feather released into his hand. "Fly!" he yells.

The bird does not fly. Its wings flutter and the two heads twist around each other. Alcaeus's legs give out and he falls to the ground. Man, and beast spiral in unison. The tips of the luminous wings start to crumble. Feathers turned to white powder and the dust fell to the ground. The hair on Alcaeus's head disintegrated as well. Chestnut brown rain fell to the ground. His knees were pulled to his chest and his arms shook. His skin turned a brilliant white. The Albino's feathers washed from head to tail in gradient white, losing brilliance on the way down. The feathered body fells, followed by the heads. One head rested on the other. Eyes closed and in moments nothing is left except white powder, smaller than daffodil seeds. Alcaeus is gone too. When Andromeda approached, she sees his eyes are missing as are his nails on his fingers. His clothing drapes over a skeletal form. He is unrecognizable. The only thing intact is one perfect Albino feather resting peacefully in his bony open palm between two skinless fingers. Andromeda knelt at his side overcome with sorrow.

"Woof! Woof! Woof!" Daniel yelps.

"Argos. Of course, the feather. I can still save him!"

Andromeda pried the feather from Alcaeus's fingers and ran to Argos.

"I am coming to you, Argos. Hold on. I am coming!" She saw a vision of Alcaeus as a young boy and shook it from her mind.

A glimmer of hope filled the space of pain. *I can make this right.* She fell to the ground ready to make any sacrifice to save him. She did not think about using the feather for herself. She thought only about saving Argos. She could see him waiting on customers with his warm smile. She could hear his voice giving quotes of hope. She could let Vexia go and work with him. She would be good to him as she had been good to her. She would visit only his shop when she went to town. She could help him be the most successful shop in Seriphos with her endorsement. She would help him find another love. She would. She tried. She was too late. Argos was gone.

Bowed heads wept for royal and canine eyes could not bear witness to what unfolded before them.

# Part III
## Re-raveled

# Chapter Twenty-Seven
## Pieces- Patmos Island

DANIEL CURLED UP next to Argos with his chin resting on his chest. A soft whimper came. Andromeda patted the dog on the head and swirled the feather around and around trying to remember what power it held. Memories of Alcaeus and Argos filled her brain. It had been years since she studied the legend. She only remembered that the Albino couldn't be used to bring anything back to life. Death was final. She saw another vision, pushed it down into the depth of her soul, looked curiously at the feather and tucked it into her hair. She wanted to believe that Argos and Alcaeus would be reunited in the stars with Calista. This would be the just thing but so would have letting them live. She left Argos and walked back to the spot where Alcaeus lay. A murder of crows was gathering around the body. Andromeda ran towards them with a bow in her hand waving it frantically trying to shoo them away. They were relentless, cawing and flapping to an unheard beat. They were trance-like in their movement. Andromeda was forced to move back from the circle they made. She climbed to the top of a rock and was able to see that in the center of the circle of crows on top of the Albino's white dust was a single crow. His torso was flush with the ground and his wings were sprawled. Each feather separated to the point that light shone between the outer veins. His pupils were set with laser focus on the ground. His head pivoted in all directions searching and scraping the dust into the crevasses of his wings. The movements were deliberate and repetitive. The murder of crows watched intensely. Their heads cocked from side to side. They spoke to each other with caws and scratched the earth. Occasionally, they lifted their wings in flight, hovering a few feet above the ground. The sound of the group of them was a hum to Andromeda's ears. The pitch varied from high to low and Andromeda wondered what they could be talking about. All were squawking incessantly except the crow in the center. He was silent. Even his movements were choreographed in a slow melodic way. He was careful to gently gather the dust. At one point he raised both wings over his head and lowered his head as if in prayer. His shoulder blades were pinched and the tips of his feathers draped to the ground. He appeared to be recovering from a past attack. His wings did not move in the same way as his peers. His beak was crooked and chipped too. With the amount of white now covering his black feathers, he looked as if he had been dredged in flour and about to be tossed into a vat of hot oil for dinner. The sounds from the circle of crows around him reached a feverish pitch, then all fell silent. Wings ceased to flap. Talons ceased to scratch. The chipped-beaked crow lay prostrate on the ground. The murder looked to the soil and began picking up the remaining specks of dust with their beaks. They walked ceremoniously to the prostrated crow and placed the remnants in between his downy barbs as close to the base of the quill as possible. After a crow deposited a speck of dust, it flew away. When they were all gone, the lone crow preened his feathers to re-align them. His eyes darted around the ground searching for any forgotten specks. Satisfied that all were collected, he too, flew away. His black wings hidden beneath a coating of Albino white.

Andromeda surveyed the scene. The Albino's visit was erased from history. Alcaeus's lifeless form lay alone. It was hard to believe it was him. She held onto the crescent necklace he had given her. It once felt like hope but Alcaeus cursed it during their last encounter. Her mind swam with torturous thoughts. *He said my touch had somehow tainted his mother's memory. That's ridiculous. People want to be touched by me. I'm royalty for Elysian's sake. He should have loved me. I thought I loved him. I thought my choices would prove my love for him. I do love him? I did love him? Why else would I have come here today? You were good people. You could have helped me become good. I tricked you into believing I was good too. I want to be good. I wanted to prove to you that I could be and now it's too late. You are the first person I ever wanted to change for. Why did you give me this heirloom if you had no intention of choosing me! It's a curse now to see it and think of all that will never be. I should throw it into the grave with you and be done with it.*

Andromeda wept but no tears fell.

*I will wear it for Argos, not for you. I will find someone who matches the love I saw in his eyes, then I will give it to her so that your mother's memory will be tainted with goodness and not held hostage by the darkness inside of me.*

In the distance she could see that Daniel was still at Argos's side. *What am I to do about this? I can't possibly carry them back to town. I have no way to dig a grave. What will I tell everyone? I cannot reveal the fate of the Albino, nor can I flaunt this feather. I need to get back to the palace records and read everything I can about the legend. Mother will know what to do about these bodies.*

"I could have loved you Alcaeus, but mother and Vexia were right. I was never destined to belong to you. You got what you deserved for not loving me. Daniel, come now. Come with me. Mother needs a new dog. I doubt you'll be a suitable replacement for Echo but if not, Vexia will love you if I tell her to."

Andromeda plucked a sea daffodil and laid it on Argos's chest. She walked away without looking back. Her mind was on the feather and what it could do for her.

ҫ℈ҏ

When Andromeda and Daniel reached the palace, no one was there to greet her. She took Daniel into her room where there were still vases of flowers sent as gifts for her wedding to Phineus. On her bed was a black dress. She sighed and walked over to the window and looked out. On the chair by her window was the dress she had worn to dinner the night of her wedding. The sight of it sent chills up and down her spine. Daniel walked around Andromeda's room with his tail between his legs sniffing everything. This space was much different than the plain floor in the one room home he shared with Argos and Alcaeus. Andromeda's room was elaborate. The entire floor was covered in colored tiles that made up a portrait of her in the garden. When Daniel got to the dress on the chair, he whimpered and tugged it off the chair. He circled it on the floor and took his nose and nudged it into a pile. He lay on top of it and fell asleep.

"Oh Daniel, of course, I'm sure you smell Argos from my time in the kitchen. Did you get to enjoy the bone he brought you? You will have plenty of bones living here. Take your nap and I am off to find mother…she's like my owner…only not as kind as your owners were to you."

With the Albino's feather stitched into the folds of her underskirt, Andromeda made her way to the palace vault. It's not that she wasn't allowed to enter, it's just that she never had except to hide from Vexia or her mother when she was up to no good. The old lock turned easily and she slowly opened the large wooden door and closed it behind her. Inside the vault were stacks of books. Glass jars with liquid lined a shelf. Small packets of parchment tied with red strings were also resting on top of a wooden box. Seeing the parchment made Andromeda smile. She saw Phineus as a threat and was just fine with him being disposed of. She walked further into the vault and saw layers of papyrus with words on them. They were in a language she didn't know. Giant pieces of silk hung from the ceiling and tapestries thick with dust covered stacks of unknown antiquities. The tapestries were heavy and she could only lift a corner by herself. After hours exploring the vault, she found a case full of double-headed eagle coins and a piece of parchment covered in wax. She carefully opened it and read.

When Zeus came into power, he let two eagles fly from the ends of the earth. One flew from the East and the other flew from the West. They met in the city of Delphi which proved Greece to be the center of the earth. Their unity represents divine power and the dualistic nature of gods and man. This is how the double-headed eagle was created. Zeus sent half of the eagles to the east and the other half to the west to build a flock and now you can only find these glorious birds in Greece. When man follows the gods, both heads work in unison and the eagles are peaceful. When there is a disruption about to take place between the gods and mortals the eagles can turn on each other and other birds.

All animals and humans used to have four arms and four legs until Zeus split humans in half as punishment for their pride. He left us destined to walk the earth searching for the other half. Legend tells us that every one-hundred years an albino double-headed eagle appears. The beast is known as Astra. One head is guided by hope and the other by fear. Together they form a communion of truth. If one head dies the other will take its own life. They cannot live separately. The heart and mind must find a balance. When Astra appears, one that hears the call and believes will be united with their half for eternity. Nothing can separate this union, not even the gods.

Although imposing in size, this bird is fragile. Even the slightest touch without invitation will destroy the animal. To approach this ethereal being, without being cursed, it must call you. The intended will hear three caws. Its voice is that of a crow.

*Once the intended hears the call, the albino has the ability to see through another's eyes to help restore light in the world and bring together a perfect union.*

*Some ancient stories tell of men who took a feather from the Astra. Their fate was sealed in death at that very moment. There are no known accounts of anyone surviving; however, it has been said that whoever possesses one has the ability to -*

The parchment was torn. Andromeda searched frantically for the remaining pieces to no avail. They were gone.

"What?! Who else could want these records? I'm the only one who saw the Albino. I need to know what to do with this feather! Mother!!!!!"

Andromeda's voice echoed in the vault. She opened the vault door and called for her mother.

"Mother, mother! Where is that women? Ugh! I need her to help me figure out what to do with Daniel's owners."

Andromeda made her way up the stairs to her room. She opened the door and then closed it and leaned against it.

"The room smells different from when I left. Daniel?"

Daniel looks up from his makeshift bed. Andromeda turns the corner to the area where her bed resides, the smell is overwhelming. She opens the shutters to the windows and light fills the space showing vases filled with sea daffodils. It makes Andromeda smile, then shudder.

"There must be five hundred blooms in here Daniel."

"There are exactly one hundred, miss," said a voice behind her."

"Vexia, when did you arrive? You startled me," said Andromeda.

"I have been right behind you for days miss, minus a few hours here and there."

"You are scaring me Vexia, stop looking at me like that. Where's mother?"

"Your parents are out planning the ceremony for Phineus's funeral. His body is downstairs for viewing."

"Oh yes, my dear Phineus." Andromeda bowed her head and shook it in dismay. "Such sorrow. When is the funeral?"

"It's tomorrow. I laid a dress out for you to wear. You'll only have to wear it to one funeral. I took care of the other two men for you."

"Whatever are you talking about Vexia? Only Phineus is gone...and Echo."

"Echo is in your mother's room. She won't let him go."

Vexia knelt and motioned for Daniel to come to her. She scratched his ears and said, "Why do you have Alcaeus's dog?"

"Oh, Alcaeus asked me to watch over Daniel, well, he asked Meda, of course. Since Argos has been so sick, he needed help. You'll help me with him, won't you?"

"That's a great story Andromeda."

"What time is Phineus's funeral?" asked Andromeda pointedly without looking at Vexia.

"They plan to bury him at sundown tomorrow night. Will you be attending?"

"What a ridiculous question Vexia. Of course, I'll be attending."

"The tears should come easily with so much loss. I don't know how you are holding up?" taunted Vexia.

"Out with it. Enough. What do you know Vexia?" said Andromeda slowly and menacingly.

"I know enough."

"What did you do with them?"

"I gave them a proper burial…unlike you who left them to rot."

"Remember who you are speaking to Vexia. I can have you disposed of in mere minutes."

"I've witnessed what you are capable of my lady and I have no fear of you. You are the one who should be afraid of me."

"No one will miss the peasant food vendor and his meek mannered son."

"Perhaps not but they will want to know what happened to the Albino."

Andromeda slapped Vexia.

"I know everything Andromeda."

Andromeda slapped her again.

"Show me the feather," said Vexia.

"What feather?" asked Andromeda.

She went to slap her again and Vexia ducked.

"You know what feather."

"Never," said Andromeda.

"Then you'll never see the other half of the parchment."

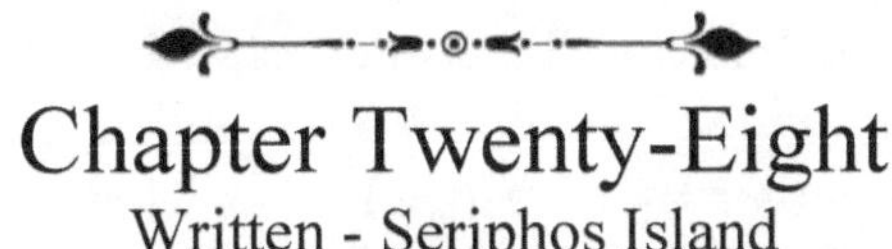

# Chapter Twenty-Eight
Written - Seriphos Island

MORNING RAIN TAPPING on castle stone awakened Perseus. The wetness that covered the usually sun-soaked palace left an earthy scent in the air. Cloud cover shielded the rays of the sun. A dull light engulfed the island as if the universe had a glimpse inside Perseus's heart. It mimicked his rumination. He awoke feeling defeated before his eyes adjusted from slumber. His heart was set but his body hadn't caught up. Putting one foot on the ground was excruciatingly difficult. It meant the next foot would have to follow and the thought that each movement he made today may be his last echoed in every cell of his body. *Is this the last time my feet will feel the mosaic tile in this room? Is this the last time my lungs will fill with palace air? Is this the last time I will see the view of my Seriphos from my window?* The path he was on today was unknown.

Perseus looked around his room. He saw the outline of the town with every lightning strike from his window. The sea beyond was churning from the storm. He lit a torch and sat on the edge of his bed staring at his feet. The flickering light made them appear to move. He kicked his feet back and forth and tried to imagine Simon walking down into the valley and up the hill to Medusa's cavern. He wondered if Simon had time to be afraid or if death came rapidly at the hand of the Gorgons. The stories differed. There were men that never returned. Their stone bodies were cast into the sea, they said, yet no one went to confirm if this legend was true for fear of being the next victim. Simon was not turned to stone. Perseus learned from the two survivors from that expedition that they never heard him scream. Medusa killed him they said, but afterwards she stood in a trance holding the pieces of what was left of him. Perseus hoped he hadn't suffered. He wondered if he spoke. *Did he have time to tell Medusa about me? How could I think of such a thing, he was overcome with terror, he wasn't thinking about me.* He wished Simon would have stayed back with him in the safety of the palace but that was not how Simon was made. He had a warrior's heart. He was a man and he kept his word with Perseus. He did not launch an arrow. Perseus felt responsible for both of their demises. He couldn't bring Simon back but he could help Medusa.

Perseus reached under his pillow and pulled out strands of dark coiled hair held together by a string. It was Medusa's hair. It was the only thing he had that belonged to her. After that fateful event with Athena, Perseus stayed in the plaza. He remembered shouting to Medusa to run. He was happy she heard him. He watched her vanish from his sight and his heart was happy. *She got away. We have a chance. I will find a way.* He watched the townspeople react in disbelief and fear. The perplexity of his thoughts overcame his ability to process what had transpired. Stone figures were scattered about like confetti in the area where Medusa had been metamorphosed. He drew his cape around his body trying to feel her warmth, trying to smell her scent, trying to comfort himself. He ran his hand along his chest trying to feel her. He couldn't remember the sound of her voice. It terrified him to think that he had just lost her and already her memory was starting to fade. He felt something tickle his hand. He looked down and there, tangled in his woven belt was a perfect strand of Medusa's hair. It must have gotten snagged there when she bit him and jerked away.

This simple strand of hair represented love and loss to Perseus. It was the first thing he reached for every morning and the last thing he touched every night. Medusa's name became his daily prayer. He walked over to his windowsill and held Medusa's locks in one hand and pressed them against his lips. He whispered her name into the sky. He placed his other hand on the windowsill. The heat from the stone was gone with the rain. It felt cool and fresh and new. *After the storm there is a rainbow.* He heard his mother's voice tell him. He was going to search for that rainbow today and at the end of it would be a curly dark-haired girl that he hoped would wrap her arms around him. If she did slay him, he was comforted by the fact that she would be the last thing he saw in this earthly world. If he had to slay her, he was comforted that he would be able to see his mother happy again in the arms of Dictys. One woman would be the victor today and Perseus was ready to pay the price for their redemption.

He left a note for his mother and placed it on his bed. He had paid a servant to ensure that it made it into her hands. He went to the tower to retrieve Scarpe but he was not there. Scarpe spent more time away now since gaining full use of his wings. He was acting differently too. He spent most of his time hopping and scratching around in the dirt. He missed Medusa. She was better at speaking crow than he was. He missed many things: his life with Dictys, his mother, Medusa and now the old chipped-beak crow. He tried to comfort himself. B*etter I do this alone, I don't need to endanger more things I love.* He walked out of the palace before another soul awoke. He turned for one last look and blew a kiss towards his mother's room. With a shield, a pomegranate and Harpe, he put one foot in front of the other towards the mountains of Seriphos.

He planted every step firmly on the ground. Each placement that sunk into the wet ground was an exclamation point saying, "Yes! Yes! Yes!" His walk became a march to the pentameter of his heart. It fueled his intention. Worry left his mind, he cared only for the process of moving closer to his beloved. What happened when he got there was up to the gods. As he exited the boundary of town, the rain became heavier. Each drop was thicker than the next and fell faster. His feet sank deeper into the earth and water ran over the rocks and covered him above his ankles. He began to tread lightly over the ground. His heart raced but his steps slowed. He used Harpe for support by placing the blade between the rocks. He remembered being rocked by the waves in the crate with his mother.

*"Perseus, my dear, lay your head on my shoulder. There are waves coming and I want to hold you closer. We can rock in them together," said Danaë.*

*"Mama, I hear thunder. Is there a storm coming?"*

*"Just a small one my love. We can look out of the cracks and watch the lightning. It will be beautiful."*

*"I'm scared mama."*

*"Have I ever let anything hurt you Perseus?"*

*"No mama."*

*"I never will. You are safe with me. Love cannot hurt and I love you Perseus. If the water comes in, we will pretend we are fish. Won't that be fun?"*

*"I love fish mama." The fear began to leave Perseus's face.*

*"We can be fish and swim right into Poseidon's kingdom at the bottom of the sea."*

*"Do you think he would let us ride on his fish horsies?"*

*"I do, we can sit on their backs and ride with the dolphins," said Danaë.*

*The sea was swelling and thunder rang out across the water. Danaë was terrified. She held Perseus closer, he held onto her necklace and she sang a song to him. Her voice was calm and she caressed his back as she sang.*

*"Rest your head my little one. Welcome all the rain. When clouds leave shadows dark as night remember somewhere the moon is shining its light. When sun returns, so shall your smile. Until then, let your mother hold you for a while."*

*The song comforted Perseus. He awakened in his mother's arms. They were soaking wet from sea and rain but they had survived the night.*

Perseus shook his head to release the memory. He was as wet as he was that night in the crate. *How did I not understand as a child how much danger we were in while bobbing up and down in the sea?* The memory of his mother warmed his heart. He felt less alone in the comfort of knowing he was loved. If his mother was able to survive that storm, he could survive this one. With the next step he slipped. The water was rushing over the rocks and down the hill. The earth washed out beneath him and he fell. His head hit a rock and he lost grip on Harpe. The rain pummeled his face and the cold mixed with something warm. He tried to sit up but the spinning in his head prevented him from standing. A warmth trickled down his cheek and red drops fell from his chin. The gash in forehead was deep. The tip of his finger dipped into the wound when he touched it. He laid back down and let the water rush over him. He lifted his arm to his mouth and tore off his sleeve with his teeth. He wound it into a ball and shoved it into the open scar to stop the bleeding. He closed his eyes and reached down to his belt satchel. His fingers worked to loosen the ties to the pouch but he began to feel dizzy. He willed himself to stay awake and find the opening. At last, the tip of his finger rested on the wet coiled hair of Medusa. One corner of his mouth raised slightly into a smile when he felt it. Medusa's fire-filled topaz eyes filled his thoughts as his eyes closed and his world went dark.

"Caw, caw, caw!"

The sun was trying to rise but leftover storm clouds veiled the light.

Scarpe cawed and chirped and scratched at a very banged up Perseus. He circled around his friend and thought of how to wake him from this deep slumber. He didn't have much time. The powdery covering couldn't risk getting wet nor was he ready to use it. With as much force as he could muster, he flew high and down hard on Perseus's chest. Perseus coughed and spat out water. Scarpe sighed with relief. He flew away knowing Perseus could carry on.

Perseus opened his eyes, his right eye would barely open from the swelling. He pinched the coil of hair between his fingers before he removed them from the pouch and pulled the cord tight to seal it back in for the journey. His head pounded when he sat up. He had made it over half-way there. Harpe had floated down the hill with the rushing water. Perseus saw him gleaming in the distance. He crawled to retrieve him and secured him on his back. It felt good to have him back. It felt right. It felt time. Perseus stood with the strength of a man full of conviction. He walked along the saturated earth. The weight of the water on the flora and fauna had a strange feel beneath his feet. It almost felt to him as if he was walking on corpses. With each foreboding step, Perseus felt the weight of what he was about to attempt but his heart was stronger than his mind. As he began his accent towards Medusa, he started to crawl thinking it would keep him hidden longer. The leaf tips nipped at his hands. The thought of death nipped at his heart.

The Gorgons sensed movement on the hill and one sister took flight. She hovered above Perseus. Claws extended from outstretched arms. Wings silently caught wind and she descended, undetected by Perseus. She waited to block his path. One hand, one knee, one thought: Courage. His fingers felt something other than leaves. He heard something sniff him. His heart pounded. He was afraid to look up. Then he saw the clawed foot. He played dead. His face planted into the mud. Harpe was on his back. There was no possible way to reach him. He took shallow breaths then felt claws reaching under his body then the sensation of floating. The leaves, which were so identifiable became a blanket of green.

They flew higher and faster up the side of the mountain. Clicks and chirps and groans echoed on the descent back to land. When they reached the cave, the Gorgon, Stheno, wrapped her wings around Perseus. Gorgon, Euryale, approached and sniffed him up and down. More chirps and clicks and then wings unfolded and the grip loosened.

He was held in a circle of wings.

He heard her before he saw her. The voice he thought he lost was as familiar as his own breath.

"Sisters, what troubles you? I am here."

Perseus closed his eyes tight and said her name over and over in his mind's eye. He visualized her walking towards him and collapsing in his arms.

Medusa exited the cave into the morning. Sunlight escaped the blanket of clouds just long enough to shine on the back of Perseus's head. Medusa saw his curls shadowed in a halo of sunlight just like the last time she saw him at sunset before that fateful evening when her world was changed forever.

"Perseus. Perseus, it's you?"

"I'm here."

"Your head, what happened?"

"I'm alright. Medusa, I'm terrified. Am I safe? Can I open my eyes? I need to see you to feel complete. If I am to die today as least let my last memory be of you."

"Oh Perseus. I wish you could open your eyes. But do not. I've dreamed of Perseus blue every moment since I left the safety of your cloak. We should have run. You were right."

"Perseus blue?"

"Your eyes Perseus. They are the color of the sky on a perfect day."

"Keep talking Medusa. I've spoken to you in a hundred silent ways. I thought I lost you. I was beginning to forget the sound of your voice and it frightened me."

"Perseus, I have been so afraid. I've lost so much of myself. The things I've done. You can't imagine." She shook her head to try and shake the memories. "I feel almost human again with you so close."

"Why didn't your sisters kill me?"

"They thought you were me. They said they smelled me."

"How?"

"I don't know. Are you wearing the cloak you hid me under?"

"I am not. It must be your hair! A small curl was caught on my belt the night you fled. I've worn it around my waist and slept with it under my pillow every night."

Medusa giggled at the irony of it all. Perseus smiled at hearing her laugh.

"That sound is music to my ears. Do I dare open my eyes?"

"There is no way for you to see me and keep your life."

"The most beautiful things about you cannot be seen. Will your sisters let me go long enough to hold you?"

"They will do whatever I ask of them." She placed her hands on each of their wings. "Sisters, please let him go."

Clicks and grunts murmured this time and the Gorgon sisters folded their wings behind them and sat perfectly still like gargoyles next to Medusa. Perseus could only hear what transpired. He didn't trust his safety yet. Medusa felt her snakes leave her head. They curled up on her sister's laps. Even snakes knew that a communion of souls was about to take place.

"Come towards my voice but don't open your eyes Perseus." Perseus walked slowly with arms outreached. "What did you wish for on that bridge Perseus?" she asked.

"To always feel the way, I felt at that moment."

"I wished for the same and I feel it now again."

"As do I," whispered Perseus.

Medusa and Perseus's hands touched and instant warmth flowed into the cold snake-like skin of Medusa. Medusa guided Perseus to the top of the cave where Scarpe gave Medusa the crescent moon necklace. Medusa laid her head on Perseus's lap. Perseus traced the lines along her face. The scales were thick where he touched them.

"Medusa, you are even more beautiful with my eyes closed. The sound of your breath, the feel of your skin, the smell of your hair, all bring hope to my heart."

His fingers traced the side of her cheek, along her chin and down the right side of her neck. There he found a familiar spot between the tendon in her neck and the base of her ear. It was smooth and free from scales and Medusa responded to his touch. She reached up and ran her fingers through his ringlet hair and pulled him down until his mouth met hers. It was a knowing kiss. Perseus's hands made their way along their descent when they rested on a familiar shape on her clavicle.

"Medusa, where did you get this?"

"Scarpe brought it to me."

"Scarpe, ha that sneak! It was my mother's Medusa. I thought it was lost forever. Do you remember the story of me being in the crate with my mother bouncing along the waves?"

"Yes, of course I do but I didn't realize that this could possibly be that necklace."

"I never thought I'd see it again. I'm glad he found it. King Polydectes ripped it from my mother's neck and threw it to the ground. I searched for it to no avail. Scarpe must have watched me and brought it to you for safe keeping. This necklace meant everything to me as a child and I hope if we ever must part again that it will be a comfort to you as it was to my mother."

"Perseus…"

"Yes, my love."

"Athena's Owl told me."

"Told you what?"

"That you were coming to take my head to save your mother."

"Medusa, I could not say these words out loud let alone act on them. To lose you by any means would be the end of me. At my own hand? Please don't think it possible."

"But how will you save your mother? I'm not changing back to human Perseus. I love you but I am no future for you."

"You are my present and my future Medusa."

"No, Perseus. Next life, maybe…but not this life."

Tears were falling from Medusa's eyes. She closed them tightly. "Open your eyes Perseus. I'm holding mine shut. You should see what I have become before you choose so carelessly."

Medusa was shaking. Perseus held her hands and sat upright facing her. He slowly opened his eyes and all he saw were darkened tangled waves cascading around a soulful expression of love, terror, and surrender. He leaned in and kissed her lips and whispered *"This life, this life, this life…"* over and over until her tears stopped and she collapsed in his arms just like his vision. He tied a cloth around her eyes while she slept and he watched her. Nothing for him had changed. She belonged to him as much as he belonged to himself. He traced the outline of her lips with his fingertips. The edges of her mouth curled up into a smile. She knew he was looking at her and for the first time in months she felt her heart warm. She was loved. Without thinking about it she mouthed. *This life.*

# Chapter Twenty-Nine
### Past Echoes - Patmos

VEXIA KEPT A short leash on Daniel during the funeral and an even shorter leash on Andromeda. Her eyes darted to catch her every move. The service was beautiful by all accounts and the new widow played her role of grieving bride with perfection. The body was laid out in the home for viewing and Andromeda had done her duty and sat with poor, old, fat-toad, Phineus, throughout the day and into the night. She dressed the body with milk and honey and placed celery and a lock of her hair on his chest. The part she dreaded most was inserting the coin of the double-headed golden eagle under his tongue as payment for the ferry into the afterlife. When she pried his lips apart all she could see were images of the wedding feast and particles of food falling out of his mouth and down onto his lap. She slipped it in and cried as if on cue but the tears were from disgust not grief.

Cassiopeia looked effortlessly polished and exhibited the exact amount of remorse to beget empathy yet not so much that she drew attention to herself. Today was about her daughter. Andromeda hadn't spoken to her mother since the dinner. It wasn't as if she was avoiding her. She had been actively looking for her but her mother was distant. Andromeda needed her mother now. The funeral procession had started and Andromeda felt the weight of all eyes on her as she walked behind the body on the way to the crypt. She wondered if Phineus would make it past Hades or if the gods had more favor on him. She didn't think much about the afterlife. She assumed that she would have a place in the stars forever alongside the gods. It never entered her mind until that moment that she may not. *How much would I have to pay the ferryman to pass Hades? Luckily my family has lots of money. They can afford my missteps. And most have been at the request of mother so she can pay for my sins.* Thought Andromeda. She caught Vexia's eyes. *Dang it that Vexia catches me every time I have a moral thought. Yes, yes, I'm sure you are right Vexia, leaving them to rot was a horrible thing to do but I couldn't bring them back to life. Let me get through this day in peace you peasant and stop looking at me and making me think differently. What's done is done. I regret nothing. You are lucky you still have benefit to me Vexia or I'd replace you too.*

The funeral was over by ten in the morning. Andromeda went back to the palace since she couldn't be seen around town for weeks now. She dreaded being locked up in her room with her thoughts and that sneak Vexia trying to infiltrate her mind. She had to get the rest of the parchment from her, but how? Andromeda tossed and turned on her bed trying to find a way to trap Vexia. There was a knock at the door.

"Mother?"

"Not mother, father. May I come in?"

"Yes father, of course."

Andromeda straightened her skirt and rose to greet her father with a hug and a kiss on the cheek.

"What brings you here father?" asked Andromeda.

"Your mother."

"Oh?"

"She's not well. Losing Echo has made her, well, not able to think properly. She has said some unbelievable things in her sleep and I wondered if you had any insight. She has mentioned you several times. She thinks you killed Echo."

"Me? Kill Echo? Really father, do you believe that?"

"I do not but you know how convincing she is. She still has Echo's body wrapped in a blanket in her chambers."

"What did she say exactly father?"

"She said, you poisoned him out of jealousy. She said you think you are more beautiful than Echo and more beautiful than her."

"How can I fix this father?"

"I'm not sure you can but she's bringing the palace under watch with the gods by touting her beauty and how she is being surpassed by you. She is saying that the two of you together are more beautiful than any goddess."

"I'm certain she is right about that father," said Andromeda.

"Well, even if she is right, she cannot say it outside of these four walls. She will have our kingdom destroyed with her blasphemy."

"I've been looking for her father, she has avoided me. I haven't spoken to her since the wedding feast."

"Best let her come to you I suppose. I don't know what she's capable of Andromeda. Her mind is not right. If I can intercede, I will."

"Thank you, father." King Cepheus turned to go. "And, father, wait, can I ask you something?"

"Of course, Andromeda."

"Was I a good child?"

"All children are good and bad Andromeda. It's a child's job to make mistakes."

"I mean, was I kind to others as a child?"

"Well, I don't know that you were ever around any children Andromeda. You spent most of your time with mother."

"Do you think mother is good?"

"I think your mother is complicated and has good intentions that don't always turn out how she expects."

"What did I like to do when I was younger? I don't have any memories father."

"I'm not sure Andromeda. You did what your mother asked you to do so you were obedient, that's a good quality." King Cepheus was grasping for words. "You liked to dress up in mother's clothes. You liked to collect dead insects. So, there we have creative and curious. Yes, you were all those things but most importantly you were beautiful so you didn't need to learn much. Your mother raised you to be a queen and that is as noble a life as one can hope for. I expect that's all the questions you have for tonight?"

"Yes father," said a sunken hearted Andromeda.

"Good night then and try not to think of things you have no control over. Some things just are."

"Good night father."

King Cepheus left the room and more doubt filled Andromeda's mind. She truly did not know who she was. She seemed to morph into whatever role was given to her. If that day, they were hunting, then she liked hunting. If that day they were going to the theater, then she liked theater. She shifted with the activities and people presented to her. She didn't even know what food she liked; she ate whatever was placed before her. The questions nagged and nagged at every turn. Argos and Alcaeus's fate was like an open wound asking her to reach deep into herself and see if she was capable of such a horrific act or if she was a product of her upbringing and simply acting upon what she had been taught. She felt something for them but didn't hurt over the loss of them…or did she and just couldn't reach into that part of her soul to retrieve those feelings. She didn't have time to figure it all out now but it haunted her and she played the events over and over and questioned her motives. For now, she came to the same resolution every time. *What's done is done and I can do nothing to change it.*

The weeks after Phineus's funeral were lonely. She spent most of her time in her room. Daniel lay at the foot of Andromeda's bed. His dark eyes imploring her to stroke him. She did not. In fact, the sight of him annoyed her. He had the same soft eyes that they did. Andromeda closed her eyes to block Daniel's gaze but even when closed she could see the faces of Argos and Alcaeus. She thought of Argos giving her the bone and how he kept smiling even when the town boys were mocking him. She saw the love in Alcaeus's eyes when he gave her his mother's necklace. She reached for it and rubbed the crescent shape between her thumb and forefinger. "I do hope you are in the stars. You deserve to be." She said out loud to herself. She wondered if Vexia had placed a coin under their tongues for the ferry. Surely, she did, she thought of everything. *I want to believe I loved you, Alcaeus. I think I did. I do not know why I abandoned you. I don't like to feel pain, I guess. It doesn't suit me. I fear if I let one real tear fall, they would never cease.*

"Come here Daniel" She patted the spot by her side. Daniel cocked his head to one side. "Yes, you. Come here." Daniel crawled a few feet up to Andromeda's side. She stroked his ears and both fell asleep comforted by each other's touch.

～ༀ～

Vexia opened the drapes in Andromeda's room and Andromeda yelled as she always did.

"Vexia! Why do you have to do that so violently?"

"You have a big day miss."

"What do I have?"

"It's your first public appearance since the funeral. You'll be going with your mother to the temple of Athena to make an offering."

Dread and joy simultaneously filled Andromeda's heart. She had longed to see her mother but after what her father told her, she was terrified.

"Thank you Vexia. Will you be accompanying us?"

"Would that make you happy my lady?"

"Yes, Vexia, it would."

"Very well then, I shall."

The chariot ride to the temple was so silent that Andromeda could hear Vexia breathing next to her. Cassiopeia looked straight ahead with a distant blank stare. Andromeda looked to Vexia with concern. Vexia simply shrugged. There was a large woven bag Andromeda had never seen before resting on her mother's lap. Her arms were wrapped around it in a protective way. *Surely that isn't Echo,* thought Andromeda. The servants helped mother and daughter out of the chariot and followed behind them with arms full of flowers and fruit to offer to the goddess. The woven bag went too, carried by Cassiopeia. She swatted any hand that tried to take it from her. *My goodness, it is Echo. How horrifying. I hope she doesn't plan on offering that furry corpse to Athen,* thought Andromeda.

The temple had Doric columns and friezes and a pediment with sculptural decorations. The structure was adorned with artwork and dedicatory inscriptions. There was a remarkably beautiful sculpture of Athena that was carved to perfection. The doors to all temples faced east to use the light of the rising sun. Temple doors never faced west as the west was seen as the entrance to the underworld. Because of their stature on Patmos, Andromeda and her mother were allowed into the inner sanctum of the temple. Cassiopeia was not allowed to bring her satchel. She had to comply with the temple rules and unwillingly gave the bag containing Echo to Andromeda to give to Vexia. Before Andromeda handed it to Vexia she sneakily removed a small jar from her pocket and slipped it into the bag.

Inside mother and daughter met the priest who greeted them with great esteem. The pair returned the greeting with a bow. The priest called for younger priests and priestesses to gather the offerings and place them on the altar for sacrifice. The servants were not allowed to go near the altar, they left and waited for the royal pair by the statue of Athena.

Mother and daughter knelt at the altar and listened to the priest say a prayer to Athena. Cassiopeia tried to focus her eyes on the ground but they kept darting toward the exit. She was lost without the security of her bag. Her body began involuntarily twitching. The moves were small but Andromeda sensed them. She could see that her mother's nerves were shattering.

"Athena, mistress of the long view. I'm calling you to show me what will be. I call you to guide me through the world's intricacies. Athena, steel-eyed goddess, I sing of your mighty strength, I praise your name, I thank you for your many gifts," chanted the priest.

A song was played on lyres. Andromeda hummed. Cassiopeia stared blankly at the altar. When the song was over so was the offering. Mother and daughter exited the sanctum and walked towards their entourage. When they reached the statue of Athena, Cassiopeia walked to retrieve the satchel from Vexia. Vexia cinched the bag closed and placed it around the neck of a shaking Cassiopeia.

"Andromeda, go stand next to the statue."

Andromeda shook her head "no."

"Come dear, stand right here." Cassiopeia was motioning to Andromeda and the palace guards and servants parted to make room for the queen and princess. Andromeda did not move. "Look at her, my dear. They say she is the most beautiful creature on the earth, but I beg to disagree. Your hair is far fairer and your eyes as green as a young olive from the very tree the goddess created. The curves of her body do not compare, nor does the sound of her voice. Even angry, you sound ethereal. It's truly unfair that one person could embody such perfection. Don't you all agree?"

The temple patrons were still. All eyes were on the ground except Andromeda's.

"Mother, stop, please." She turned to the people. "Forgive her. It's Echo, her dog, he has passed and she's not thinking clearly." She turned to her mother, "Please mother, let's go home and see father."

"Your father cares for me about as much as you do my dear. Ever since my looks began fading, so did his care for me."

The priest and priestesses were just now leaving the inner sanctuary. They began their descent down into the courtyard just when Cassiopeia said...

"Does anyone here disagree? Andromeda, my daughter, is more beautiful than any goddess on Olympus as was I in my prime."

"My queen, get control of yourself. What you say will get you killed," said the priest.

"I care not of my fate nor do I care of the thoughts of a goddess who changes anyone who beats her into spiders and snakes and such. What do you think she would do to me. . . turn me into a Gorgon like she did to that peasant in Seriphos?"

"You dare speak against Athena in her temple? Have you gone mad? The gods are listening in this sacred space. You came to make an offering and now you slander the very one who vowed to protect this kingdom?" said the priest.

Andromeda looked for Vexia. She saw her in the back of the group of servants but her eyes were glued to the ground. Andromeda willed her to look up, *please look at me, what am I to do Vexia? If only I had brought the feather.* Vexia broke her gaze and looked up just enough to catch Andromeda's eyes. She motioned with a quick tip of her head towards the priest. Andromeda didn't know what it meant. She watched Vexia start to move towards the ground and then back up. *Yes, Vexia, thank you.* Andromeda knelt to the ground and held her hands over her eyes and asked for forgiveness.

"Please, my mother does not know what she is saying. I beg your forgiveness kind priest."

Silence filled the room, no one dared raise their bowed heads.

"Don't bow to anyone Andromeda. Stand up. You are going to be a queen. Let them bow to you," said Cassiopeia.

With that statement, the priests and priestesses went back to the inner sanctuary and began to pray for guidance. Andromeda rose, walked to her mother, took her hand, and tried to exit. Cassiopeia did not move. Andromeda let go of her hand and walked to the chariot. Cassiopeia yelled after her.

"You know, Andromeda, when you were little, I called you Echo because you never left my side. Then you got your own ideas and you fought me and I had to do the things I did to you to make you mind. I regret nothing Andromeda. Everything I ever did was for you. Everything!"

The queen collapsed clutching the bag containing Echo. Andromeda did not turn around as the queen spoke, but she heard every word. The servants helped get Cassiopeia into the chariot. Andromeda and Vexia walked home in silence. The doom-stricken air thickened their lips and trapped the thoughts each held in their minds from escaping.

# Chapter Thirty
## Solstice Seriphos Island

THE SUMMER SOLSTICE was upon them. Perseus awoke blindfolded next to Medusa. He titled his head back just a bit so that the gap in his blindfold allowed him to peek. By now the snakes were used to having him around. He gently moved one that was covering Medusa's face so he could watch her sleep. Her head was on his chest and the morning light illuminated his mother's necklace. Perseus had seen this necklace in the best of times and worst of times but no other memory would ever compare to the one he was creating now. His hand caressed her cheek and he thought of every moment he dreamed about while they were apart. *This moment is the most perfect,* he thought. All moments with Medusa felt perfect to Perseus. He closed his eyes in wonder of her. How could it be that the most beautiful things about her were things that one could not see? He knew the depth of her thoughts without speaking. He knew the serenity of her soul without praying. And, he knew, from the first time he saw her, he belonged to her completely. Words and sight were pointless in her presence.

Medusa yawned and reached around Perseus's chest.

"Are you awake Perseus?" she whispered.

"I may be or I may be dreaming. What have I done to deserve to awake with you by my side?"

Medusa laughed. "Is your blindfold on?"

"Yes, I do not need eyes to see you."

"Well, you will need eyes to see what I want to show you. My eyes are covered. Remove your blindfold, sit up and look at the ground."

Perseus did what Medusa asked and was astonished by what he saw. Inside the cave was a mosaic of a bridge, a girl, a boy, and a bandaged-up crow.

"Did you do all of this Medusa?"

"I did. Do you like it?"

"I love it. How did you capture it so perfectly?"

"The distance between us was only a blink and a thought. I could see you perfectly every night in my dreams, but I could not touch you. I wanted to make something I could see with my eyes open and touch with my hands. I used pebbles and shells I found and created this from my memory. The stone at your heart is the pellet I kept from your friend, Simon. I'm so sorry Perseus. I didn't know. I vowed never to kill again after I learned he was your friend."

Perseus knelt and kissed the pellet that belonged to Simon.

"How did you know I knew him? Wait, don't answer that question."

There was a long pause before Medusa spoke, "I suffered knowing I hurt you. I often thought, if they did come to kill me, at least maybe they would see this and know I had feelings. I never imagined that I would get to show it to you, but here we are." She leaned her head against him.

"Yes, here we are." He kissed her gently, knelt and ran his fingers over the pebbles that made up their figures. The scene was just how he remembered it. It felt like they had always been together and he was happy.

"Being with you is the best birthday present I could ever ask for. Today is the first of many birthdays we will share together. I don't know how I lived without you for 17 years. My heart is so full of you that there is no room even for the blood in my veins to rest within."

Medusa wrapped her arms around Perseus. A smile extended across her face.

"What do you want for your birthday, Medusa?"

"I have everything I want right here." She nuzzled his chest. "What do you want for your birthday?"

"This moment on repeat for eternity."

"You will bore of me in time."

"There will never be enough time with you. Surely there is something your heart desires that I can give you. I could run back to town and fetch a new dress for you or a sapphire necklace."

"I do not want you to leave Simply Perseus, simply stay with me."

He loved it when she called him Simply Perseus. It described him *perfectly,* she had said with a flirtatious tone, that day in the meadow.

"I wish Scarpe was here, he would be up for the adventure of going to town and acquiring something that shimmers for you."

"The only shimmer I want to see is the one in your eyes."

She was smiling when she said this but he felt her sadness knowing she could never look upon his eyes again.

"The first time we met I felt heaven and earth meld into one at the sight of you. I do not need to see you to know that we are one."

Her love for him grew and strangled her heart with every word he said.

"What did I do to deserve you Perseus? I am broken and cursed. I murdered your friend. How can you love me? Look at me. I am destined to walk alone in this world. We have no time. We are not aligned. I could not ask you to live this life, in the dark, in a cave, waiting in fear for someone to come and kill you. The depth of me was taken away. Make no mistake Perseus, I am dark and cold and only feel light and warmth with you. I cannot use you to fuel my light. I need to find that, if it's possible, on my own. I do not want to shatter the good in you. You have not seen what I'm capable of Perseus."

"Medusa, I am equally as broken. Our brokenness matches. Together we are one. The song is complete and enchanting when I'm with you. I tried to forget about you but ignoring my heart is a betrayal against myself. I cannot live without trying to make us whole."

"You are more tangled into my soul than these snakes are in my hair."

"I love you Medusa."

"I love you Perseus."

A kiss began their day. A kiss that transcended all logic and reason. Perseus and Medusa explored each other until the evening sun began its descent against a crystal blue sky. Perseus took Medusa by the hand and guided her out of the cave.

"Do you trust me?" he asked.

"Yes."

"Let's walk to the sea. I will guide you."

Medusa took his hand and kissed the spot she had bitten under the cape just months ago. The clouds under their feet effortlessly carried them to the shoreline. Time and things of this world do not apply to those in love. Even the consistency of their mistakes was flawless in each other's eyes. Perseus began to hum. He pulled Medusa close and rocked her back and forth. The sound of his humming vibrated against her cheek. Each beat of his heart and note of his song lulled her further in love. They danced and took turns with the blindfold, so each could see the harmonious vista of birds coming in, to roost for the night. Their black silhouettes dotted between clusters of trees and looked like black lace against the pink and purple sea of colors.

The sun had not yet fully set when they heard the screams. They turned to look towards the sound and watched as flames skipped into the sky. The trees looked like torches from where they stood.

"My sisters!" screamed Medusa.

Without a word, she sprang to the hill. Her speed was other-worldly. Perseus could not keep up. He watched as the Gorgons carried bodies into the air. He saw arrows flying and fires burning all around the cave. The king's army had arrived and there was nothing he could do to protect his Medusa. They were all there for one purpose, to slay the monster.

The smell of blood overtook Medusa's senses and overwhelmed her reason. Her snakes guided her. They did not leave their host for this war. She needed their eighteen additional eyes on the battlefield. Their heads were on a swivel as they extended their bodies as high as possible to survey the chaos. This time there were more than fifty men and with them were animals that Medusa had never seen. Lions lurched in cages. Bears were shackled to cargo wagons. Groups of men carried huge battling rams that she had only seen on war ships. The Gorgons kept to the air. Fire-lit arrows sailed into the sky. The blind and winged sisters hovered just above their reach. Medusa slithered into a group of men. She found a branch and snapped it over her thigh. The men turned towards the sound and before they could move more than their gaping jaws, they were stone. Medusa was wild-eyed. She could not see her sisters. More men were approaching. Some wore metal visors that covered their eyes. She felt the heat from their bodies and tasted their scent. She struck with precision. Their bodies slashed with teeth and talons. Blood stained her face and dripped from her lips. The metallic taste soothed her adrenaline. She licked the sweetness from her lips. It nourished her focus. She felt whole in a new way. Each kill felt better than the last. The animals were no use to the men. They knew when they were outmatched by a predator and ran. Medusa heard Euryale call for her. She dodged flaming arrows and rocks launched by men to find her. Stheno had been hit with an arrow. Her wing was singed by flames and useless for flight. Medusa told Euryale to fly her to safety. The battle had just begun.

Perseus approached with trepidation. He was frozen in his own thoughts. He watched from a distance in a tree. Terror filled his soul. He could hear more than he could see. Men he knew were dying and possibly at the hand of Medusa. He thought of Simon. *Could he have known his death was eminent? Had he watched his friends die before he succumbed to Medusa?* Perseus searched the land for her. He could not find her. He climbed down from his tree and moved to a closer one. He saw Euryale flying with a wounded Stheno. Medusa was alone in the battle for her life. There was nothing he could do. He opened the pouch and pulled out the lock of curls. He brought them to his lips and prayed for guidance. Simon's words lingered in the air mocking his conflicted mind…" *When the time comes, I will have to ask myself whose love is more worth dying for.*"

"Simon STOP," Perseus said while covering his ears and shutting his eyes. *I can't possibly choose. I would rather die myself than watch my mother or Medusa take their final breath.*

The fires were growing and Perseus could see more with the light. Men hobbled and crawled along the ground. Some were fleeing with the animals. In the distance, Perseus saw the outline of a small tree alone on a hill. Its branches bare from the fire. The trunk of the tree was stagnant but the branches were moving. Men approached and stopped in their tracks. *Was this some sort of a look-out post for the battle below?* Perseus squinted to make out as much as he could. He watched a man run towards the tree. He was holding a blade and had it extended above his head ready to strike. On his head was a helmet that covered his eyes. Perseus could hear his battle cry. "Ahhhhhhhhhgggggggggrrrrrrrr." The man bellowed into the field of men at the base of the tree. He went to strike at the tree when the branches came to life. They moved up and around and grabbed the man. Perseus could see the outline of the branches well enough to count them. There were nine that appeared to be all the same length and two a bit longer. Together they raised the man above the trunk. There were hissing and gurgling sounds. Some branches let go but two pulled the man closer. There was silence and then the branches lifted the man up again. Liquid poured out of his chest and fell over the tree. The nine smaller branches tangled themselves into a nest at the top of the tree trunk. The tree began walking down the hill.

"Medusa, no." A shocked Perseus whispered, "*No, no, no…*" over and over as the tempest of tears fell onto his hands which held the lock of Medusa's hair.

Her wrath was not over. He watched as she turned men to stone with her eyes and slaughtered those who had their eyes covered with her fangs. There was no sign of the Medusa he loved. There was no sign of love within her. She was more animal than human. He thought about what his mother had said to him under the willow tree…*Whatever she was, she is no more Perseus. She will never be what you want her to be now. You must understand.*

Perseus inched closer and heard a whimper. Medusa rolled onto her stomach and slithered towards the sound.

"Shhhhhhh, shhhhhh, shhhhhh," a voice murmured among gasps of air coming from an injured fighter.

"Ahhhhh, my leg, help me Cal, my leg."

"Shhhhh, please, she will find us. Play dead or we will perish."

Cal heard rustling in the weeds.

"I can't save you mate." He slid away from his friend.

When he looked back, Medusa had the injured man in her grasps. Her eyes were closed. He could hear her taunting him.

"What is your name? Are you who launched an arrow at my sister?" she asked with a raspy voice.

The boy just screamed, "Stop, no, please stop, you are hurting me."

Medusa took her talon and dug it into the wound on the boy's leg. She twisted it and brought her blood-soaked hand to her mouth.

"Don't worry, I won't kill you now." She placed the boy back on the ground. She sped as quick as light to the one called Cal. She tracked him by scent and brought him back to his friend. Both boys were wailing in terror. Perseus watched as she bit off part of Cal's arm, then his cheek. The injured boy was silently rooted in fear. Medusa turned away from Cal and opened her eyes. A ghastly sound came from the depth of her dark soul and echoed across the battlefield. She opened her eyes wide then narrowed them and straddled the injured boy. His eyes were closed but she pounced on his chest and the startled boy opened them. Cal watched his friend transform. His blood dried, his tears stopped flowing, his mouth stopped moving, his lips turned the color of his teeth, his chest stopped heaving and finally, the light in his eyes left as the last bit of his humanity turned to stone.

Medusa closed her eyes again and snapped Cal's neck with one hand. She fell to the ground as his body fell under her force. Perseus watched as Medusa surveyed the carnage. She ran her fingers over her snakes and called for her sisters. They did not come. No one came. Not even Perseus.

"I understand now, mother. I choose you. I will be the one to slay Medusa," said Perseus.

Perseus held Harpe close and weaved his way towards Medusa by hiding behind the stone columns that used to be men. No signs of life were left on the battlefield. Medusa was laying on her back looking up to the sky. Perseus took the helmet of a fallen soldier and placed it on his head. There was a slit just big enough to see straight ahead. He moved as silently as a falling feather and thought only of his mother. He hadn't thought of her while he had been in Medusa's arms but now the images of Polydectes hurting her fueled his mission. He told himself that he would be freeing Medusa from the horror of her life. The Medusa he knew wouldn't want to live this way. She embodied love. He thought of the way she cared for crow. He had watched her become forlorn over a broken wing and her vulnerability and kindness touched him deeply. She loved all. She wanted to save the weak. Now she killed them, savagely, without remorse. She had tried to warn him but his love for her hid the truth. She was a monster. She knew it and now he knew it too.

The greatest battle Perseus would fight was the one against his own soul. His body moved but his mind still doubted. Soon he would be too close to hide his approach from Medusa. He withdrew Harpe and lowered his helmet. He turned it to the side so one eye was completely covered and the other was mostly hidden. His breath warmed the inside of the helmet. Under the helmet he could smell what was left of her on his chest. The feeling of her there mere hours ago made him shiver. He started to panic. His breath was short and his chest was tight. He raised the helmet, looked to the sky, and inhaled deeply. The moon was rising. A perfect crescent. He thought of his mother and the necklace and the moonlight bouncing off its surface. He thought of seeing it on Medusa and how perfectly it fit around her long, elegant neck. He thought of dancing and Dictys and an old, chipped-beak crow. His life was flashing before him. He was sure he would die. He bowed his head and cried. He felt her touch on his back. He wasn't startled. He resigned. She spoke but he heard only his mother's voice.

*Whatever she was, she is no more…*He gripped Harpe tightly and turned to end her.

She was looking up with her eyes closed. She looked like an abandoned child. The delicate features on her face were scratched and ripped. Varying stages of fresh and drying blood covered her completely. She was panting from exhaustion.

"This is what I am Perseus."

Perseus tried to shake the love from his heart. He soaked her in. Every scar tore at him but the blood that covered her was that of many. Was her one life worth saving over the next hundred men that would come to kill her? They would come. He knew the battle for Medusa's head was just beginning.

"Say something Perseus. I can't look upon you."

"I don't know what to say Medusa."

"Then tell me what you see."

"I see the love of my life standing in a pool of blood under a darkened night with my necklace around her neck. A necklace that perfectly matches the shape of the moon tonight."

Medusa reached to touch the necklace.

"That necklace gave me hope on my darkest days. I feel no hope now Medusa. Nothing I have ever seen compares to what I saw tonight. I want this darkness to end."

"Then end it."

Medusa reached for Harpe and ran her hand down the shaft until she found Perseus's hand. She squeezed her hand around his.

"I cannot understand my place in the world. Why this happened to me is beyond reason. All I know is that if I cannot be with you, I do not want to be. This moment is part of our story. I had two visitors before you came. Owl told me to only trust Scarpe and Scarpe told me there would be a way to help you on the summer solstice. My death is the only way for you to live and for me to be free. I see no other way. Hope has been pried from my hands tonight. Take my head and save your mother. There is nothing more to say."

They sat in silence as their thoughts melded.

"I would choose my time with you again even knowing I would only be left with grief and memories. You are worth more to me than you will even know. How am I to take your life? There must be a way, Medusa. I cannot kill what I love."

"Then kill the monster and free me. I know you have thought about it, Perseus. You had Harpe drawn. Love cannot conquer some things. It wants to move mountains, but the mountains still stand. You tried Perseus. Your love cannot save me."

"I wanted to leave my mark on the world but not in this way. I will forever be known as the man that slain Medusa instead of the man that loved her."

"The only true way to leave a mark on the world is to truly love. You loved me completely without question. The only one who needs to know this is me."

"So, we have already won the lesson of this earth?"

Medusa nodded yes.

"Then why can't I go too?"

"Please Perseus, I have killed so many. Don't ask me to take you. I cannot."

They held each other in silence and time ceased to exist. Perseus spoke first.

"How do you want me to do it?"

The snakes coiled a little tighter with those words. Medusa felt lightheaded and broken but she did not let Perseus feel her hollowness.

"Tonight, I will drink a tea of Hemlock, when I am asleep is when you will do it. I would rather fall at your hand than be tortured by the men that will come."

"I will do what you ask but please may the end be away from this horror. I want our final moments together to be beautiful."

Medusa nodded and placed her arms around his neck. He cradled her and carried her to the sea. There he washed her stained body and dried her with his cape. He held her and whispered all the beautiful parts of their story. They made plans for the next life. She would hold a place for him and wait.

"My final wish in this life cannot come true. To look upon your Perseus blues."

"We can look together upon the moon. You stand in front of me and I will hold you in my arms and on the count of three we will open our eyes at the same time. It's the moon of hope for me. When you are gone, I will be able to look upon a crescent moon and think of you. Surely you will see it too from your place in the stars. One day, I will join you there and we can sit on the edge of that moon and dangle our feet into the sky. We will joke about time and how long it took to be alive and forced to walk the earth wondering *why*. We will know it was preparing us for dangling nights on crescent moons and all the things unknown to us now. My love for you is real, this is the only thing I know for certain."

"I will wait for you."

"My eyes are closed, are yours?" asked Perseus.

"Always, to protect you."

"Are you ready?"

"Yes Perseus."

"On the count of three. Say it with me."

"One…two…three…"

They opened their eyes and took in the light of the moon. *"Perseus was right, the shape was exactly the shape of the necklace and exactly the shape of Harpe. A shape of hope and pain,"* she thought. Her body switched. The crescent around her neck turned hot and a flash illuminated the surface of their world for a second. Medusa collapsed and Perseus knelt beside her.

"Medusa, Medusa!" he yelled.

She sat up and pushed him away.

"Who are you? Get away from me! Where am I?! ARRRGGHHHH! What has happened? Vexiiiiiaaaaaaaa!!!!"

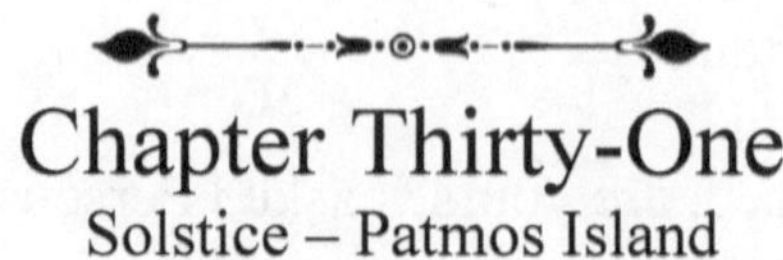

# Chapter Thirty-One
### Solstice – Patmos Island

THE SOUND OF swishing fabric revealed the morning light. Vexia opened the window with such force that the fabric was still swaying when Andromeda sat up.

"Ughhhh, I thought I asked you to open them less violently. It's my birthday…remember?" She hoped Vexia had remembered. Her mother surely wouldn't.

"Birthday or not, it's time to rise. Your mother has plans for you."

"Mother?"

Andromeda had very little feelings about seeing her mother. She had retreated into her room after the incident at the temple. Vexia came only in the mornings to annoy her by forcing daylight into her room; otherwise, she saw no one. When Andromeda left her chambers to walk down to find her mother, the palace seemed cold. She wished to relive the night of her wedding when every room was covered in white and light. She took a detour and went into the garden before meeting her mother. The peacock was there preening about regally between the Oleander trees and red roses. Andromeda had always loved the story about how red roses were created. Her mother told her that Aphrodite went looking for her lover, Adonis. She found him wounded and bleeding from an encounter with a wild boar. A mixture of her tears and his blood produced a red rose. Her mother loved red roses. Vexia told her they were the symbol of secrets. The garden was filled with red roses. *A garden full of secrets,* thought Andromeda.

She walked about looking at the roses and had to stop herself from thinking about sea daffodils. She shifted her mind to her plans for the day. It was her birthday after all and the summer solstice. She would stay up and watch the sun go down. She was certain that the palace help would remind her parents of her birthday and plan a great feast as they did every year. She walked and thought of birthdays past then stopped at the reflecting pool. Her flaxen hair and green eyes throbbed in the water. In the pool she could see herself and the vines of climbing roses on the garden walls.

*Even the perfect red roses fade around my beauty. What good is all this? Am I doomed to walk alone with only my reflection to comfort me and opulence surrounding me? Does beauty mean anything without love?* she asked herself.

Andromeda was admiring her reflection with Cassiopeia approached.

"Good morning my dear," said her mother in a sing-song voice. She opened her arms. The bag containing Echo was still hanging across her body. Andromeda faked a smile. She curtsied to her mother and attempted a hug.

"I have wonderful news for you."

"What's that mother?" she asked with hope.

"I'm taking you to the seaport for your birthday gift."

*She remembered,* thought Andromeda.

Cassiopeia looked over Andromeda's shoulder into the reflecting pool.

"More lovely than a rose," she said.

"I was just thinking that mother."

"We are more alike than you think. Come now, the carriage is waiting."

King Cepheus was at the side of the carriage. He helped Andromeda in and patted her on the leg. A guard got in after her. Cassiopeia stood next to the king.

"Goodbye my dear," said Cassiopeia.

The king turned to go. The queen followed. Her father said nothing. A tremble ran down Andromeda's spine.

"Wait. Mother? Father? What is happening?!"

They kept walking. Andromeda moved to leave the carriage and the guard stepped on her chiton to stop her and used his arm to push her back into her seat. The horses began moving and Andromeda screamed. She watched for them to turn around, to stop this, to care, but they did not. Their figures faded into the courtyard and the palace gates were shut.

The guard placed a gag in her mouth and put a cover over her head. He forced her down to the bottom of the carriage so she was hidden as they made their way through Patmos. Evey time Andromeda fought, the guard put his foot on her head. The bumpy ride over the cobblestones ended at the sea. Tears did not fall. Anger set in.

Andromeda could smell the scent of fish and salt water. She was hoisted out of the carriage and into a cart. They covered her with a blanket and rolled her into a ship. She heard men chanting in a foreign tongue. She heard wood crunching beneath feet. She could barely breathe out of terror and angst. She wanted to taste the air. *How could you mother? How father? Vexia. Vexia will save me. The feather?!* Andromeda could feel that the ship had left the port. They were gently swaying from side to side. The chanting continued and the sound of the oars hitting the water kept the beat of the song. It was hypnotic. It may have been five minutes of five hours later when a man removed the hood covering her face.

"I am King Menik of Ethiopia."

The man was African and was not much bigger than Andromeda. He looked young too. His voice was meek and unsure. Andromeda still had the gag in her mouth and could not respond. He did not frighten her. She looked at him inquisitively.

"Your parents betrothed you to me to save Patmos. Your father was visited by Poseidon. Your escapade at the temple outraged the gods. He promised that Patmos would be destroyed if he didn't make a sacrifice. Your father chose you over your mother. Together they devised a plan to fake your death and save your life. You will be hidden by me in Ethiopia. Andromeda cursed him through her gag. He placed the bag back over her head and said, "Do not fight. You are legally mine now. When we arrive at my palace you will be in my care. I will marry Estrale, the love of my life. She is an ethereal beauty but unfortunately not suited to fulfill my legacy. You will keep your life under my care and bear the children my wife is unable to have. I hope you have a son in there for me." He poked her belly with the tip of his little finger and left.

Andromeda stared into the cloth covering her head. Specks of light seeped through the fibers. She wanted the light to go out. She closed her eyes. Alcaeus's face appeared. *I would be honored if you would be my wife and wear this necklace as a symbol of our love.*

The memory of his sweet smile warmed her. She had made a mistake with Alcaeus. She still had time to make amends. She wanted love to win even if it was not her own.

*No,* she said to herself. *No, no, no. I will not end this way. I have the feather. Help me Alcaeus. Tell me what to do.*

She shook her head and lashed about until the hood fell off. The wheel barrel she was in was next to several amphorae. She sat up and tipped her legs over the side of the barrel and slid onto the wooden floor. She was in the ship's hull. She sat quietly memorizing the beat of the chant and at the loudest moment when voices rose and oars slapped water, she tipped over an amphora. She backed up against a sharp edge and placed the ties that bound her between stone edges. With effort, she was released. She removed the gag from her mouth and took a deep breath. Inside she was screaming. *I'll scream later,* she thought. She grabbed a chard of broken amphora and freed herself from the rope that had bound her wrist. She felt her way around the dimly lit guts of the ship until she saw an opening above her with a ladder leading up.

The beat continued. One, two, three and the oars hit the water. With each slap on the sea, she took another step up the ladder. Determined eyes peered out and into the rows of men working together to move the ship. The holes of the oars pierced the side of the ship. They were bigger than she expected. *Big enough for me to squeeze through,* she thought.

There was one man to the right of the opening. He was leading the chant and commanding the men. He had an oar in one hand with the blunt end resting on the ground between his feet. His feet were spread in a wide stance and both hands were gripping the shaft like he was holding an unwilling partner in a dance. Andromeda waited. She pounced just when the oars took a beat. Her gag was placed in his mouth and the rope that held her wrists was twisted around his neck. Before blood could flow from the cut she made across his neck with the chard of amphora, Andromeda escaped.

She felt the kiss of freedom when she hit the water. She had taken the commander's oar and used it to float. The current was strong and the sea dark. Clouds covered the sky and sprinkles of rain began to fall. Andromeda rested on the oar and watched the ship bob up and down on the waves. Rain began to fall and the sea took an angry turn. Unpredictable waves struck from every direction. The sea lashed at her. It was so dark she could only see her hands on the oar. The waves took them under over and over. She felt something brush her feet. It was hard and jagged. She turned her head around and saw a rock jutting out of the water. She stretched her legs as long as she could and reached her toes for a footing. Every time she touched a rock, the waves took her up. She let go of the oar and dove under the churning water. It was calm below the surface and quiet. The roar above sounded more like bubbles popping. She kicked and swam with all her might until her hands reached the rocks. She lodged them into crevasses and pulled her way along the rim of the shelf until her head emerged above the surface. There she was able to rest under an outcropping of rock. Lightning flashed in the distance and she could see the outline of the ship. She watched it hard trying to determine if it was still looking for her. The next flash hit the boat. Before long Andromeda could see a glow in the distance. An orange orb on the dark carpet of water. She watched it until the fire was swallowed by the sea. She smiled. She had survived.

A stronger wind came and tested Andromeda's strength. The rock was small and the waves tried to lick her off. She held on and finally the clouds parted, the sea calmed and Andromeda rested her eyes for the first time in hours. She could feel the moonlight washing across the water. She took a deep breath. *When I open my eyes, I'm going to make a wish on the first star I see. I'm going to wish for a new birthday.* Tears fell from her eyes. Tears that held the past seventeen years of birthday wishes left unfulfilled. She wiped the last tear away and looked to the sky. She searched for the stars that pierced the night sky until she found the moon. A perfect crescent. Just like Alcaeus's necklace. Her hand went to reach for it. A flash of light engulfed her and her body convulsed. She fell to the rock clutching a glowing crescent moon necklace.

She awoke by the sea in the arms of Perseus.

## Day 1 of 17

### Seriphos 4:00am

"I SAID, WHO are you? How did I get here? Why are your eyes closed? Open them!" ordered *Medusa*.

"*Medusa*, what is wrong? Your voice sounds different."

Andromeda pushed Perseus with both hands on his chest. "*Medusa*? I'm not that monster. Look at me! Tell me where I am!"

Just then a rustling was heard nearby. It was a soldier; he must have climbed down the fire-blistered hill seeking refuge. He was weaponless and hiding in a bush.

"Don't go to him. Don't look at him. Please, *Medusa*."

"Stop calling me *Medusa*. My name is Andromeda and I am the daughter of King Cepheus of Patmos." She walked towards the soldier. He was too terrified to move or speak. "Who are you and where is the rest of your army?" Perseus peeked out of the corner of his eye and could see her looking at the boy. She was looking directly at him and he was looking directly at her. He did not turn to stone.

"Please, please don't hurt me," he said with quickened breath.

"Hurt you? Why would I hurt you? I don't know you. You've done nothing to me."

"*Medusa*, stop. Leave him alone!" said Perseus.

"I'm not hurting him and my name is NOT *Medusa*!"

Perseus looked to the sky in disbelief. The clouds began to cover the moon. The soldier and the impostor *Medusa* locked eyes. He did not turn to stone. When the clouds covered the last speck of the moon, there was a great flash. This *Medusa's* arms and legs shook. She fell to the ground. Within seconds, she began to move more fluidly. The snakes, which went limp on her head, began to squirm. Perseus moved back. He turned his head away from her and wrapped his eyes with the cloth. The soldier looked on perplexed by what he saw. Petrified by fear he locked his eyes on Medusa. She opened her eyes and his breath was stilled. She stared at the man, touched his hardened hand, and called for Perseus.

"Perseus, Perseus? What happened? Where was I? How did I get back?"

"Medusa, it's you. Your voice. I thought you were gone. You told me you were called by another name."

"I had a dream Perseus. A vision. I don't know where I was but you were not there. I was alone on a rock in the middle of the sea. I was wearing clothing fit for royalty. I could hear a dog barking on the shore."

"Medusa, a minute ago you looked upon this man and he didn't turn to stone."

"It wasn't me Perseus. I was in the sea. My hair is still wet. I saw this soldier for the first time only a second ago."

"This man, he looked right at you and didn't change. There was a flash and that girl was gone and you were back. When you looked upon him a second time, he became a monument to your power."

"How Perseus? Where is she now?"

"I don't know. You replaced her. This girl looked like you but she didn't sound like you. She was confused. I'm confused. What is happening? Medusa, can you tell me what you saw?"

"I was here with you. I remember the moon. I saw the moon there too. I was cold and wet and clinging to a rock. I know it was me because I was holding your necklace in one hand. I felt like me too but more human. I felt determined. I don't know what I was trying to do there. I don't know how I got to the rock but the dog started swimming out to the rock. It was a long way but the dog kept coming. He was gray. I was happy to see him. The sea was calm. The moonlight cast light along his path to the rock. I slid down the rock and reached out to the dog. He was helping me to shore. I was almost there when I saw a flash of light, I went under the water and I ended up back here, with you. I can still smell his wet fur on me. Was it real Perseus? It seemed so real but it was a dream. Surely it was a dream?"

Perseus held her closer. "I don't think it was a dream Medusa. It was real. The girl that was here was real but it wasn't you. She called herself, Andromeda. It must be a sign Medusa, a sign of our salvation. Scarpe predicted this. You told me Scarpe scratched out a message to you. What did Scarpe tell you again?"

"He said to wait until the Solstice. That I could help you on the Solstice."

"Maybe this is how you are helping me, helping us. There is no me without you Medusa."

The clouds parted. Medusa shook, this time more violently. Perseus held her.

"Medusa, Medusa, I'm here. What's wrong? Tell me. How can I help you?"

Her eyes closed and she went limp. The snakes on her head fell to one side. Perseus was too afraid to uncover his eyes. He felt energy surging through her body. What was once resting was now engaged. She gripped his arm with force.

"My name is Andromeda," she said pulling off his blindfold. Their shocked eyes met.

"I was just underwater. How? How did I get here and why are you looking at me like that? Where's Daniel?"

The girl looked like Medusa but her eyes were sea-foam green. There was fire in them but not the topaz-filled fire of Medusa's eyes. This girl was cold. Her voice was high and sharp. Medusa's voice was mellifluous. She barked orders and flailed her arms about.

"Get me out of here. Why are you staring at me? Do something!" she whimpered exasperatedly.

Perseus stared more intently at *Medusa*. The snakes seemed different too. They coiled tightly against her scalp. *Medusa* was too busy thinking about how to get back that she didn't realize she wasn't herself.

"Well, you are no help at all. Where is your king? I demand you take me to him at once," she quipped.

Perseus didn't answer. He needed guidance. He tried to piece together the state of his surroundings with each of her arrivals. He wished for Medusa to return.

"If you won't help me, I'll find him myself." *Medusa* pivoted on her heels with her nose slightly in the air. She was fumbling about trying to decide which direction to go when she saw him. The reflection of the moonlight off the water was rippling onto his shoulder. The moon's shadow flickered in pools of light. It was the soldier. He was stone. His face contorted and frozen in agony.

"What happened to this man?" she demanded.

Perseus went towards her. He reached out his hand. She slapped it away.

"Who sent me here? My father? What are your intentions with me?"

"I don't know who you are but you look like…you look like…"

*Medusa* interrupted him, "Who? Who do I look like?" she screamed.

"Follow me," said Perseus.

"I follow no one. You follow me." She scoffed at him. "Where am I leading you?"

"Towards the sea."

"Towards the sea, what?" She asked, as if he should know what to say next.

"Towards the sea….my lady?" he asked.

"That's better. Come now." She walked towards the sea with Perseus close behind. He rolled his eyes at her entitlement then smiled thinking about how she would react to seeing her reflection in the water.

Patmos 4:00am

The waves slapped *Andromeda's* face. She could not swim and she struggled to keep her head above water. Her clothes kept getting tangled around her legs. The dog treaded next to her and she used his body to keep her afloat while she discarded the outer layer of clothing. Under the second layer she felt something in the lining. She tore it open at the seam. It was a white feather. *Andromeda* took it as a sign of hope and kept it. When she went to tuck it into her hair, she saw an image of two men laughing. She attributed this to exhaustion. With a lighter load, she knew she could make it to shore. This dog was a good help too. The two trudged along as best they could and finally made it to land.

"Thank you, dog," said *Andromeda*.

The dog thanked her by shaking all the water off his body. *Andromeda* reacted as if she were dry. She put her hands up to block the spray of water, turned away and giggled. It felt good to laugh. The happiness lasted only a moment before her thoughts turned to Perseus. She wondered if she would ever make it back to him or if she was now destined for a new life with this dog. She took her hand and brushed the hair off her face. The snakes were gone. She reached for her neck. The necklace was there. She lifted her skirt and the scar from Poseidon's trident was gone too. Royal clothes, no snakes or scales or scar…Who was she?

A girl's voice was calling in the distance.

"Daniel, Daniel!" she yelled.

The dog's ears perked up. He tugged at *Andromeda's* skirt.

"I see you boy, I mean Daniel. I'm coming. I'm glad to know your name and will thank your owner in person for your bravery in helping save my life."

She patted his head and he kept by her side as they made their way towards the voice. The sun was rising behind them over the sea. The light engulfed the hill in a warm glow. There was a girl, in a field of flowers walking toward them. She looked as if she had seen a ghost.

"*Andromeda*, my lady," the girl gasped. "How did you get here?"

*Andromeda...My name is Andromeda,* Medusa said to herself. "I swam. From the rock. Your dog rescued me."

"My dog? "Yes, my dog, Daniel," said Vexia concernedly. "What about the boat? Were you on it? What will you tell your mother?"

*Andromeda* thought quickly and asked, "I don't know what to tell her. What do you think I should say?"

"Did you hit your head out there?"

"Maybe, I'm not sure. I don't feel quite like myself. What are you doing out here in the dark?"

"You know exactly what I am doing. I'm visiting them. You should pay your respects as well," Vexia said curtly.

*Andromeda* got a sense that she was about to be found out as an impostor. This girl knew her and knew her well. She had to find out more.

"Yes, yes of course I will."

*Andromeda* saw two raised patches of earth. She knelt and removed the white feather she had found in the dress and laid it down between the two graves. Vexia's eyes widened. *The feather,* she said to herself...*she's gone mad, like her mother.*

*Andromeda* saw the dog again in her memories. He was here in this exact spot barking at the Albino. She pondered this but could not make sense of it.

"We should go miss. You can hide in my quarters. Your parents haven't been seen since you disappeared. I'm sorry about your birthday miss."

*Disappeared?* she thought. "How did you know it was my birthday?" *Medusa, think before you speak,* she thought.

"I've known you since you were a child miss. A servant keeps track of all things."

*Oh, I'm saved. I share the same birthday as this Andromeda,* she said to herself. "Servant? You are my same age."

"Yes, I am and I have been at your side for every moment of your life up until yesterday when you disappeared. Do you remember the day at the temple?"

Vexia could see that she did not. *The day at sea, however she got there, must have taken a toll on her,* she thought.

"Which way to home?" asked *Andromeda*.

"That way miss." Vexia pointed North, up the coastline. "Come Daniel, let's take Andromeda home."

*Andromeda* walked with a head full of thoughts. Vexia bent down as if to fix her sandal.

"I'll catch up my lady. Daniel knows the way."

*Andromeda* was too preoccupied to respond. Vexia gently picked up the feather and tucked it under her servant's cap. When she touched the feather, she saw Medusa in the arms of a boy.

Seriphos 6:15am

*Medusa* marched ahead of Perseus. She reached the waterline alone.

"What are we doing here?"

"I brought you here to show you something. This may be a bit of a shock to you but you are not who you think you are."

"Of course, I'm me you fool. I'm just in different clothing and I plan to change that as soon as I meet your king."

The light from the sun was peeking over the horizon. Perseus bent down at the water's edge. He motioned for *Medusa* to join him. The sea was as smooth as glass. He looked out over the surface and tossed a double-headed eagle coin into the sea and made a wish. The same wish he always made.

"Why did you throw that coin? What did you bring me down here for? I see no palace, no boat, no horses. Is this a trick?"

"I brought you here to see your reflection."

*Medusa* gathered her skirt into her hands and began walking towards Perseus. The sunlight rose just enough to reveal her hands in the light. At the end of her fingers were claws. Her hands were bent and crooked and the nails were sharp and dirty. *Medusa* dropped the cloth and raised her hands in front of her face.

"Arrrrrrrgggggggggggghhhhhhhh, no! No! No! NO!!!!!" she yelled.

"What happened? Who did this to me!!!!????" She made her way to the waterline. She looked at her reflection and hit the water with her fists. "Was it you Poseidon?" she shouted out to sea. "Isn't taking me away from my family enough?!"

*Poseidon? Who is this Andromeda and what could she have done to cause such wrath from a god,* thought Perseus.

After fits of rage and storming about, *Medusa* calmed.

"What is your name boy?"

"Perseus."

"Well, Perseus, if I'm *Medusa,* where is she and what were you doing with her?" she asked condescendingly.

"I pray she is alive. I hope she is where you were and I am with her because I love her and I'm trying to save her."

"Love her?"

"Yes, I love her."

"How can you love a monster?" she said in a mocking tone.

"I loved her before Athena changed her and I love her even with her curse. A body is just a body. Beneath the surface lies a beauty that transcends the external. Love sees beyond what the eyes perceive."

"You are some fool. She has nothing to offer you. You can't possibly think that you can live like this forever?"

"I know we cannot but I would choose one day with her over 40 years without her.

"What's wrong with you? I could never choose what you chose. Choose power. Love isn't real. Being loved fleetingly by all is better than being loved completely by one."

"Tell me about your life then. Why is it better?"

"My life has been filled with privilege and opulence. I was married and my husband died on our wedding night."

"Oh, I'm so sorry."

"Don't be. I couldn't stand him. My mother made me marry him to build the empire and save me from being a priestess to Athena. That is love Perseus. The more powerful you are, the more loved you are."

"I beg to differ. A love based in power means you are either feared or controlled. It's not free. There is a price."

"You have a price for loving her. Staying here sleeping under bushes isn't my idea of a beautiful life."

"When you are in love the cold doesn't feel so cold, the ground feels like laying against a lamb, the night feels like daytime, love is enough. There is no need to look for anything else to fill the spaces of your soul."

*Medusa* thought of Alcaeus and how it felt to lay in his arms dressed as Meda. She was happy at that moment even though she was dressed as a peasant. She shook her head to forget the memory and said, "Well, I've never been in love then."

"What exactly did you do to be exiled?"

"The gods overreacted to a statement made by my mother. Poseidon wanted a sacrifice. My parents used me to make amends. She faked my death and sent me away to live in another country but I escaped. I was making my way back when I ended up here."

"What did you plan to do when your parents found out."

"Honestly?"

"Yes, that's the way I prefer my questions to be answered."

"Hmmm." I prefer to not answer that yet. If there is another switch, there's something I need you to tell your Medusa to get when she is me in Patmos."

"Do you think she's safe?"

Andromeda was touched by his sincerity. She could see he loved her. "I do not know. Is she wise and quick? A dog I know was barking on the shore which means Vexia, my servant, was nearby. Vexia knows everything about me. She had to do what I told her to do before I was exiled. I'm not sure of her loyalty now. She stole something of mine before I was sent away. I need to get it back. With it, I can make everything right again."

"What did she take from you?"

"Something that may be able to undo this curse we are under and return your Medusa to you."

"Are you asking me to ask her to steal?"

"I'm asking you to ask her to kill."

"I cannot ask her to do that."

"Do you want her back? I can make it safe for you to live together."

"How? They will be coming for her any day now."

"Do you know the legend of the Albino double-headed eagle?"

"I do. Medusa dreamed of flying away on its wings one day."

"I can make that happen."

"How?"

"I have one of its feathers."

Perseus gasped, "How?"

"How I came to possess it is of no consequence to you. I need her to find Vexia and convince her to give your Medusa the torn piece of the parchment she took from me and then kill her (Perseus shook his head) Very well then, I'll do it later. The parchment and the white feather are the most important things. I need them to overthrow my father and settle the gods. Do you think you could ask her for it if she makes her way back to you?"

"If it will give us a future together, then yes."

Patmos 6:15am

Vexia twisted *Andromeda's* hair into a knot at the base of her neck. She applied dirt to her face and thought about Meda. There was no need to switch clothes now. *Andromeda* looked every bit a peasant. Her clothes were torn and dirty from her escapades at sea. All she had to do was hide that flaxen hair and she could go unnoticed.

They entered the town's agora through the eastern gate between two massive columns topped with statues of Athena. A chill ran down *Andromeda's* spine. The statues here were much larger than the ones on her island. She was reminded of Athens and how today would have been the first full day of her service to Athena. Poseidon ruined that life for her. She wondered what the friend she made, named Daphne, was doing today and who was helping her stitch the cloth. In a year her life path had changed dramatically; from a young girl committed to serving Athena as a priestess, to a girl that rescued a crow and found the love of her life, to the most feared monster walking the earth, and today, she walked as an unknown girl with a dog and a servant. She couldn't begin to imagine what could happen to her next.

The girls slipped through narrow passages and crumbling alleyways blending perfectly with the townsfolk. The echoes of conversation and laughter reverberated off the stone. There was freedom in not being known and *Andromeda* relished the moments of ambiguity. A malnourished donkey called to them as they passed by. Andromeda stopped and petted him on his nose.

A flabbergasted Vexia said, "*Andromeda,* how hard did you hit your head? Petting farm animals? What will I see next, dish washing?"

"It's good to step out of your comfort zone every now and then."

*Remember, you are royalty,* she thought. "I promise, it will *never* happen again," said *Andromeda* in her best authoritative voice.

The owner of the donkey came out of his door.

"Hello Vexia, are you here to retrieve eggs for the queen?" he asked.

"No, kind sir. I will return this afternoon. We simply stopped a moment to give your donkey some attention," said Vexia.

*Vexia...her name is Vexia,* thought *Andromeda.*

"Have you happened to see Argos? He hasn't been by in few weeks. I'm missing his quick wit."

"I miss him too," said Vexia glancing at *Andromeda.* "We can discuss Argos when I return this afternoon for eggs."

"Very well Miss Vexia," said the farmer as he waved her off.

Vexia led *Andromeda* into the palace grounds through a remote garden. They made their way into a concealed courtyard. There was a small stone structure with ivy covering it. The door was wooden and the structure had no windows on the front. Daniel went immediately to an earthen bowl filled with water and quenched his thirst from the long walk home. There were bunches of sea daffodils dotting the courtyard. Vexia opened the door. The place was modest but tidy. Much homier than that cave *Andromeda* had been living in. Inside was a cot, a small table and one chair. There were flowers in a bowl on the table. Vexia pointed to the single window on the back wall.

"The entrance to the palace is just through the oleander trees in the back." She shut the window. "You must promise me that you will keep this window shut and stay here. I'll leave Daniel with you. Do not try and enter the palace my lady. I will hide you here until I figure out what to do with you. If they find you are alive, I fear it will not be for long."

*Andromeda* tried to conceal her ignorance. She had so many questions that she didn't dare ask.

"I need to report to the palace. I'll try and find out what I can about Poseidon's threats and if danger has passed," said Vexia.

Just hearing his name made *Andromeda's* stomach drop.

"Yes, thank you. I will stay right here. When will you return?"

"I hope to be back by nightfall."


*7:00pm - Patmos*


*Andromeda* rested with Daniel all day in the cottage. There was barely room for the two of them on the cot. When she woke it was already dark outside. She fluffed the saggy old pillow and under it she found a piece of parchment. She carefully opened it and saw that it was written in ancient text and torn across the top.

*- see the truth through another's eyes.*

*Astra is believed to be connected to Athena's white crow. The Albino double-headed eagle was there the day she banished her crow for finding her secret, a son. Legend says that Athena's intended punishment for the crow was to turn him into metal and place him at the bunt of her spear for all to see as a reminder of what happens when you cross a god. When she went to strike him with her lance, Astra cawed and distracted Athena. The tip of her weapon struck a stone column which snapped the point. When the lance struck, it missed the bird's heart and hit only his beak. It went clean through both sides. Two pieces, now metal, fell to the ground. Athena's blind rage over the event allowed the crow time to fly away. Athena looked at Astra's interference as an omen and allowed her once beloved crow to go, but turned his white feathers black and cursed him to an eternal life in exile. Athena, fearing the omen, gathered the two metal pieces of beak and launched them into the sky. She proclaimed that if the crow could retrieve the pieces and find a way to bring them back together, his curse would be broken.*

*When this account was written down the pieces of metal had not been found and the crow had been wandering Greece in search of his beak for 100 years.*

*Andromeda* gasped and placed the parchment back under Vexia's pillow.

"Daniel it's about the Albino." *Andromeda* peeked through the slits in the blinds searching for Vexia. "Where could that Vexia be?"

"This means that the legend is true. Astra could come any day now. If he does, I'll take you with me and we will fly to Perseus and start a new life."

*Andromeda* paced the floors and thought about the words on the parchment. *If I can dream it, it can happen*, she said to herself. After hours of pacing, she peeked out the window again. There stood the brightest moon she had ever seen. A silver sideways smile, larger than the one last night but still a crescent. She thought of Perseus and her body shook. Her necklace felt warm. Daniel barked when she fell to the ground.

"Daniel?" The pup howled. "Where are we now?" asked Andromeda.

She felt around the dark space. It was small. She contemplated what she should do next. Daniel sat in front of the door and growled at her every time she went near. She leaned against the wall and wrapped her arms around her body. She rubbed them. They were thin. She rubbed her legs. Her skirt felt different. There was less of it. "The feather!" she exclaimed. She searched the layers of fabric and found nothing. The feather was gone. "Medusa has it. That rat!" *What good was it anyway? I don't have the other half of the parchment to know what to do with it,* she thought. Memories flooded her mind's eye. Memories she hadn't told anyone.

It was daytime in a field of sea daffodils.

*She watched as Alcaeus turned to dust. She went to him and pried the feather from his fingers, she ran to Argos. As she ran, she saw a memory that wasn't hers. A young boy sat on his mother's lap. She saw her eyes and heard her laugh. Argos walked in and the woman ran to him while holding the boy, the three embraced.*

When she approached Argos to try and save him with the feather, she saw Alcaeus again…

*It was her wedding feast and Alcaeus was holding his father, Andromeda walked in and saw him look at her. He knew it was her but the depth of pain he felt did not allow him to acknowledge this fact.*

That afternoon it happened again, this time in the library while searching for the Albino's legend.

*Andromeda held the feather between her thumb and forefinger. She twisted it back and forth while reading through ancient scripts. A scream echoed in her heart but it did not escape. She was Alcaeus and he was looking at his dead mother. His arm was around Argos and the old man looked at his son with eyes swimming in tears. She saw his hand wipe them away and hold onto his father.*

She placed the feather between the pages of a book and left the library.

That night, after Vexia taunted her about the parchment, she opened the book and took out the feather. She saw herself this time.

*Alcaeus's head was in her lap and he was looking at her. He loved her. She could feel the love he had for her. As his eyes searched her face, she saw herself smile and she heard herself lie to him and she felt him believing her lies.*

She slammed the book shut, walked to the dresser, grabbed a needle and thread, and stitched the feather in between the layers of her skirt where it would be safe and she would be safe from the hurt of the truth that she had killed them both.

"This place is of no good for me Daniel. Move, I'm leaving."

"Grrrrrr," Daniel growled.

Andromeda tried to shove Daniel away from the door. He wouldn't budge. She ripped off the bottom fabric of her skirt at the hem. She sat by Daniel and half-heartedly stroked his head. He continued to growl at her. Infuriated, she stood up.

"I said move!"

"Grrrrrr!"

She backed away and felt a counter. On it was a jar. She could see Daniel's shadow against the door. She launched the jar at him. It met his head and he fell to the floor. She used the fabric from her skirt to tie his legs together. She opened the door and stepped out into the night.

She saw the palace flag in the light of a torch. She was home and soon it would belong to her. She needed to find Vexia, get the other half of the parchment, overthrow her father, find the feather, and use it to get Poseidon to forget about the error of her ways and begin her reign over Patmos.

# Chapter Thirty-Two
### Revenge - Patmos Island

THE PALACE WAS quiet. Andromeda crouched in the oleander trees and waited for the night guard to ride past. When he passed, she mimicked the hoof beats of his horse and made her way across the stone path and into a door on the southern wing. The library was right above the entrance. She made her way in and crawled along the floor avoiding the open-air windows. It was dark and she couldn't dare light a candle but the torch lights and moon illuminated a section of the room which was bright enough for reading. She fumbled about grabbing books and artifacts and bringing them into the light to inspect.

She felt a solid object and brought it close to the window. It was a sculpture of a snake and in its mouth was a bird. On the bottom the artist had carved their name. She held it up a bit to catch more light and see the name. When she did the light caught her crescent shaped necklace and bounced around the room. Fearing that a guard would sense an intruder, she tried to take the necklace off. It wouldn't budge. She couldn't untie the leather strap holding it nor could she remove it by bringing it up and over her head. She hunted for something sharp and found a shard of broken glass. When she tried to cut it off, it wouldn't cut. The necklace remained.

Frustrated, she moved out of the light completely and felt around searching for something sharper. She climbed on top of stacks of antiquities covered in various cloths. The muted colors of foreign places cast a warm glow in the space. *Where could Vexia have put the other half of that parchment? Surely, she wouldn't have kept it in that hovel she lives in knowing that I would have it searched. She must have it on her.* Andromeda contemplated sleeping in the library and waiting for the day to light the room but opted to go and retrieve the first half of the parchment that she hid. Surely her mother was asleep.

Andromeda stepped out into the hallway and slowly closed the door behind her. The hallway had a series of open windows that flanked the garden on one side and the central courtyard on the other. She crawled along the mosaic tiles dodging the light. When she arrived at the end of hall, she decided to go right towards her room, instead of left towards her mother's room. She wanted to see it. She silently opened the door. With each step she felt hollower. She expected to see it exactly as she left it but in the back of her mind she prepared for disappointment. She always had a plan for disappointment since it so often wandered into her life. She was not prepared for what she saw. The room was empty. She had been gone only a day and they had erased her from their lives. She walked about the space picturing her bed and her clothes. She could see Vexia opening the drapes and she could hear her scolding her for all manner of things. The memories flooded her mind. An overwhelming feeling set in, loneliness. She had always been alone. She had always felt unloved. The emptiness of her room felt comfortable. It felt right. Emptiness felt like home.

What she did now didn't matter. If they could forget about her so easily, she could do the same to them. Anger rose from her heart. She imagined watching her mother fall at her hands. With each imagined cut she felt a release of pain. Her father would have to go too. It would be harder to take his life but he was just as guilty. It would be done. The depths of her thoughts were interrupted by a voice. It was coming from the garden. She peered above the windowsill and saw her mother walking in the moonlight. She was singing. She was happy. *How could she be singing and happy? She thinks I am dead. Doesn't that hurt you, mother? Don't you miss me? I thought you loved me?*

Andromeda doesn't know how to feel hurt. Every emotion comes out as anger. It's what she knows. Each tear that doesn't fall, each sunken heartbeat, rises to block out the pain, each memory is shifted to solidify her narrative. It's easier to feel angry and want revenge than feel the hurt from a lifetime of abandonment.

Andromeda recognizes the song. It's one her mother used to sing to her as a child. Now, she sings to a satchel. She is cradling the bag containing Echo and rocking it back and forth as she walks. The other animals are making their nightly routine. Bunnies nip at verdant blades of grass and the peacocks sit together along the fountain admiring their reflections and sipping water. As her mother walks, a toad hops on her skirt and takes a ride. Lambs, still wearing the white bows from the wedding, are curled up for the night. Andromeda leaves her room and crawls along the hallway until she is above the fountain.

She peeks over and sees her mother transfixed on Echo. She's walking towards the fountain. She kisses the spot where Echo's head must be. She holds it against her chest. She walks slightly under the spot where Andromeda is which causes Andromeda to lean out further to continue watching her mother. Andromeda is laser focused on her mother. Her hair loose and down her back shining in the torchlight. Her doll-like features dot her face like an artist placed them there. Everything about her was perfect. Andromeda loved her but it's foolish to love something that can't love back. The scar is too deep to fill. *If they were gone, I would have space to learn to love.* She leaned further over. Her mother was staring into the fountain now. She gasped and clutched the satchel tighter. She turned her head to look up. Andromeda ducked. She heard her mother say.

"There, there, Echo, it's my mind playing tricks on me. Andromeda is not there. It is only some shadows playing tricks on the water."

Andromeda slowly rose up and leaned out over the window as far as she could. She could see her mother's reflection in the fountain. Her eyes were closed and her face looked peaceful. She leaned even further out and thought about jumping and tackling her to the ground. She could drown her in the fountain and retrieve the parchment she hid in Echo's bag that day at the temple. Before she could decide, she stared into the fountain's water a little too long. The moon was passing over and she saw its crescent shaped reflection in the basin of the fountain. A surge of electricity ran over her limbs. She fell and Medusa appeared.

MEDUSA WAS LOOKING through Andromeda's eyes now. She blinked several times to clear the scene. Andromeda had been looking out the window. *Andromeda* searched the view to see what could have drawn her attention. *Andromeda* sensed sorrow. She looked down into the garden and saw a figure kneeling in the grass. It was a woman and she appeared to be crying?

*Andromeda* didn't think. She left the room and wound around the halls of the palace until she found the entry into the garden.

"Andromeda, what are you doing here? Let me be! How did you get back here? You drowned? Are you a ghost?" asked Cassiopeia.

"I came to help you?"

"Help me, you are the one that killed him!"

*Andromeda* didn't know what the woman was talking about but she had to pretend that she did.

"Where is he now?" she asked.

"Here of course. With me as he always will be. And now you are here. The ghost of my dead daughter comes to haunt me. I deserve it. You used to follow me around and do whatever I asked you to do. You loved me as only a child can love their mother and I tried to love you. But you grew up and you were strong and you stood up to me and your beauty, oh your beauty is otherworldly. When I realized I couldn't compete with you, or completely control you anymore, I got Echo. He loved me more than you ever could. Look what love got him!" Cassiopeia held up the woven bag and shook it.

The reality started to sink in for *Andromeda.*

"Do you care for me at all, Andromeda?"

"I do."

"I've been so horrible to you and now we may all perish just like Echo." Cassiopeia's voice was eerie and distant. The words had no weight, they simply fell out of her mouth slowly and landed on the earth.

"What do you mean?"

"Poseidon. He's threatened to flood our entire island if we don't make another sacrifice. We already sacrificed you. I suppose I'm next."

Just the sound of his name sent chills down Medusa's spine. She saw him hunched over her and heard his voice…*at least this moment will leave you immortal in a small way.* Her body tightened and her lips quivered trying to get out the next words.

"What kind of sacrifice? When?"

"Whenever he chooses. He's a god and no match for your father, a measly king."

A cloud covered the moon and, in a flash, Medusa was back on Seriphos.

Cassiopeia was so engrossed in herself that she didn't notice *Andromeda's* necklace turn to white and her body going limp.

Andromeda surveyed the scene and stared intently at the bag in her mother's hand waiting for her to speak.

"What do you have to say about this predicament you've gotten us into?" asked Cassiopeia.

"I, um, I."

"That's what I thought. I'll have to think of something, like I always do. I knew having you would be the end of me. I've carried you for seventeen years, why should the next seventeen be any different. Except you are already dead. My ghost daughter comes to haunt me, pay no attention to her Echo."

Andromeda allowed a single tear to fall from her eye. That tear held every ounce of heartache, doubt and pain but willed her conviction to the surface. She wiped away the tear and anger fueled by years of believed lies ripped open a fury unseen, except in stories of the gods.

"You've tortured me for the last time mother," she said with calm and steady eyes.

Andromeda lunged at her mother and grabbed the bag containing Echo and ran. She ran into the palace and up to the tower. Cassiopeia was right behind her.

"Stop, Andromeda, stop!"

Andromeda did not stop. She went faster and faster up the twisting staircase holding the bag containing Echo. The bag flung from side to side with every step.

"You're hurting him. Give him back to me!"

At the top of the tower was an opening that led to a balcony. Andromeda went to the edge of the balcony and leaned the arm carrying Echo out over the ledge. The night sky began to brighten. The clouds were sashaying south with the wind. The tip of the crescent let itself been seen, then the curve of its back and finally the point at the top.

～ຽຽ～

The jolt sent Andromeda on her heels and *Andromeda* entered and fell forward clutching the bag containing Echo. *Andromeda's* head was spinning. She bent down to settle and gather her senses and stood up rapidly. She didn't see Cassiopeia until it was too late. She was running towards *Andromeda* with wild eyes and hands that looked like weapons. She clawed at *Andromeda's hair* and *Andromeda* rose up

158

quickly to defend herself. She didn't know she had left the garden; she was still adjusting to the shift. Cassiopeia snatched up Echo just as *Andromeda* stood and the force of the impact hurled her over the side of the balcony. *Andromeda* looked at her bare hands and turned bewildered around the turret balcony trying to piece together the flurry of what just happened. She peered over the edge and saw the body of Cassiopeia sprawled in the garden with the bag containing Echo resting, as if gently placed, on her chest. She looked flawless except for the stain that was forming on the mosaic floor from the blood that was pouring out of the back of her head.

*Andromeda* turned in horror and slid her back slowly down the side of the balcony wall until she sat. She crossed her arms and pulled in her knees. With a heavy heart, she placed her head on them, and wept.

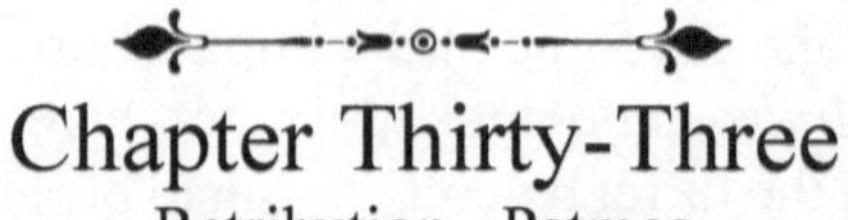

# Chapter Thirty-Three
## Retribution - Patmos

A DISTRAUGHT *ANDROMEDA* entered the garden and walked over to the lifeless Cassiopeia. She opened the bag and gasped in horror when she saw the remains of a small dog inside. She dropped the bag and when it hit the garden stones something shattered. It sounded like pottery. This puzzled *Andromeda* and she held the bag up once more and felt the bottom. There was something small and hard in the bag. She moved the vessel up the side of the bag and opened it when it reached the top. She retrieved a small broken amphora. Something was hidden within. *Andromeda* was about to retrieve it when she heard a voice.

"What has happened. What did you do to the queen?" A shocked servant ran towards her. "Andromeda? How did you get here? Guards! Guards! Alert the king! The queen has fallen at the hand of her daughter."

*Andromeda* was terrified. Unbeknown to her, one of her snakes made the switch with her. He grabbed what was hidden in the amphora. It was a folded piece of parchment. The snake held it in his mouth and pulled himself deep into her braided hair. She was midway through the garden when she realized she was trapped. Guards stood at every doorway. She knelt to the ground and looked up to the sky. Her eyes met the moon and her neck turned warm. A flash of light fell upon her as she said, "Perseus, save me."

Andromeda was surrounded when she came back into herself in the garden. The guards were chastising her. She couldn't see around them. The last thing she remembered was holding Echo over the balcony ledge.

"What have you done miss?" said one guard.

"I always knew you were born with a dark heart," said another.

"Your own mother, our queen."

"We will all pay for this."

"My mother?" asked Andromeda as she tried to break free and look around the guards.

"Her blood is on your hands."

"Mother," she whispered as she looked around the courtyard.

She saw her mother's lifeless hand laid palm up in the distance. The bag containing Echo was next to her and opened. Her face, still flawless. The stain of blood oozing around her looked like a red velvet cape. Even in death she was regal.

"There was an impostor. She did it!" said Andromeda.

"Silence. Your father has been alerted."

Two whistles blew, a sign of the king's beckoning. The guards took her to her father's inner sanctum. There she was locked in until his arrival. When he entered, he was holding the bag containing Echo.

"Father—" Andromeda began but was interrupted.

"Do not speak Andromeda. I have no choice now. Your mother and I tried to save you by sending you to live with King Menik in Africa. Poseidon wanted me to sacrifice both you and your mother for retribution for your blasphemy at the temple. I convinced him of taking only one, you, and only because your mother had it arranged to fake your death and let you keep your life. When we heard the ship caught fire and sank the night you departed, we grieved. Your mother sunk deeper into despair. Her mind was shattered with pain over losing you and Echo. To see you here now leads me to a painful choice. I want to ask for forgiveness but I deserve none. Poseidon has decided for me. There are no other options Andromeda. All our servants saw you here. They all think my Cassiopeia's demise was at your will. Poseidon will destroy our island and all its inhabitants by flood if I do not do what he asks of me."

"What is it he asks of you?"

Father and daughter stood silently looking at each other. Tears fell from all eyes but no words were said.

"Guards," King Cepheus said.

Four guards entered and took Andromeda away. The king turned his back as she was escorted out. He could hear her screaming for him but he did not succumb to her heart-wrenching plea for help.

Andromeda was blindfolded and taken by boat to a large rock formation which could be seen from the shore so that the citizens of

Patmos could see the king's sacrifice to Poseidon. There she was tied with a chain around the waist and both wrists to a pointed spire of stacked stone at the top of the formation. She spit at the guards as they secured the chains.

"You'll pay for this!" she said.

"You've done enough damage to the people of Patmos, miss. We have all suffered greatly due to your actions," said the Commander.

"When I get off this rock, you will suffer at my hand. Your fate will be worse than my mother's!"

The guards entered the rowboat and began their way back to shore. Andromeda kicked rocks in their direction and continued her hateful rant.

"Should we tell her?" a baby-faced guard asked the commander.

"She'll find out soon enough," he replied.

"It's a sorrow to see a beauty like her destroyed," said the young guard.

"Beauty comes from the heart not the flesh," said the commander.

"You speak the truth yet I do not want to be near when Cetus comes to take her," said a guard with salt and pepper hair.

"How long before the sea serpent comes?" asked a usually introverted guard as he looked back at Andromeda.

"Cetus lives in the waters surrounding Patmos but only comes to the surface at the request of Poseidon. Row faster if you do not wish to watch," the commander said feeling the weight of their task on his crew. "Regret nothing about tonight men. We served our king and our god. What's done is done."

The men rowed the rest of the way to Patmos with conflicted thoughts. One focused on seeing his wife and children, one thought about the king and if he would be rewarded for his obedience, one thought about saving Andromeda and one secretly wished he could watch her flesh being ripped from her bones and devoured by Cetus.

# Chapter Thirty-Four
Legend – Seriphos Island

WHEN MEDUSA FOUND Perseus back on Seriphos she was talking so fast he couldn't understand her.

"I made it back to you! I don't want to go back there Perseus. I killed her mother."

"What? Whose mother Medusa. Who did you kill?"

"Andromeda's mother. It was an accident but I think she was trying to kill her own mother. I awoke on a balcony and when I stood up, her mother was running towards me and the force of our impact launched her over the balcony where I stood."

Medusa was pacing and thinking.

"Her servant's name is Vexia. She has a dog named Daniel that saved me by swimming with me."

"Slow down Medusa, breathe. The sun is rising. I think we have time. The last time you left you were looking at the moon. There must be a connection."

"You may be right Perseus. I was looking at the moon when guards were coming to take me away and I ended up here with you."

"What else happened when you were Andromeda?" asked Perseus.

"Vexia concealed my identity and I pet a donkey and walked in the town as a human, not a monster. She hid me in her quarters just outside of the palace. Andromeda's parents are angry with her. I rested with the dog all day and I found proof of the Albino in a note hidden under her pillow. The Albino is real, Perseus. His name is Astra and he should be arriving any moment now."

"How do you know this Medusa?"

"I'm guessing, I'm hopeful. I don't know for sure. The parchment was torn in half."

"Torn in half? I believe you. Andromeda told me about the Albino as well and said she had half of the parchment and Vexia had the other half. She asked me to have you help get the parchment and a feather. She said the feather was white and came from the Albino.

There was a long pause before an excited Medusa said, "I had the feather Perseus. It was sewn into Andromeda's skirt. I found it and left it on a grave as an offering."

"What else do you remember? Can we get it back?" asked Perseus.

"I saw two men laughing when I held the feather. I didn't think too much of it then. One was young and the other was old. Father and son perhaps? They were cooking together. I tucked it into my hair and continued swimming to shore with the dog."

"Do you have any idea where the first part of the parchment is?"

"I do not," said Medusa.

"Andromeda told me she thinks the feather can be used to break your curse. If you end up as Andromeda again, do you think you could get to the feather?"

"I will try."

"We cannot possibly figure this all out now but if there is a chance we can end your curse, we must try. For now, let me look upon your face."

Perseus and Medusa spent most of the day and night in each other's arms with their eyes shielded, soaking up every moment they had together. Simply breathing next to each other felt like a gift. They knew their time together was coming to an end, they just didn't know how it would end. Eight of Medusa's snakes were coiled on rocks next to them, bathing in the sun. One stayed coiled on her head. Perseus took the moment to cradle Medusa in his lap. He rubbed her temples and spread his fingers wide to move her hair and expose as much of her face as possible.

"Keep your eyes covered my love. I'm going to look at you."

Medusa smiled and used her hands to seal the edges of her blindfold more tautly around her eyes. Perseus stroked her face and hair gingerly. He looked upon her as if she was made of lace. The slightest movements intended to glorify her existence and etch her into his memories. He began to unbraid a section of hair on the side of her head. The snake coiled more tightly.

"Medusa, there's something here in your snake's mouth. It's a piece of parchment."

"Open it Perseus."

A reluctant snake opened his mouth and released the note. Perseus studied the parchment as he unfolded it. He smoothed the damp edges and his eyes pulled words from the page.

"It's about the Albino. The parchment is torn. It's the other half!

Listen Medusa. You are right. The legend is true."

*When Zeus came into power, he let two eagles fly from the ends of the earth. One flew to the East and the other flew from the West. They met in the city of Delphi which proved Greece to be the center of the earth. Their unity represents divine power and the dualistic nature of gods and man. This is how the double-headed eagle was created. Zeus sent half of the eagles to the east and the other half to the west to build a flock and now you can only find these glorious birds in Greece. When man follows the gods, both heads work in unison and the eagles are peaceful. When there is a disruption about to take place between the gods and mortals the eagles can turn on each other and other birds.*

*All animals and humans used to have four arms and four legs until Zeus split humans in half as punishment for their pride. He left us destined to walk the earth searching for the other half. Legend tells us that every one-hundred years an albino double-headed eagle appears. The beast is known by the name, Astra. One head is guided by hope and the other by fear. Together they form a communion of truth. If one head dies the other will take its own life. They cannot live separately. The heart and mind must find a balance. When Astra appears, one that hears the call and believes will be united with their half for eternity. Nothing can separate this union, not even the gods.*

*Although imposing in size, this bird is fragile. Even the slightest touch without invitation will destroy the animal. To approach this ethereal being, without being cursed, it must call you. The intended will hear three caws. Its voice is that of a crow. Once the intended hears the call, the albino has the ability to see through another's eyes to help restore sight in the world and bring together a perfect union.*

*Some ancient stories tell of men who took a feather from Astra. Their fate was sealed in death at that very moment. There are no known accounts of anyone surviving; however, it has been said that whoever possesses one has the ability to -*

Medusa listened as she put the pieces together.

"Perseus, this is the beginning of the legend I found in Vexia's room. If I go back, I can retrieve it and put it all together. We may have a chance. This princess, Andromeda, who comes to replace me, has she said anything?"

"She says a lot, but nothing of significance."

"If a switch happens again, see what you can find out. Do not tell her we have this. Her mother must have been hiding it for a reason."

"If a feather and the legend have been hidden with such care, what power do you think they hold?" asked Perseus.

Medusa saw herself gliding through the sky on Astra with Perseus. She gripped his hand tighter and replied, "Freedom."

# Chapter Thirty-Five
### The Rock – Patmos Island

IDNIGHT SITS ON guard. A half-moon shines down on golden hair now a tangled mess of sea-spun sorrow. Moonbeams hold her secrets. She wonders who would save her now. Once upon a time, Alcaeus may have saved her. Her mother would have if it had benefited her but she was no longer an option. Curiously, she didn't miss her or Alcaeus. Vexia? Yes, maybe the poor fool, Vexia, would show up. Andromeda imagined her waving from the shore trying to distract a sea monster. The thought of it made her laugh, then cough and the coughing made the chains dig into her torso. She was bound at the wrists and waist. She couldn't move her arms enough to reach her mouth to cover up. Wet clumps of hair stuck to her cheeks like leaches. The salty waves tore at her legs and the thin chiton clung helplessly to her body. The creases folded into the crook of her elbows and sprawled out like a web over the rock.

She looked at the moon and wished for a switch to happen. She wanted Medusa to be strapped to the rock and eaten by the sea serpent. She stared at the moon on and off all night waiting for Alcaeus's necklace to warm her skin and for her to fall into Seriphos as Medusa. She cursed the night sky and wondered how she could force a shift to happen. The shift always happened when the moon was shining. What was she missing? She needed Vexia's parchment and the feather.


6:00am Patmos


When morning came, there was still no sign of a sea monster. Calm waters, as blue as the lapis stones that decorated the palace walls, lapped playfully on the rock. Andromeda was thirsty and hungry. Her eyes searched the shore for any signs of life. Surely someone would come and rescue her. Her father wouldn't leave his only child to die just to please a god…would he? Surely this gesture of leaving her out tied to a rock all night was enough. If there was truly a sea serpent coming, wouldn't he have come by now? *I'm sure he's getting hungry too,* thought Andromeda.

Time moved slowly on the rock. The sun scorched Andromeda's skin. She was beginning to lose faith in being rescued. It was too much effort to keep her head up, she was weak from the toll of the night and the sea and the sun. Her mind started playing tricks on her. She spoke to her mother as if she was right there with her.

"Was this in your plan mother? When you had me did you envision this future for your only child? Are you happy now? You are finally more beautiful than me. Look at me! Scorched and wind whipped. You win! You win…you win…you…win," the words tripped out over her tears.

Vexia returned to her home to find the door open. She peered into the space and saw Daniel tied up in the middle of the room.

"Daniel! Are you hurt? Daniel, please wake up."

She shook the dog gently and looked him over. He whimpered and tried to open his eyes but he was too weak. There was a wound on his head but it wasn't bleeding anymore. She untied his legs and the pup stretched.

"There, there Daniel. You are fine. I'll take care of you sweet boy."

Vexia stroked his head and took off her servant's cap where she had hidden a bone from the kitchen. When she went to grab the bone, she touched the feather. She saw the boy she saw from the last time she touched the feather and heard a girl's voice.

*"Then kill the monster and free me. I know you've thought about it Perseus." Vexia could see blue eyes destroyed at the thought of what he was asked to do.*

Vexia dropped the feather. That voice. She knew it. She picked up the feather again and held it in her open palms. This time she saw Athena and heard her say.

*"Quod Obstat Via Fit Via!"*

*Vexia was under a cape next to a girl and when she spoke, she heard that familiar voice, "The obstacle becomes the way," She watched as the girl grabbed a hand and bit it, then dashed out from under the cloak.*

*"I'm here your highness!"*

*"You dare to address me as one of my priestesses?" Athena cackled. "Medusa, your transgression has broken an oath promised to me. You owed me a life of service but now I will take your life for what you have done."*

*"I did not pursue Poseidon. HE took me. I tried to run! I tried! I have always been loyal to you, Athena. Please, I beg you. I must live!"*

*Vexia saw the crowd and when her eyes locked with the boy with blue eyes, she dropped the feather.*

"Medusa?" she questioned. "Daniel, who did this to you? Andromeda?"

Daniel was lethargic but made a low growl when he heard the name Andromeda.

"Don't worry, she can't hurt you again. She has been taken away for killing the queen. She is tied to a rock in the sea."

Vexia didn't dare leave Daniel but she couldn't wait to get her hands on Andromeda. She sat and thought about what she saw. She wanted to touch the feather again but was terrified at what she would see next. She held the bone for Daniel to lick and tried to piece together everything that had transpired. She went to her cot and took out the parchment. Only one line made sense to her. The very first line…

*- see the truth through another's eyes.*

She needed the first part of the legend. Something was happening she couldn't explain. She looked at the feather resting on the floor next to Daniel. It was tempting her and she couldn't resist. She picked it up…*waves were crashing around her. She saw Daniel swimming towards her. She heard her own voice calling his name.*

She dropped the feather. She took a few deep breaths and picked up the feather again and held it tightly this time. She was at a pond.

*Caws and chirps, squeals, and flapping were coming from a tiny island just below a bridge. Vexia saw a frightened girl with long dark hair running towards the sound. A double-headed eagle held a crow in its talons, its beak gripping feathers and tugging at black wings. Two more were flying in to help destroy the crow.*

*"Stop! Stop please! Somebody! Help!" she heard her say. "Shoo!"*

*Vexia watched the girl wade in but she could not get close enough to reach the crow. One of the eagles left the scene and flew straight towards her. He brushed past the top of her head. A warning. The girl grabbed a branch and swung at the bird. During its next descent it plucked the branch from her hands and flew off. The girl was crying now and screaming for them to stop. The crow was bleeding and his cries had lessened.*

*"Help, help. Anyone! Please help!" she wailed through desperate breath.*

*Out of nowhere, an eagle fell silently just steps away from her. His heart pierced with an arrow. Vexia heard the next arrow flying above. It came from the bridge. Vexia looked to the bridge and saw the boy with blue eyes, his hand holding a quiver taunt against his bow. He let go and dove from the bridge into the water. The arrow downed the second eagle. He swam to the crow who was still being held by the last surviving eagle. He grabbed the eagle with his hands and choked him until he released the crow. He reached back for his sword. It was different from any she had seen before. It was curved at the end like a sickle. He wielded the sword and pivoted around searching for other offenders.*

*The girl wiped tears from her face as the eagle flew away. The boy placed the wounded crow on the nape of his neck and swam to the shore. He handed the wounded crow to the girl.*

Vexia gently placed the feather on the ground.

*- see the truth through another's eyes.*

Vexia read the legend over and over. The images she saw played on repeat. She knew she saw Medusa but who was the boy and why was she seeing them? Daniel laid his swollen head on Vexia's lap. Vexia moved the feather with her foot. She saw nothing. She removed her shoe and tapped the edge with her toe. A flash.

*She was standing in a pool of blood. The boy was there but he was wearing a blindfold.*

Vexia moved her toe. The vision stopped. She put her shoe back on and tended to Daniel. She had to know more. When Daniel was asleep, she moved out from under him and crawled over to the feather. She was on her hands and knees and the feather was just below her face. She studied the feather and saw nothing unusual about it. The quill was white, stark white. The pearlescent surface seemed to glisten, even in the dark. Vexia laid down next to it. She closed her eyes and slowly placed one finger at a time on top of the feather. She started with her pinky.

*She saw a young Medusa being mocked by a group of girls.*

She placed down her ring finger.

*She saw an owl circle Medusa at Athena's temple.*

She placed down her middle finger.

*She saw the boy with blue eyes and heard him say, "I am not much of a warrior, yet. I, and my sword, Harpe, have just begun our adventures. I have plans to be many things Medusa, but for now, I am simply Perseus."*

*Perseus blue, she heard Medusa's thoughts. The sky matches his eyes. The sky is Perseus blue.*

She placed down her pointer finger.

*Vexia watched as Medusa walked out of a cave. Her skin was gray and marred. Snakes twisted between her dark hair and around her head and neck. Medusa turned and saw her sisters holding the boy. She heard her speak.*

*"Perseus. Perseus, it's you?"*

*"I'm here."*

*"Your head, what happened?"*

*"I'm okay. Medusa, I'm terrified. Am I safe? Can I open my eyes? I need to see you to feel complete. If I am to die today as least let my last memory be of you."*

*"Oh Perseus. I wish you could open your eyes. But do not. I've dreamed of Perseus blue every moment since I left the safety of your cloak. We should have run. You were right."*

*"Perseus blue?"*

*"Your eyes Perseus. They are the color of the sky on a perfect day."*

Her thumb was the last to land on the feather.

*Vexia saw a confused looking Perseus and Medusa. Medusa was sopping wet. Vexia looked at her inquisitively. The snakes uncoiled themselves from around her neck and Vexia saw something familiar. A crescent moon necklace just like Andromeda's necklace, hung around her neck.*

*"What is happening Medusa? Can you tell me what you saw?" asked Perseus.*

*"I was here with you. I remember the moon. I saw the moon there too. I was cold and wet and clinging to a rock. I know it was me because I was holding your necklace in one hand. I felt like me too but more human. I felt determined. I don't know what I was trying to do there. I don't know how I got to the rock but the dog started swimming out to me. It was a long way but the dog kept coming. He was gray. I was happy to see him. The sea was calm. The moonlight cast light along his path to the rock. I slid down the rock and the dog held me and swam me to shore. I was almost there when there was a flash of light, I went under the water and I ended up back here. I can still smell*

*his wet fur on me. Was it real Perseus? It seemed so real but it was a dream. Surely it was a dream?"*

*Perseus held her closer. "I don't think it was a dream Medusa. It was real. The girl that was here was real but it wasn't you. She called herself, Andromeda. It must be a sign Medusa. A sign of our salvation. Scarpe predicted this. You told me Scarpe scratched out a message to you. What did Scarpe tell you again?"*

*"He said to wait until the Solstice. That I could help you on the Solstice."*

*"Maybe this is how you are helping me. Helping us. There is no me without you Medusa."*

*The clouds parted. Medusa shook. Vexia blinked at the sight of it all and then Perseus was gone and, in his place, she saw a crazed Cassiopeia charging towards her.*

She lifted her fingers from the feather.

She took a deep breath as she spread her fingers wide and hovered them across the length of the quill. She dropped them gently onto the feather and tapped them up and down the spine like she was playing a lullaby on a harp. With each tap she saw something new.

*Tap...Medusa playing with her sisters...Tap...Medusa laughing with Daphne at the temple...Tap...Medusa kissing Perseus...Tap...Medusa laughing at the crow...Tap...Medusa seeing her reflection in a mirror around Poseidon's neck, she felt pain...Tap...she saw Medusa laying in a field with the crow and Athena's owl...Tap...she watched the face of a child slowly turn to stone...Tap...she saw the face of a boy right before his eyes were ripped out...Tap...she saw Medusa making a mosaic out of pebbles...Tap...she saw crow bringing Medusa a crescent moon necklace...Tap...she saw Perseus, she felt love...Tap...she saw a soldier crying for help, she watched him die...Tap...she saw the moon, she felt heat and light then darkness...Tap...she was in the palace courtyard and saw blood coming out of Cassiopeia's head...Tap...she saw Medusa adrift in the sea wearing Andromeda's clothes...Tap...she saw Daniel...Tap...she saw herself.*

She hovered her fingertips again. The images ceased. Vexia's hand was shaking. She grabbed it with her other hand and lay on the floor motionless next to Daniel and the feather with a swirling head of thoughts and fears.

"Daniel, gather your strength. We are taking this feather to the rock."

# Chapter Thirty-Six
## Harpe – Seriphos Island

PERSEUS AND MEDUSA sat quietly unmasked staring out into the sea. Their tranquil embrace was interrupted by the sound of wings cutting through the air. They turned their heads to look and saw nothing. When they turned back, she was standing in front of them. White wings expanded. Her head darted between their faces. The look on her face was calm but her eyes told Medusa that something needed immediate attention. Owl lowered her wings between her legs and there was Scarpe. He was limp and covered in white powder.

"Owl. Can I hold him? What happened?" Medusa asked while tears streamed down her cheek. She knelt to her friend and stroked his head.

"He has given a valiant effort towards a task nearly impossible to complete. His work has been all consuming. I have helped him all I can. He has one more tremendous feat to accomplish tonight. I planned to bring him to you later but I brought him now because time is running out. For him….and for you. They are coming for you."

"How can we save him?" asked Perseus.

"You saved him once. You can save him again. Look through his eyes Medusa. When it's time, you will know what to do. Remember what I told you when I visited you at the cave." Owl lifted off into the night and flew towards Athens.

Medusa held Scarpe under her chin to keep him warm. Owl's message gave the night air a slight chill. She sat on the ground against a tree. Perseus secured his blindfold and joined her.

"What did Owl tell you at the cave?" asked Perseus.

"He said help him fly to the moon."

Scarpe's wings moved slightly.

"Do you want to fly Scarpe?" asked Perseus.

His wings fluttered.

"Did you see that Medusa?"

"I did. Scarpe, do you remember when Perseus jumped off the

bridge and swam to save you?" asked Medusa.

The crow moved a bit more. Medusa wasn't sure if it was a response to the memory or an involuntary twitch. His eyes were fixed to one spot. He did not make a sound but he was breathing.

"I carried you in my shoe and you looked just like Hermes," chimed in Perseus.

"They say love can heal all things Scarpe and I love you," whispered Medusa.

"I love you too," said Perseus. "We have fought so hard Scarpe. We will fight again for you. We have nothing to lose."

"Except each other," said Medusa.

The crow blinked.

"Scarpe!" Medusa stood up and Perseus followed.

"Perseus, put the blindfold on me and help Scarpe like you did after we found him."

Perseus held the old crow in the palms of his hands. He lifted him up and down. His wings caught wind but they could not flap on their own. Even after a few minutes, he could see that the exercise was taking a toll on Scarpe. He placed him in Medusa's care and walked down to the sea. In the distance he saw a flock of birds. Black wings against the sky fluttered. They flew without sound and low to the ground. When they glided over Perseus's head, he saw that Owl was leading them. They dipped lower near Perseus and they each dropped a feather. Perseus smiled and gathered the feathers. He ran back to Medusa and Scarpe.

"Medusa, give me some of your hair."

"Perseus, your voice sounds like hope. Snakes, take Perseus some of my locks."

"Hold Scarpe, Medusa. The Owl has helped us again."

Perseus took the strands of Medusa's hair and wove the new feathers into Scarpe's frail wings. Medusa sang and stroked his head.

"Do you remember the day in the meadow Medusa?" asked Perseus.

"I do."

"We were so entertained by Scarpe hopping around catching bugs between his chipped beaks."

Medusa laughed at the memory.

"You would have eaten all day little fellow." Perseus tied the last of the feathers. "There now Scarpe. I am done. Let's see how your fortified wings work. I'm turning around now Medusa. Look at what I've done."

Medusa removed the blindfold and held Scarpe up to her face. She could see her reflection in his black eyes. He looked like something hand-made, like tattered origami or a tangled-up marionette. The white powder wouldn't rub off his scraggly wings. The new black feathers were shiny against the dull black ones hidden under the white dust. She looked deeper into his eyes and willed herself to see something, she needed a sign. He was in there. He had to be. She strained to see more. *Look through his eyes,* Owl had said. The longer she looked, the more she saw. There was life in the depths. She saw flecks of gold and white and light. She knew he had it in him to fly.

Their joy was short lived. The hills to the south of them had a halo of glowing amber.

"Perseus, it is time. They are coming," said Medusa.

Perseus reached for Medusa's hand and said, "It's too soon Medusa. The moon is half. We need to wait for a crescent."

"We don't have time. Now Perseus," said a resigned Medusa.

"Medusa, I can't live without you. What if it doesn't work? If the shift doesn't happen, I will slay you instead of Andromeda."

"I trust it will work. We have nothing to lose. They are coming for me now. We can't live running forever. There are no absolutes in life but I can promise you this…Love transcends the boundaries of this life. If it doesn't work, and I fall at your hand, I'll go and prepare the next life for us."

"My love for you is more than should be allowed. You are my perfect path, even in this tragedy."

"And you are mine."

Medusa paused and caressed Perseus's face. She nuzzled his chest with her cheek. Their hands were intertwined at Perseus's heart. She took in the sound and felt his quickened beats against her cheek.

"We cannot shelter each other from our souls. What touches me, touches you. Even if we hide from each other, we will be together. It will be the same after I'm gone. Not storm, or gods or blade can separate us. Only through this darkness can we live in light Perseus. Your eyes see darkness but my heart sees light." Medusa's speech was calm and convincing.

Perseus gripped her hand tighter. His shallow measured breaths were dotted with these words, "I will see you in the sea, in the wings of birds, in the smallest of pebbles, in the snakes on the rocks, in the ripples of tossed coins in fountains, in the fire on a hillside and every night I will see you and hold you in the depths of my dreams."

"The sacred space between heaven and earth will be filled with our love," she whispered.

Her eyes were tightly closed under the cloth trying to visualize what it would look like if she could see that space filled with their love. She was surrounded by a vibrant blue dripping with peace. *Perseus blue. Even the universe knows that love is the color of Perseus blue,* she thought.

"Convince me that I do this out of love," these staccato laden words left his trembling lips.

"You hold our love in your hands," she said.

"I hold your life in my hands."

"A life that I ask you to take for love," she implored.

"My heart has no words left."

Perseus watched tears escape her eyes like sap dripping from a tree. They rolled slowly out from under her blindfold and became thicker as they made their way down her cheek. Hardened tears dropped to the ground.

"Perseus, what is that sound? It's as if I tossed a handful of pebbles onto a frozen pond."

"Medusa, it's the sound of your tears."

"If I can turn my own tears to stone, my heart is next. Take me now while there is still life in me. I would rather die in love than let my curse extinguish the life I love. I do not have much time left. They will come for me or the curse will. You will watch me die either way. Let love be the victor Perseus."

Perseus placed Scarpe in her hands. The snakes coiled into a triumphant crown. Perseus kissed Medusa and turned her to face the sea and the glowing moon. He untied the material covering her eyes. It was wet from her tears.

"My broken heart feels the purest love. I surrender you to the stars that brought us together. May divine mercy shine through them onto us tonight. When you are ready, lift Scarpe to fly and open your eyes."

Medusa looked down at Scarpe. He turned his head up so he could look at her. His eyes had a strength that resonated with her own battles. She felt hope when she looked at the dusted white crow.

"I need to know you will be able to go on when I'm gone Scarpe. I need you to fly and guide our Perseus to whatever lays ahead for him."

The crow nodded. Medusa smiled. Perseus prayed.

She raised the crow and loosened her grip. Her fingers spread wide to give him space to move. He did not flap them. She didn't know what to do next. Owl's words lingered in her head. *Help him fly to the moon and back.* She didn't know what it meant. She had done everything she could.

"Fly Scarpe, fly," she cried.

A gust of wind swept across his limp wings and lifted them. His wings flapped and an elated Medusa tossed him into the night sky. The breeze turned him. Each quill transcended the air between earth and heaven in an arch that covered part of the moon.

"A perfect crescent," said Perseus. He exhaled and felt himself take a breath for the first time in months. Air filled his lungs and joy filled his heart. "Forgive me," he said as he swung Harpe above his head and watched the blade come down on Medusa. She opened her eyes as he raised the blade. The reflection of the moon rested on fire-lit topaz with a hint of green. She closed her eyes before the blow hit. Her head fell to the ground. The crown of snakes left their host. His mother's necklace lay between the head and body in a sea of red. Perseus brushed the hair away from her face. His thoughts were swirling between disbelief and hope. The eyes were closed. He placed the head in a satchel and placed the necklace around his neck. *I cannot cry now,* he tells himself. He must try to move through the next chapter of their story. He feels the light shift from above. A great shadow has fallen over the moonlit path between Perseus and the sea. The sky becomes so dark that he cannot see its source. He searches the sky and slowly the shadow passes across the moon and begins its descent. The light from the moon reveals undulating white wings that cast shadows over the glistening sea. The beauty of the bird was blinding.

"Nothing in my dreams has ever compared."

As the bird descended, the light surrounding it penetrated every ounce of darkness of the night. Every beat of the wings created more light. So much so that daylight overcame the night. Perseus watched in awe as the gentle beast landed at the edge of the shore. The eagle cawed three times. *He sounds just like Scarpe.* Perseus thought about the parchment, *He who hears the call and believes.*

"I heard the call. Medusa, I'm coming for you," he said as he walked towards the beast as if on a familiar path.

He called for Scarpe. He called for Owl. Neither came. He held the satchel with the head of Medusa and approached the legendary albino. The bird lowered its heads and turned them to one side to look into Perseus' eyes. One head had an eye of sea foam green. *As green as the girl that called herself Andromeda,* Perseus thought. The other head had a topaz eye that was more ablaze with fire than that of his beloved Medusa. Perseus smiled. The bird turned its heads and eyes of blue, the color of the Adriatic sky, starred back at him from both heads. *Medusa would call these Perseus Blue*, he thought.

"Astra," said Perseus and then he paused. Astra knew he believed. He knew him and he knew Astra. Perseus smiled. The bird nodded and used its beaks to nudge Perseus to mount its back. Perseus placed the satchel across his chest, strapped Harpe to his back and climbed onto a mountain of white feathers.

Together they flew over Seriphos towards Patmos.

# Chapter Thirty-Seven
For the Ferry – Patmos Island

VEXIA DOVE INTO the dark expanse of sea. The force of her impact knocked her servant's cap off her head. The cap that concealed the feather started drifting. Just as she was about to retrieve it, Daniel saw a seagull and his thrashing paws stirred up the sea so much that she lost sight of the cap.

Vexia screamed, "Stop Daniel, come back! Please Daniel!"

Daniel didn't listen. Panic filled Vexia's eyes. The feather was drifting away towards Andromeda.

Andromeda heard Vexia's voice and perked up. "Vexia! You found me!"

Vexia's panic thwarted her energy. Daniel was way ahead of her. The seagull flew away. It was then that he heard Andromeda's voice. He swam excitedly towards her.

"Daniel, stop!" yelled Vexia.

"Good boy, Daniel. Here pup," called Andromeda.

Daniel made it to the rock. Andromeda watched Vexia struggle in the water. She was about to send Daniel to help her when she spotted a sinking servant's cap. A buoyant white feather released itself from the folds. She watched as it rose. Yes, it was the Albino's feather and now it was floating atop waves.

"Vexia, that rat," she said under her breath. "Here Daniel. That's a good boy."

Daniel approached the rock.

"Fetch Daniel."

Daniel looked for a tossed ball, found nothing and looked back to Andromeda.

"There Daniel, fetch that feather. Do you see it?" she asked.

Daniel, eager to please Andromeda, paddled around the water looking for something to bring her.

"Daniel, Daniel!" Vexia shouted as she swam.

Daniel eyed something floating on the surface. It was the feather.

He grabbed it in his mouth and turned to take it to Andromeda.

"Good boy Daniel. What a good pup. Come and I'll give you a treat," said Andromeda.

An exhausted Vexia continued to scream, "No Daniel. Here boy."

It was too late. Daniel was at Andromeda's feet shaking the sea water from his body.

"Drop it Daniel," Andromeda said.

He dropped the feather. Andromeda kicked him off the rock back into the water. Daniel swam back and climbed up the rock. She kicked him again. Vexia saw the second kick.

"Andromeda! What are you doing? Stop!" pleaded Vexia.

Andromeda sneered at Vexia. She had the feather now. She didn't need Vexia. She would make a wish and save herself. Vexia could drown for all she cared. She went to reach for the feather and realized she was still bound to the rock. She couldn't bend to reach and pick it up. She looked helplessly at the feather thinking of what to do next.

Daniel swam to Vexia and together they reached the rock. Daniel cowered behind Vexia. She picked up the feather and tucked it into her sleeve. She saw a flash. *Medusa holding a crow. Andromeda.* She knelt and rubbed Daniel's ears and kissed him on the forehead. She looked up at Andromeda.

"We are your only friends miss. How can you be so cruel?"

"Forgive me Vexia. Look at me. I've been tortured for days out here. I've always been good to you." She started to cry. "Help me one last time. Please Vexia."

"Why should I help you?"

"You have no one else Vexia. If I am to perish tonight, you will as well. What future do you have without me?"

"What future do I have with you?"

"If you give me the feather and the other half of the parchment, I will overthrow my father and rule Patmos on my own."

"The feather has a power that you could never understand," said Vexia.

"The feather will understand what I need Vexia. Give it to me, now!"

"I cannot."

Andromeda kicked Vexia and she tumbled into the sea. Daniel helped her to the back side of the rock. The two climbed up and composed themselves. The moon was rising over the water. It was a half-moon now. Vexia and Daniel sat quietly listening to Andromeda try to win back their favor.

Vexia whispered to Daniel, "Daniel, Andromeda didn't hit her head. She's Medusa and she's not a monster. She helped a wounded crow. She is who stopped to pet the donkey."

Vexia removed the feather and held it close to her heart. The images were confusing. She let go of the feather and watched it float down to her lap.

"Daniel, sit here with me. I'm going to close my eyes for a while. Don't be alarmed."

Daniel laid his head on Vexia's lap. She placed one hand on his head and gave him reassuring strokes. She picked up the feather with the other hand and placed it on her chest. She spread her fingers wide along the spine and pushed the feather with her just her thumb against her chest. She saw *Andromeda*…

*She was in Vexia's room sleeping with Daniel.*

She pressed her thumb in tighter against the feather.

*She saw Andromeda reading the parchment and heard her speak.*

*"Daniel it's about the Albino." Andromeda peeked through the slits in the blinds searching for Vexia. "Where could that Vexia be?"*

*"This means that the legend is true. Astra could come any day now. If he does, I'll take you with me and we will fly to Perseus and start a new life."*

*Andromeda paced the floors and thought about the words on the parchment. If I can dream it, it can happen, she said to herself. She peeked out the window again. There stood a bright silver sideways smiling moon.*

*She watched Andromeda's body shake. Her necklace glowed. Daniel barked when she fell to the ground.*

Vexia placed her first finger against the feather. She saw Cassiopeia.

*"Andromeda, what are you doing here? Let me be! How did you get back here? You drowned?*

*Are you a ghost?"*

*"I came to help you?"*

*"Help me, you are the one that killed him!"*

Vexia placed her middle finger against the feather.

*Cassiopeia was running towards Andromeda with wild eyes and hands that looked like weapons. She clawed at Andromeda's hair and*

*Andromeda rose up quickly to defend herself. Cassiopeia snatched the bag containing Echo from her hands just as Andromeda stood. Andromeda looked at her bare hands and turned bewildered around the turret's balcony. She peered over the edge and saw the body of Cassiopeia sprawled in the garden with the bag containing Echo resting on her chest. There was blood pouring out of the back of her head.*

Vexia placed her ring finger tight against the feather. She saw Perseus and heard Medusa speak.

*"I made it back to you! I don't want to go back there Perseus. I killed her mother."*

*"What? Whose mother Medusa. Who did you kill?"*

*"Andromeda's mother. It was an accident but I think she was trying to kill her own mother. I awoke on a balcony and when I stood up, her mother was running towards me and ... she fell ... her head ... I tried to help her but the guards came and then I looked at the moon and I was back."*

*Medusa was pacing and thinking.*

*"Her servant's name is Vexia. She has a dog named Daniel that saved me by swimming with me."*

*"Slow down Medusa, breathe. The sun is rising. I think we have time. The last time you left you were looking at the moon. There must be a connection."*

Vexia placed her pinkie finger along the tip of the feather's quill. She saw Medusa and Perseus in each other's arms. Perseus was unbraiding Medusa's hair. She saw a snake coiled tightly between her curls.

*"Medusa, there's something here in your snake's mouth. It's a piece of parchment."*

*"Open it Perseus."*

*A reluctant snake opened his mouth and released the note. Perseus studied the parchment as he unfolded it. He smoothed the damp edges and his eyes pulled words from the page.*

*"It's about the Albino. The parchment is torn. It's the other half! Listen Medusa. You are right. The legend is true."*

*When Zeus came into power, he let two eagles fly from the ends of the earth. One flew to the East and the other flew from the West. They met in the city of Delphi which proved Greece to be the center of the earth. Their unity represents divine power and the dualistic nature of gods and man. This is how the double-headed eagle was created. Zeus sent half of the eagles to the east and the other half to the west to build a flock and now you can only find these glorious birds in Greece. When man follows the gods, both heads work in unison and the eagles are peaceful. When there is a disruption about to take place between the gods and mortals the eagles can turn on each other and other birds.*

*All animals and humans used to have four arms and four legs until Zeus split humans in half as punishment for their pride. He left us destined to walk the earth searching for the other half. Legend tells us that every one-hundred years an albino double-headed eagle appears. The beast is known by the name, Astra. One head is guided by hope and the other by fear. Together they form a communion of truth. If one head dies the other will take its own life. They cannot live separately. The heart and mind must find a balance. When Astra appears, one that hears the call and believes will be united with their half for eternity. Nothing can separate this union, not even the gods.*

*Although imposing in size, this bird is fragile. Even the slightest touch without invitation will destroy the animal. To approach this ethereal being, without being cursed, it must call you. The intended will hear 3 caws. Its voice is that of a crow. Once the intended hears the call, the albino has the ability to see through another's eyes to help restore sight in the world and bring together a perfect union.*

*Some ancient stories tell of men who took a feather from Astra. Their fate was sealed in death at that very moment. There are no known accounts of anyone surviving; however, it has been said that whoever possesses one has the ability to -*

Vexia tucked the feather between the folds of her dress and mouthed into the night air.

*"To see though another's eyes."*

Vexia thought about the legend and all that she had seen. Medusa had been wronged and she thought she could be saved by the Albino. She didn't know that the Albino had already come and gone. Andromeda had killed it too. Andromeda had hurt so many. She wanted to help Medusa and Perseus. It would be a way to make up for the deaths of Alcaeus, Argos and Astra.

*Think Vexia, think. What can you do to make this right?* she said to herself.

"Astra? Argos? Alcaeus? Anyone who's listening. Please guide me." Tears began to cascade down Vexia's cheek.

"Stop saying those names Vexia!" screamed Andromeda. "They are gone. Forget about them."

"I'm not made like you miss. I do not forget."

"Vexia, know your place. You cannot see the future as I can see it. When I have power, you will have everything you've ever wanted. Once the moon rises over this rock and I can see it, a switch will happen and Medusa will be the one on this rock with you, waiting to be devoured by a sea serpent."

Vexia did not answer Andromeda. She waited, watching the moon slowly rise over the sky. It reached the pinnacle and began its descent over Andromeda's head. The night was cloudless. Vexia watched the moon through wet eyes which distorted the edges and made the moon appear to bob and sway around the stars. It looked to be tethered there. She wished someone would cut the tether and she could watch the moon fall into the sea. Then a switch would never happen. She knew Medusa was with Perseus now and she wanted to keep it that way. Andromeda would be able to see the moon any minute now. Vexia held onto Daniel bracing for the inevitable.

"I can feel the light coming Vexia. I'll be back to take my place as queen. You'll get nothing from me if you don't give me that feather now," protested Andromeda.

The moon was directly above Andromeda now. She bent her head back as far as she could and strained her eyes upwards. She caught a glimpse of the light. Nothing happened. She didn't dare blink as she continued to look for several minutes more. The expanse of the moon was visible now. Nothing.

"Vexia! What did you do? It's not working! Give me that feather!"

Vexia sensed hope. She reached into the folds of her dress and grabbed the feather with both hands, laid all ten of her fingers across the spine and held it tight against her heart. She saw Medusa and Perseus. They were together by the sea. The moon was the exact same shape as the moon that was shining down on her right now. She heard Perseus speak.

*"Convince me that I do this out of love."*

*"You hold our love in your hands,"* Medusa said.

*"I hold your life in my hands."*

*"A life that I ask you to take for love,"* she implored.

*"My heart has no words left,"* Perseus said as he watched tears roll out from under Medusa's blindfold. Hardened tears dropped to the ground.

*"Perseus, what is that sound? It's as if I tossed a handful of pebbles onto a frozen pond."*

*"Medusa, it's the sound of your tears."*

*"If I can turn my own tears to stone, my heart is next. Take me now while there is still life in me. I would rather die in love than let my curse extinguish the life I love. I do not have much time left. They will come for me or the curse will. You will watch me die either way. Let love be the victor Perseus."*

*Perseus placed an old crow into her hands. Vexia watched as snakes coiled into a triumphant crown. Perseus kissed Medusa and turned her to face the sea and the glowing moon. He untied the material covering her eyes.*

*"My broken heart feels the purest love. I surrender you to the stars that brought us together. May divine mercy shine through them onto us tonight. When you are ready, lift Scarpe to fly and open your eyes."*

*She saw Medusa look at the old crow.*

*"I need to know you will be able to go on when I'm gone Scarpe. I need you to fly and guide our Perseus to whatever lays ahead for him."*

*The crow nodded. Medusa smiled.*

"NO!" cried Vexia. She climbed to the top of the rock and held the feather above her head. "NO!!!!!!!!!" She saw Medusa toss the crow into the sky.

*"Fly Scarpe, fly," she heard Medusa cry.*

*She watched the crow turn in the air. A gust of wind opened his wings just enough to cover part of the moon.*

*"A perfect crescent. Forgive me," he said as he swung a sword above his head.*

"A perfect crescent. The moon must be a crescent," Vexia said and she knew what she must do.

"What did you say Vexia?" asked Andromeda. "Enough of your babbling, give me the feather."

Vexia held the feather just above Andromeda's head, when Andromeda went to reach for it, Vexia turned it sideways. The arch of the feather perfectly shadowed a portion of the moon. The half-moon turned crescent. She let the tip of Andromeda's fingers touch the feather. Andromeda saw Perseus raising a blade. She screamed at Vexia who was now, eye to eye, with her. She watched as Vexia held a coin in front of her. Andromeda's eyes were lit by the light of the moon but all Vexia could see was darkness inside them.

"Get that out of my face and move peasant, the switch is about to happen. I'll be back. You'll pay for this disloyalty. Just you wait and see what I'm going to do to you."

Andromeda's body began to shake. The necklace around her neck turned a brilliant white. The sea began to rise and the sound of mer-music trickled in off the waves. Vexia took the coin and placed it into Andromeda's mouth.

"For the ferry my lady," Vexia said solemnly as she held Andromeda's mouth shut until her body went limp.

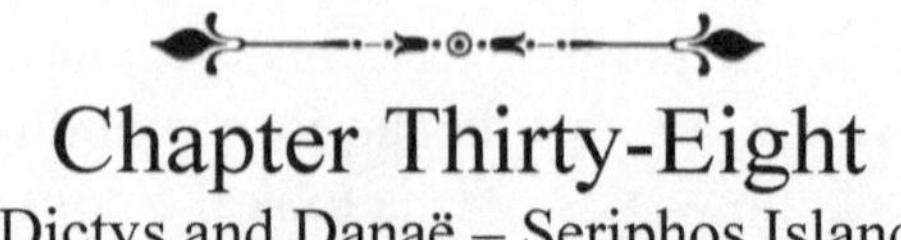

# Chapter Thirty-Eight
### Dictys and Danaë – Seriphos Island

THE ALBINO SOARED low over Seriphos. Perseus looked down over the island he loved. When they reached the other side, a lone fisherman was casting a net into the sea.

"Dictys," said Perseus. "*My mother.*"

The Albino instinctively knew to descend. Dictys watched in disbelief and fell to his knees when Perseus climbed off the bird and into his arms.

"Perseus? How?" he asked.

The two embraced and Perseus said, "Dictys, we don't have much time. Come, we need to rescue mother."

"Perseus, we are too late. She is married."

"It doesn't matter. I know how to save her. Please, come with me. I'll explain everything later."

Dictys climbed up next to Perseus. The sky was now full of sunlight and the palace courtyard was brimming with soldiers. They all looked to the sky and knelt in respect of the legend that was flying towards them. When the eagle circled to land the force of its wings cutting through the air sent a burst of wind that blew hats off men and silenced all sound. Perseus called for his mother, "Mother, mother!"

When Perseus dismounted the eagle, the men rose to defend the king. Perseus braced for what was coming. King Polydectes entered the courtyard with fury in his eyes. When he saw the Albino, he was stuck by the ethereal beauty and stood mesmerized. The mythical creature was real and Perseus, who he believed to be dead, approached him.

"Where is she?" Perseus demanded.

The king tried to think of the words to say. The longer he took to answer, the brighter the light became emanating from the Albino. Perseus was also glowing as if he was a messenger from Olympus. The king raised his hand and called for his guards. Perseus opened his satchel and retrieved the head with one hand. He held the Medusa by the hair and used the other hand to pry open her eyelids. He directed its petrifying gaze toward the king. Polydectes succumbed to the power of Medusa's stare. A wave of silence washed over the king's supporters.

"Who else dares to keep me from my mother?" Perseus covered Medusa's eyes with his hand and walked among the men in the courtyard. No one dared to look in his direction. Guards on towers raised bows and prepared to attack. The eagle cawed and Dictys yelled, "Perseus watch out!"

"Shield your eyes!" he yelled back.

Perseus removed his hand and held the Medusa and pointed her eyes to the guards. They froze as did any man who chose to look towards him. Dictys took cover under the Albino's wing. He peered out and saw Danaë. She was being held by guards on the lower level in the shadow of an arch. Her eyes were pried open and her mouth was gagged. She was fighting them with all her might. *"Danaë,"* Dictys ran between statues of fallen men towards Danaë. Perseus was fighting. He kicked and used the Medusa to destroy any man that stayed. Arrows began to come from all directions. Astra cried and flew away. Dictys and Perseus locked eyes. Dictys motioned towards the archway, in that split second an arrow pierced his flesh. His leg gave out and he fell. Perseus looked towards his mother and at that moment an arrow arrived and penetrated his arm, the Medusa dropped and rolled. It landed face up and a guard went to pick it up. He charged towards Perseus. Perseus drew Harpe and began swinging with his eyes closed. He could feel men approaching.

"Perseus! I love you!" echoed in the courtyard. It was his mother's voice.

"I'm coming mother!" he yelled. "Hold on."

Perseus's mind flashed to being trapped in the chest. He saw a crow looking through the cracks between the wood planks to see his mother's shining necklace. He felt her arms around him and warmth overtook his fear. *The necklace*, he reached and ripped the cord from his neck. He clasped the metal pendant in his uninjured hand and held it straight out in front of his face. He kept his eyes sealed shut. The man holding the Medusa yelled for guards to seize him. No one approached for fear of turning to stone. *He's close*, thought Perseus, *come closer.*

When the guard inched closer, the crescent began to warm. The pain in his injured arm was excruciating. He willed himself to stretch his good arm out even further. He moved the crescent between the tips of his thumb and index finger to expose as much of the metal surface as possible. When the guard was close enough to see the crescent, his fate was sealed. His eyes beheld the reflection of the Medusa's eyes shining back at him. He was frozen holding the head. Perseus ducked down low below the Medusa's gaze and crawled to the guard. He reached up from below the statue to retrieve the head. It was permanently wedged between two stone hands now. Perseus rose up to the side of the figure, unsheathed Harpe and slashed at the stone arm until it released the Medusa. He placed it in the satchel and called for Dictys and his mother.

"Dictys?" Danaë said with disbelief under her breath.

The guards holding her secured her tighter. She could not move her head to look for him. She couldn't see that Dictys was approaching behind her. He had shuffled on his wounded leg and managed to loop fishing rope from his pocket into a noose. He stealthily approached a guard and wrapped the noose around his neck. When one guard was subdued, Danaë had enough strength to fight the one left. She bit him and kicked. The lone guard kicked back and Danaë fell. Dictys was choking the man he held and as he slumped to the ground he held on tighter until no life was left. Danaë was crawling away from her captor.

Perseus yelled, "I've got him, mother. Go with Dictys."

"Dictys?!"

"I'm right here," he said. He was crawling towards her. She helped him up. She smiled and the two embraced. The union was short-lived.

"Grab him Dictys!"

The guard was getting away. Dictys leaped into action. He removed the rope around the downed guard and charged the one getting away. He raised the rope over his head as if casting a line and launched it hard towards the guard's feet. The rope met its mark and the man toppled over. Perseus straddled the man across the chest, pulled out the Medusa and ended his life. Danaë ran to her family.

"I promised you mother," said Perseus.

"I will never doubt you again son," she replied.

"With the king removed from power, you hold the crown now mother. I need to right another wrong. I will return but now I leave to save Medusa."

Danaë nodded and embraced her son. Pride filled her eyes.

"Go Perseus. Follow your heart. It will not leave you astray."

"Thank you, son," said Dictys.

"Anything for you father," he replied.

Perseus grabbed his satchel and called three caws. The Albino swooped down as Perseus climbed the stone king. He leaped from the top of the statue onto Astra. Together they soared over the sea to find Medusa and set her free.

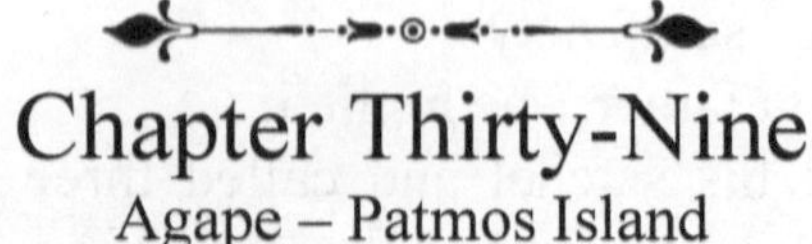

# Chapter Thirty-Nine
## Agape – Patmos Island

"MEDUSA, MEDUSA?" VEXIA spoke softly. Her body was limp against the restraints but she was breathing. Vexia stroked her hair and watched as the crescent moon around her neck dimmed from white to gunmetal gray. Daniel "yipped" when Medusa moved her head.

"Perseus?" she called out. Her voice was soft and weak.

"You are on Patmos miss, you made the shift," said Vexia. Daniel and I know everything. We are going to help you."

Medusa began to smile then her senses went on high alert.

"That music. Do you hear it?"

"Yes, it started only moments ago," said Vexia.

"You need to hide. Take Daniel and hide. NOW!"

"We can't leave you alone. We tried to untie you but the chains are too strong, they will not budge."

"I know this music. Please go and find a place to hide on the other side of this rock. No matter what happens, do not come to try, and save me. Save yourself Vexia. Swim away when he is distracted."

"When who, is distracted? The sea monster, miss?"

"Worse. Poseidon."

Medusa wilted against the restraints. She held her gaze down and waited. Soon the sea began to rise and waves splashed up onto her gown. Medusa prayed for Perseus to arrive. Poseidon's seahorses emerged first. The mer-music was overtaking Medusa's senses. She pushed down fear and thought, nothing *can be worse than what I've been through, not even death.*

Poseidon swam onto the back of a seahorse; he circled his trident into the sea and made the tide rise so that he was positioned right in front of *Andromeda's* face.

Poseidon spoke with eerie calmness. "So, we finally meet. I have heard so much about you. Your claims have disturbed the gods but your claim of beauty over that of my wife has been your worst offense.

I'm sorry about your mother. She was a great beauty."

*Andromeda* turned away from him. Vexia inched father away and clung to the rocks, the waves from his arrival threatened to drag her into the sea. She hung on every word and buried her face in Daniel's neck.

"Are you frightened?" he asked.

*Andromeda* didn't speak.

"The sea serpent is a gentle death. The wait is worse than the bite. I have a gift for you before you go. The seahorses lifted Poseidon so he was face to face with *Andromeda*.

"An angelic face but where are the sea-foam green eyes I've heard so much about?" She turned her head and closed her eyes. He scolded her. "Eh, eh, eh, don't close them, I want to see," he whispered.

He took his trident and brought it towards her face. The tip grazed her cheek and pried open her right eye. Fire-filled topaz stared back at him. Poseidon's mind traveled to a moment in a mirror. "Medusa." His eyes narrowed and he hissed. "How? It is you. Those eyes have been drenched in my memory since our encounter."

His words fell out of his mouth like a fresh cut and seeped into her heart until she could feel it no more. She tried to think of Perseus but in the terror of his presence she couldn't even remember how to say his name.

The clouds parted the sky and the top of Poseidon's head covered the moon just enough to make it a crescent. There was no switch. Medusa exhaled. Perseus must have been successful. He couldn't come soon enough. She raised her head to meet Poseidon's and willed herself to look directly into his eyes.

"I don't know how this is possible, nor do I know what to do with you," said Poseidon.

"It matters not. There's only one thing that matters."

"What is that?"

"That I was loved," Medusa choked on the word *loved*.

There was a rush of wind as a silent wing cut through the air above Medusa's head.

*Owl,* she said to herself. *Owl.*

A roaring thunder followed and a golden chariot descended from the heavens. Poseidon slid back into the safety of the sea. It was Athena and her arrival unleashed a thousand unresolved feelings deep within his heart.

"Athena," Poseidon nodded, his voice echoing over the waves. "What is of such importance that you felt the need to leave Olympus and venture into my realm?

Athena's chariot stopped above the waves. Owl returned to her shoulder. She paid little attention to the mortal on the rock. She was focused on Poseidon. Medusa turned away from the blinding golden armor.

"I never thought it possible but your latest escapade shocks me Poseidon," Athena quipped. "Meddling in mortal affairs will win you no favors with me."

"I quit trying to win you a long time ago Athena."

"Your mortal whims have consequences. Consider your path before you act."

"I have already acted Athena," said Poseidon as he gestured towards Medusa.

Athena glared at the girl on the rock. Once she recognized her as Medusa, Poseidon made a swirling motion with his trident. Colossal waves clashed fiercely around the rock. Medusa could barely see the gods through the crashing water. Athena countered by raising her lance and manifesting a storm with thunder and lightning that shook the sky. Medusa was caught between the oceanic and celestial dispute. With every lightning strike, she looked to the sky for signs of Perseus. During one strike she made eye contact with Owl, who sat stoically on Athena's shoulder. His look encouraged her strength. She thought the worst must be over but the tumultuous waves intensified as did the gods impending clash. The sea pounded at her legs and twisted the fabric of her chiton around her ankles. The raw fabric edges lashed at her legs. The more she tried to free herself, the more bound she became. She was one with the rock now. There was no escape.

"Vexia? Are you here?" asked Medusa.

Vexia didn't answer.

With the next lightning strike, Medusa saw it. The sea serpent's body worked its way effortlessly though the pounding surf towards Poseidon. The flesh was obsidian black and fangs protruded upwards from an extended jaw. There were no eyes, just a long, twisting, shining, slug of imminent death. She searched the water with every wrathful strike that launched from sea and sky. The water was ominous. She couldn't make out sea from serpent. Every movement looked snake-like, every crashing wave, a hiss, marking a step closer to the end.

Between the bellowing surge of sea and strikes from divine fury, Medusa heard a familiar sound. A caw. Her mind told her Scarpe was nearby. She heard the crow caw two more times. Her head swiveled to confirm what she heard. *Three caws*, she thought. The gods were caught in their own dispute. They showed no sign of hearing anything other than their own intentions to outperform each other.

*Caw, caw, caw,* echoed in the depths of her memory. It was Scarpe, there was no mistake. His voice was ingrained on her heart.

"Scarpe." She said his name into the storm as lightening cracked the sky.

The clouds parted and Astra emerged. The blinding white contrasted against the darkness of the thunder clouds. Medusa saw it briefly before it hid in a sinister cloud.

*Astra, Scarpe, Perseus,* she said with the reverence reserved for a sacred prayer.

The light was not lost on Athena's wisdom. She sensed the presence of the Albino. She intensified the lightning and with every strike she lit the clouds until she found white feathers starkly outlined against the dark clouds. Then the white turned to black. She saw a crow. The Albino dipped into another cloud. She raced to light the sky. She thought Poseidon had enchanted the heavens but that was not his realm. The vision must be real. She launched more lightning and with every burst of light, she saw black wings, protruding from white. Astra was there, but so was crow. The Albino skillfully outmaneuvered the lightning strikes. Perseus was cradled deep within the base of the neck. He gripped Harpe. As the lightning intensified and streaked across the darkened sky, the blade's polished surface caught and reflected Athena's charged bolts casting an ethereal glow around the rock holding Medusa.

Poseidon and Athena were faced with the unexpected alliance of mortal and eagle. Poseidon called for the sea serpent and sent him to taste his prize. With the swish of his tail, he bolted, jaws agape, towards Medusa.

"Perseus! He's coming! HELP!" screamed Medusa.

Athena sent bolt after bolt into the atmosphere. Perseus moved with the force of a hero. He emerged from the abyss of clouds, wielding Harpe. The razor-sharp edges of the blade sent arcs of light dancing through the air. Perseus skillfully navigated the sky above the treacherous waters. With divine agility, Astra dodged Athena's wrathful strikes. Harpe gleamed overhead. The clash between mortals and gods intensified with each lightning strike and surge of the sea. Perseus, fueled by determination, pressed forward using Harpe to redirect the hits. Once he had a moment between strikes, he looked to Medusa. The serpent was on approach. Its tail wrapped around the back side of the rock. Medusa was looking for him to come by way of sea but the beast was climbing out of the water and onto the rock. He would take her from behind. Perseus searched the sky for lightning strikes. Athena was holding back now. The sky was pitch black. He knew she was watching him. In the dark, he could not see her but she could see the white wings of Astra. The eagle did a barrel roll and pitched to the right. He dove straight down towards Medusa. Poseidon sent another surge of sea. One could not tell where sea and sky began. They were engulfed in black. Astra made another turn, this time, his wings turned black. They hovered, shrouded in darkness, waiting for a sign. Astra turned his heads to look at Perseus. His eyes were solid black, just like his wings…just like Scarpe's. Perseus hid Harpe under his cloak. Perseus felt a vibration in the air. A burst of light followed. Astra opened its wings to full expanse and glowed white. The bolt came and ricocheted off Harpe, the light was sent towards the serpent but missed by a hair. In the light Perseus saw Medusa tied to the rock. He also saw a girl clutching a dog on the backside of the rock. The sea serpent slithered past them, his tail thrashed and sent the pair into the sea. He heard Medusa scream.

"Perseusssssssss!"

Astra made another turn this time on black wings. They suspended in midair just behind the serpent over the swell of the sea. Stealthily they waited. Perseus raised Harpe. Astra turned upside down and Perseus dropped onto the back of the monster. He used Harpe to carve a gash all along the creature's back as he ran towards its head. Poseidon's pet opened his jaws and the smell of rotted sea escaped into the damp air. An ear-piercing screech was the only thing Medusa heard as Harpe met its target. She watched the eyeless creature's head roll past her and into the sea. Medusa did not make a sound. Poseidon had his trident under her chin.

Perseus stood at the crest of the rock. Harpe was covered in blood. He pointed it directly towards Poseidon. The sea around the rock calmed. No more lightning strikes came. Astra was shrouded in the night sky. Between cracks of thunder, Perseus heard Medusa whimper.

"Turn back Perseus, please turn back."

Perseus's neck started to warm. He reached for the necklace and felt heat. The crescent started to glow. He saw a light coming from Medusa's necklace as well.

"Make that stop," demanded Poseidon.

Medusa did not answer. She closed her eyes and tried to imagine flying on the wings of Astra. The crescent around Perseus's neck began to glow brighter the closer he got to Medusa. Poseidon looked up and saw the gleaming crescent that matched Medusa's. Poseidon used his trident and tried to cut it off Medusa's neck. The leather would not snap. With every attempt, it grew brighter. Perseus leaped from the peak and landed next to Medusa.

"I'm here. I'm here." He took her trembling frozen hand. "You are safe now. Open your eyes. Look at me…look…at…me."

Silent wisdom settled upon Athena as she observed the reunited pieces of her spear connecting Perseus and Medusa in a bond that transcended the enmity of the past. The curses she enacted, once a symbol of her power, now bore witness to the intricate threads of destiny woven together by wind and wing. Time and myth intertwined. The crow had won.

Athena called off the storm and Astra glided in over the rock. His eyes were solid black. The heads worked in unison to remove the crescents around Medusa and Perseus's necks. Owl whispered into Athena's ear. She called Astra to her side. He cawed a haunting melody that spoke of reunions and the passage of time. In the eagle's beaks, two shimmering crescents, relics from a wayward curse, swung like pendulum.

Athena was silent. She closed her eyes and nodded to Astra.

Astra let out a loud, "CAW!"

Owl whispered, "Well done crow."

Athena cast a blanket of light over the island. Poseidon remained above the surface. Astra flew over to Medusa and Perseus and nudged them with his beaks to mount. Perseus lifted Medusa into his arms. Their eyes never broke sight of each other as they flew on alabaster wings to the shore.

"Perseus blue," she whispered.

"My guiding light," he whispered back.

"My face, it is not mine."

"The things I love about you cannot be seen Medusa."

"I'll never leave your side."

"Then my wish from the coin I tossed on the day we met has come true," said Perseus.

"Mine has too."

Athena and Poseidon listened in on the reunited lovers from the rock. A single white feather dipped up and down in the sea. Owl left Athena's shoulder to retrieve it.

"That was quite a show you put on today, Athena," said Poseidon.

"I could say the same to you."

"The mortals and your crow won. Does that anger you?" asked Poseidon.

Before Athena could answer, Owl landed on her shoulder with the feather. She placed it against her cheek and in a flash, Athena saw and felt everything Vexia had witnessed. A wave of understanding washed over the goddess.

"No, it does not anger me. I gained wisdom today. They have something we can never have," replied Athena.

"What do they have?"

"Love."

Poseidon looked perplexed. Athena gathered her thoughts and looked into Poseidon's eyes,

"They are willing to die for it."

"I fight for love," said Poseidon.

"You fight for victory, not love, and you fight without risk. We are immortal. We know nothing of what it means to love something enough to die for it. I took everything my crow and Medusa loved away from them and yet they risked the half of a life I left them with for love. Love is the only thing more powerful than the gods."

"Then our fight is over," said Poseidon.

"Our fight for Medusa is over. You and I will always find a battle. The legend of Astra has been fulfilled. We cannot undo what he has brought together."

Owl whispered again. Athena nodded and lowered her helmet. As she ascended into the clouds she motioned over the sky with her lance and undid the curse she had placed on the crow.

Poseidon used his trident and swept a new memory into the inhabitants of Patmos leaving Medusa to freely live as Andromeda.

# Chapter Forty
### Next Life

**A**STRA LANDED ON a shoreline dotted with sea daffodils. Perseus, Medusa and a once banished crow, now an immortal legend, were one against the setting sun. Their silhouettes, outlined, by golden rays.

Bowed feathered heads wept with joy as their eyes bore witness to what was unfolding before them. Perseus and Medusa embraced and disappeared into each other until the only thing left was love. Astra used his beaks and scratched at the earth before he flew away. A single black feather fell from white wings as he disappeared into the sky…

* * *

www.ingramcontent.com/pod-product-compliance
Lightning Source LLC
Chambersburg PA
CBHW020658160726
47991CB00003B/1248